PAYMENT IN FULL

"Six years, Georgianna. That's what I gave up for you. One night doesn't come close to compensating me for that."

"Compensating you?" Her eyes flashed, anger bubbling up, making the depths sparkle. "Tonight isn't—"

"Six nights. One night for every year." Ivo cupped her jaw, ran his thumb along her cheek, savoring the softness of her skin, the slight tremble of her whole body in response to the caress. He leant in, setting a hot, open-mouthed kiss to the delicate skin just below her ear. "You owe me at least that much."

BOOK YOUR PLACE ON OUR WEBSITE AND MAKE THE READING CONNECTION!

We've created a customized website just for our very special readers, where you can get the inside scoop on everything that's going on with Zebra, Pinnacle and Kensington books.

When you come online, you'll have the exciting opportunity to:

- View covers of upcoming books
- Read sample chapters
- Learn about our future publishing schedule (listed by publication month *and author*)
- Find out when your favorite authors will be visiting a city near you
- Search for and order backlist books from our online catalog
- Check out author bios and background information
- Send e-mail to your favorite authors
- Meet the Kensington staff online
- Join us in weekly chats with authors, readers and other guests
- Get writing guidelines
- AND MUCH MORE!

**Visit our website at
http://www.kensingtonbooks.com**

LORD SIN

KALEN HUGHES

ZEBRA BOOKS
Kensington Publishing Corp.
www.kensingtonbooks.com

ZEBRA BOOKS are published by

Kensington Publishing Corp.
850 Third Avenue
New York, NY 10022

All Kensington titles, imprints, and distributed lines are available at special quantity discounts for bulk purchases for sales
promotion, premiums, fund-raising, educational, or institu-
tional use.

Special book excerpts or customized printings can also be created to fit specific needs. For details, write or phone the office
of the Kensington Special Sales Manager: Attn. Special Sales
Department. Kensington Publishing Corp., 850 Third Avenue,
New York, NY 10022. Phone: 1-800-221-2647.

Zebra and the Z logo Reg. U.S. Pat. & TM Off.

ISBN-13: 978-0-8217-8149-4
ISBN-10: 0-8217-8149-9

First Printing: May 2007
10 9 8 7 6 5 4 3 2 1

Printed in the United States of America

For my grandparents, Elbert and Mildred,
who always believed I could do anything.

My parents, Stephen and Cheryl,
who raised me to believe in myself.

And my godmother, Amanda,
who supported me along the way.

Acknowledgments

There are so many people to thank beyond those in my dedication:

Lisa, who gave me my first romance novel.

Nance, who introduced me to Georgette Heyer.

Jess, who challenged me to write a romance in the first place.

Meghan, who copyedited my dyslexic ramblings.

Scott, master of obscure facts.

Issa, god of comfort food.

Kristie and Amie, who supported me in this, as in all things.

Cathie, who got me hooked on the eighteenth century.

Siobhan, who doesn't mind doing dishes and feeding my dog.

The members of the San Francisco Bay Area RWA chapter, especially Monica, Jami, Nyree, and Doreen.

The members of the Beau Monde RWA chapter, who shared their knowledge and resources so generously.

The Wild Cards (my fellow 2005 Golden Heart finalists) for their endless support and unflagging optimism.

My agent, Paige Wheeler, for guiding me through the woods.

And my fantastic editor, Hilary Sares, for helping me make this the best book it could be (and unleashing the great hounds Whine and Scream to make sure we got a HOT cover!).

Thanks, gang, I couldn't have done it without you.

Chapter 1

*London once again finds itself enlivened by the presence
of the handsome Lord S—. If only we could discover
what has kept him from our shores for so many years . . .*

Tête-à-Tête, 6 October 1788

She'd haunted his dreams for years.

Auburn curls and sherry-colored eyes. A singularly
wicked smile, tilting up higher on one side to expose
a dimple. A spray of freckles across her bosom: a con-
stellation designed by God to tempt a man's thoughts
below her décolletage.

Another man's wife.

Of all the unfortunate things Ivo Dauntry had
learned about himself over the years, the fact that he
could lust after someone else's wife should have been
minor. Should have been nothing beside the fact that he
could kill a man, thwart his grandfather's will, break
his mother's heart, and never look back. But it wasn't
the face of the man he'd killed or the

mother he'd disappointed that swam through his dreams night after night.

It was hers.

Mrs. Lionel Exley's.

In his dreams she was nothing like the proper newlywed who had actually existed, barely more than a girl, excited to be flexing her wings on her first visit to Paris. No, the siren in his dreams had eyes that brimmed with the shared knowledge of lust. Her smile seeming to promise everything he'd ever wanted. But she always remained just out of reach.

A temptress. A tease. A practiced coquette.

None of it was real, but he'd had the same dream so many times now that it felt real. Her seduction had become the clearest of memories, as treasured as his first lover, as sensual as the first time he'd plunged naked into the warm water of the Mediterranean.

Mrs. Lionel Exley. The woman standing across the prizefighter's ring at this very moment, casually clinging to the arm of a man who was certainly not her husband.

The only woman whose virtue he'd ever defended. An action which had cost him dearly. Career. Family. Friends. He'd lost them all. No, not lost. He'd sacrificed them for her, like a lamb on an altar to a biblical god.

And all this time he'd thought it had been worth it.

His fist clenched around his purse, coins biting into his palm. The sea of humanity pressing in on him blurred and spun momentarily before the pain in his hand grounded him again.

Nothing in his dreams had been real, but watching her now, it was as though he'd somehow conjured her, given the dream form. She turned and said something to the man on the other side of her, the column of her neck twisting, swanlike, elegantly pale against the dark fur tippet wrapped around her throat.

He swallowed thickly, lust rushing through him, liquid fire from heart to groin.

Where the devil was her husband?

She shone like a beacon, her red habit blazing out against the dull blues and browns of the greatcoats surrounding her like the breast of a pheasant when it launches itself into the sky.

Magnificent.

Her breath escaped in a white cloud, mingling with her escort's reply. She smiled, and Ivo could swear he heard the accompanying laugh carry over the dull roar of the crowd. It reached right inside him, grabbed hold until he could hardly draw breath.

He wrenched his gaze away, forcing his attention to the combatants as they prepared for the match.

She wasn't any of his business.

The champion, Tom Johnson, was bantering with the young Prince of Wales, while his challenger stood by like a lump. It didn't look as though Johnson had much to worry about. The upstart was large, but beefy and slow. Ponderous, like a dray horse.

Ivo shifted his weight, stamping his feet on the cold ground. The damp was seeping up uncomfortably through the soles of his boots. He'd almost forgotten what autumn was like in England. A riot of color in the trees. Frost on the ground like sugar dusted on a pastry.

He was home again. Reluctantly returned from Italy to the not so welcoming embrace of his family, with the uncomfortable status of heir to his grandfather. He was the Earl of Somercote. A courtesy title for the Marquis of Tregaron's heir.

He simply couldn't get used to it. Nor did he want it. He'd been plain Mr. Dauntry for almost thirty-five years, and no matter how much he tried, he couldn't seem to answer to anything else. Couldn't step into his cousin's shoes without feeling the pinch, without his grandfather reminding him how unfit he'd already proved himself to be.

And the proof was right there across the ring.

All around him bets were being furiously laid as the two combatants stripped to the waist, shucking coats, waistcoats and shirts, tying their cravats about their waists to hold up their breeches. Routine enough for a prizefight, but it suddenly seemed highly unsuitable with Mrs. Exley present.

What on earth was she doing here? What kind of lunatic brought a woman to a mill? Any woman, let alone a respectable one.

Unless she wasn't.

Respectable anymore, that was. He hadn't seen her since Paris, and a lot could change in six years. He didn't want to believe that she could have. He couldn't.

His friend Bennett jostled his arm. "You didn't follow Rivers's advice and put your blunt on the challenger, did you?"

"No." Ivo rolled his shoulders, trying to relax, to keep his attention away from the woman across the ring. "But what odds will you give me on that great lump going at least ten rounds?"

Bennett looked the challenger up and down, assessing. "Not a chance. I'll bet you fifty pounds he doesn't make it even to three. Johnson has a punishing left."

While Bennett loudly sized the pugilists up, arguing the finer points with the men surrounding them,

Ivo's gaze slid back to Mrs. Exley, back to the rakish buck who was watching over her with a proprietary air. The man wore his cocked hat angled low over his brow, gilt trim winking as he dropped his head to hear her over the crowd. His leather greatcoat gaped, revealing a flash of a puce coat beneath embroidered in darker browns and gold.

The way she stood, arm tucked into her gallant's, was an affront to the sacrifices he had made. She had no right to flaunt herself like a fallen woman. No right to be such. If nothing else she owed him purity.

As he studied the pair of them, she glanced across the ring and her eyes met his for the briefest of moments. Her face paled, then she looked away, turning her attention back to her cicisbeo.

Ivo's stomach clenched. Fury rushed through him—a hot, burning tide—mingling with an almost violent repulsion. What had she become?

He was barely aware of the match as it commenced. The combatants, the din of the crowd, the jostling, raging, swirling humanity surrounding him, it all simply faded away, nothing but a fantastical stage set for the woman standing across the ring. She was the only thing that was real. The only thing that mattered.

Fifteen rounds later the match was over, the challenger bloody and beaten. Howls of anger mingled with cheers. Fights broke out in several places, causing the mob to shift and push. Across the ring, Mrs. Exley's companion wrapped one arm familiarly about her waist and turned to escort her from the field.

Ivo shut his eyes for a moment, resisting the urge to plunge into the crowd after her. He'd given up everything for her, and it stung to realize that sacrifice didn't give him the right to demand an explanation today. It didn't give him any rights at all.

As he collected his winnings, he glanced surreptitiously over his shoulder, trying to catch one last glimpse of her.

"She's gone," Bennett said with a sly smile, thrusting a wad of bank notes at him.

"Who's gone?"

His friend's smile widened, revealing the perfect teeth for which he was justifiably famous. "The only woman out here. The one you've been staring at for the last hour or more."

"You know her?"

It didn't matter that Bennett knew her. Didn't matter that he'd seen her again. Or that some man had succeeded in giving her husband a pair of horns. It didn't matter that their attraction was every bit as strong as he remembered.

He ran his tongue over his teeth. His mouth was chalky and bitter. He needed a drink. A very large one.

"Everyone knows her." Bennett tossed back the ruffles at his wrist and pulled a flask from one capacious pocket. "That was Georgianna Exley. One of the most outrageous widows in England." He removed the top and took a drink before holding the flask out to Ivo. "It's rumored she has rules for taking a lover, the most pernicious of which is that she only grants the men she chooses as many nights in her bed as they roll on a die."

"Widow?" Ivo swallowed hard, heart hammering in his ears. That single word reverberated through his whole body, echoes cascading like a stone dropped into a well.

"Widow," Bennett repeated absently, thrusting the

flask into Ivo's hand. "You can meet her tomorrow if you've a mind to. She's sure to be another guest at Lord Glendower's shooting party. The earl's her father-in-law."

Ivo stared hard at the crowd, searching to no avail for her fur-trimmed hat in the sea of humanity headed back toward the village. He glanced down at his hand, realized he was holding Bennett's flask, and tossed back what was left of the brandy. The heady fumes filled his nose and the liquid burned a slow track all the way down into his belly.

A widow.

"George, who the devil is that man across the ring? The tall fellow staring at us."

Georgianna Exley glanced up before following Gabriel Angelstone's gaze across the straw-strewn ring where the two prizefighters were being helped from their coats.

Her eyes met those of the man Gabriel was glaring at and she glanced away immediately, her hands suddenly cold. Her head buzzed as though she might faint.

Dauntry. His name was Dauntry.

Her breakfast swirled about in her stomach and she swallowed convulsively. She was not going to throw up. She was not going to faint. Not here.

"I haven't the slightest idea," she replied, pressing slightly closer to Gabe, burrowing into his reassuring warmth. Around them people eyed her and Gabe askance. Dauntry's look of disgust was reflected in many other pairs of eyes.

She didn't belong here. No woman did. And her oldest friend was not well liked. Too handsome.

Too foreign in a myriad of subtle ways: honey skin and almond eyes from his Turkish mother, an air of French dandification from his ambassador father.

He was her rock. The one constant in her life. The only man she'd ever known who hadn't deserted her in some way.

George tilted her head, peeking around Gabe's shoulder, and studied Dauntry for a moment. He looked very much as she remembered: tall enough to be imposing, his own black curls tied back in a queue, eyes that seemed almost as dark. His face was lean, the planes angular, the features sculpted. He was only saved from the epithet pretty by his sheer size and the thin scar that cut down along his left cheekbone. A swordsman's scar, received in her honor. . . . She bit her lip and looked away.

She didn't want to remember Paris or anything about it. She could have handled Blanchot herself. Lord knew she'd fended off enough drunken advances over the years, but Dauntry had stumbled upon them, and without so much as a word, he'd pulled Blanchot off her and knocked him to the ground, sending the older man's wig flying.

What began with fists had ended with swords, the flash of steel wicked in the scant light provided by artfully placed lamps. Blanchot's lips had been wet with blood-flecked foam by the time the ambassador and the rest of Dauntry's party had arrived on the scene and her world had spun out of control. She could still picture Blanchot's wig lying abandoned on the ground, sullied and trod upon.

As ambassador, Lord Fitzherbert might have been able to arrange everything to keep that night's events quiet—it was amazing what money, power, influence, and sheer force of will could achieve—but his machinations hadn't prevented the worst of it: the look of disquiet in her husband's eyes. Just because no scandal had broken over her—over them— didn't mean she'd forgotten or forgiven the events of that night.

Chapter 2

The beautiful Mrs. E— has been seen leaving Town escorted by none other than the Angelstone Turk. Could it be that he's given up a certain yellow-haired opera singer?

Tête-à-Tête, 8 October 1788

On the second night of Lord Glendower's annual shooting party, Ivo stole out of the overheated billiard room and secluded himself on the terrace. The room inside, overflowing with the cream of the sporting set, had become stifling.

The night was cold, the air holding a hint of frost. Perfect hunting weather. One of the many things he'd missed while he'd drifted through country after country, always telling himself there was nothing left in England worth coming home for. Nothing waiting for him but the possibility of resurrecting a long-cold scandal and a family that wanted nothing to do with him.

He blew a cloud of blue-gray smoke from his

French cigarito out into the garden and tried not to think about Mrs. Exley. It seemed like the only thing he'd done since the mill was try not to think about her during his waking hours and dream even more vividly about her each and every night.

She wasn't the same woman he'd been so enamored of, but he couldn't figure out the changes. It made his head hurt to try.

After dinner she'd disappeared, probably off with one of the two men who appeared to be vying to be the next man in her bed: her companion at the mill, whom they all called Brimstone—apparently to differentiate him from his cousin, who was also an Angelstone—or with the Viscount St. Audley. As far as he could tell, she was the spoiled and petted darling of every rake in England and it made him sick.

But not sick enough.

He still wanted her so badly his hands shook with the need to touch her.

Ivo froze as the subject of his thoughts suddenly appeared, walking up the gravel path that wound through the garden with her long, masculine stride. Aside from that walk—and her rather colorful vocabulary— she was utterly feminine. Nothing but soft, inviting curves from the mass of auburn curls that she never powdered, to the swell of breasts and flare of hips, to the surprisingly dainty ankles visible just below the hem of her petticoat. Curves. Lush, ripe, disturbingly erotic.

He straightened as she ran lightly up the steps. Leaned back against the balustrade, glad for the cold bite of the stone against his hip, for the grounding the discomfort gave him in the moment. This wasn't one of his dreams.

She didn't look particularly happy to see him. Up

until now, she'd been fairly successful at avoiding him. And she was avoiding him. He was sure of it.

"Good evening, my lord." She paused at the top of the stairs, tense as a feral cat. She pulled her shawl tighter about her shoulders, hugging herself.

"Mrs. Exley." He inclined his head, ever so slightly. "You've been down to the barn?"

She glanced briefly toward the house, her expression guarded. He could hear their fellow guests just inside the open French doors, but so far none had been inclined to join him on the terrace. Probably disgusted by the smoke from his cigaritos. Smoking anything but a pipe was a habit mostly confined to the riffraff of France and men who'd spent long periods in the hot climes where tobacco was grown.

"Yes," she said at last, "one of my father-in-law's setters is whelping, and he's down there, nervous as an expectant father."

Ivo swallowed thickly, doing his best to keep his gaze from locking on her lips. She was so tall he wouldn't have to do more than bend his head to kiss her, and that too-full lower lip of hers had clearly been created for kissing. He'd thought so years ago . . . apparently so had Blanchot. And look where that had gotten them all: an exile, a corpse, and a woman teetering on the verge of ruin.

She looked pointedly at his cigarito. "Can I bother you for one of those? It's a habit I picked up from my husband, and I suddenly find that I miss it. I could smell the smoke drifting down through the garden, and I don't think any flower could have smelled so sweet to me tonight."

Ivo did his best to keep his expression neutral as he withdrew a second cigarito from their case and passed it to her. Outrageous. That's what she was. Blazingly, unforgivably outrageous. No one said no to her, ever. She was surrounded by the most masculine, cocksure, sport-mad gentlemen in England, and they let her lead them around by their noses. By their cocks, more likely.

Very much as he was doing now. He ground his teeth together. He should have refused her request. Someone ought to attempt to keep her in her place.

She let go of the shawl and put one ungloved hand out to take the little cigar. Her finger brushed his, and his whole body quickened with anticipation. In that instant he could have sworn the air around them thickened and began to crackle.

"The other guests seem to have been very fond of your husband," he said, making a bid to mask both annoyance and attraction. "All their stories seem to start and end with 'Lyon.'"

He shifted his weight, ruthlessly ignoring the way her presence pulled at him. He had trouble thinking around her. Everything always spiraled back to a hasty duel, a dead man, and a woman he'd wanted desperately, but couldn't have. To the husband who'd stood in his way, whom he'd have sworn she'd loved.

"Everything always did," she acknowledged while smelling the cigarito with her eyes closed, a small smile flickering across her generous mouth.

Ivo's groin throbbed and he quickly took a puff of his cigarito. Why this woman? He didn't want to be attracted to her. Why couldn't the reality of her present mode burn out the infatuation he'd harbored for so long?

Why had he brought up her husband? Why was that subject lodged so firmly in the forefront of his mind? It didn't seem to be in hers.

She wandered away from him to light the cigarito from one of the wall sconces that lined the terrace. She took a short puff, then strolled back to him, her shawl slipping down off her shoulders to trail from her elbows, exposing her chest and shoulders. Light and shadow played across her skin, emphasizing the swell of breasts, the clean line of collarbones, the hollow of her throat.

Ivo risked another glance at the open doors. It had been all he could do not to make a fool of himself since he'd arrived. Even now all he could think of was how it would be to kiss her. To simply drag her down into the garden and do every wicked thing he'd ever dreamed of. To awaken her. Engender a response to his own desire and watch it radiate out of those arresting eyes of hers.

If she was going to be a fallen woman, it ought to be with him. Some part of him even felt she owed it to him. A part that felt small and cheap. An ugly bit of himself he didn't want to acknowledge fully. His grandfather might call him a fool, and he might even have been one if he was to judge with the clearer vision of hindsight, but up until now he'd always been proud to have been the knight who'd rescued the lady from the dragon.

She took a long drag and let it out slowly, smoke drifting up to obscure her face. She sighed again, blew out another cloud, and bit her lower lip, obviously thinking. Remembering. Her eyes were shadowed, almost vacant.

She smiled a bit wistfully. Torchlight haloed her hair. One side of her mouth quirked up. It was that smile that had gotten him in trouble all those years ago. At the time, he'd have done anything to see it again. Seeing it now sucked the breath right out of him and set alarms ringing in his head. He should go. Now. The fey creature beside him simply wasn't the woman he'd given up everything to save.

Reason struggled with want, with need. Desire slipped its leash and he felt himself lean in. It was impossible not to answer that smile. That sly invitation.

She didn't step back. Didn't twist aside. Her eyes didn't drop in maidenly anticipation, but he hadn't expected them to. This wasn't the girl from Paris. No. This was the woman from his dreams.

"Hey, Georgie!" The Viscount St. Audley's voice, loud and eager, erupted from inside the house. Ivo jerked himself upright and turned to stare out into the garden, nerves jangling, heart racing with the spark of unfulfilled lust, with the rush of near discovery. He gripped the balustrade with his free hand, bearing down until his knuckles whitened, and took a slightly unsteady breath.

"I've been looking all over for you," the man yelled from the doorway. "Lord Glendower wants to hear about the race you won last week."

Mrs. Exley took one last puff on her cigarito, her eyes teasing him, full of the knowledge that he'd been about to kiss her—that she'd been about to let him—and then excused herself, striding quickly across the stone terrace, skirts sushing loudly with every step. A nightingale who'd overstayed the season trilled in the dark recesses of the garden, lost and lonely.

He shouldn't have done that. Shouldn't have been so weak. He and his family were barely on speaking terms as it was. If did something as profoundly stupid as to entangle himself with the source of his original downfall, his grandfather would have an apoplectic fit. And rightly so.

Ivo stared down at his hands, willing himself to breathe, watched as the ash fell from his forgotten cigarito. He stubbed it out and flicked the remains down into the garden.

He shouldn't have come.

As soon as Bennett had said that Mrs. Exley would be here, he should have made his excuses and escaped into the next county.

A crack of male laugher burst out of the billiard room, rolled over him, and scurried off into the night to cause havoc as it might.

The cosseted darling of rakes. The *bona ropa* of at least one gentleman inside that very room. He shouldn't want her. He shouldn't.

George let her breath out with a rush as she crossed the terrace. The light shining behind St. Audley beckoned. Offering warmth, sanity, reason. She'd thought she'd learned to overcome the flicker of awareness Dauntry called up in her. She'd hadn't experienced it since she'd seen him last: blood trickling down his cheek, down the blade of the sword still in his hand, eyes burning. She'd been bundled out of the garden while the ambassador had set his lackeys running . . .

It had been wrong then, and it felt that way still, but she couldn't seem to damp down the flutter of attraction. Of recognition. It had been there the first time she'd met him. It was there still, a blood-stirring surge she couldn't escape any more than driftwood could escape the tide.

There was simply something in the way Dauntry watched her. Something almost raw . . . and it made her feel like a wanton. Or at least, it made her feel as if she'd like to *be* one.

Something basic—primal—in her responded. An

embarrassing and alarmingly sexual response. She'd taken lovers since her husband's death, but only infrequently, and always on her terms. One night only. That was the rule. One night. But none of the men she'd shared her bed with evoked the blaze of lust that Dauntry did. Or evoked the knowledge that here stood a man who truly saw her, saw and wanted her.

Even as she rushed toward the viscount she could feel Dauntry's eyes on her. She shivered, a trickle of fear combined with the illicit thrill of desire working its way down her spine. She should stay away from him. She wasn't herself when he was near, and she didn't much like the person she became in his presence.

She stepped into the light and slid her arm through St. Audley's, giving him a practiced, flirtatious smile that invited him to laugh about the little tête-à-tête he'd just broken up. The viscount smiled back at her, but it didn't reach his eyes. His lips had a white edge to them. He cast one last hard look over her shoulder and led her back into the house.

Brimstone offered uncomplicated laughter and unconditional love. Audley was another beast altogether. Quick to anger. Possessive of her even with their other friends. Far more the elder brother than her own ever had been—Lucas would have teased her. The viscount clamped his hand over hers and marched her rather stiffly over to where her father-in-law waited.

Just for a moment out on the terrace the night had become charged. It had been clear Dauntry was going to kiss her, and in the moment, she hadn't had any desire to stop him. Something feral had clawed its way through her, possessing her. She certainly hadn't been looking for rescue. She'd been almost sorry when they'd been interrupted. Almost sorry, and terribly relieved.

Saved from him. Saved from herself.

Dauntry was the last man on earth she should be considering as a paramour. He didn't even like her. She was sure of it. He looked at her with disgust, with anger, just as often as lust. And lust was hardly all that flattering a response. But her body couldn't seem to grasp what was so clear to her head. Her nipples hardened whenever he entered a room. The bottom dropped out of her stomach and her whole lower body throbbed.

If he were to touch her, she didn't know what she'd do. Shatter into a thousand pieces. Melt into a puddle. Something climactic. Something that she was afraid wouldn't be settled by one night.

She shouldn't have joined him on the terrace, but her curiosity had gotten the better of her. What had happened to him after the duel? Where had he been since? Had he thought of her as often as she had thought of him?

Disloyal. Unworthy. Abandoned in thought if not in deed. All the things Dauntry made her feel, made her remember feeling. Not because Blanchot had touched her, but because she'd wanted Dauntry to. Not because Blanchot was dead, but because Lyon was, and Dauntry still had the power to stir her.

Chapter 3

It seems Mrs. E— is currently enjoying the hospitality of her husband's family. A country house party . . . what better place is there for an illicit assignation?

Tête-à-Tête, 10 October 1788

A sudden rush of feathers announced the eruption of a large grouse, closely followed by two more. They fled upward, streaking away from the excited spaniels. Ahead of Ivo the hunters watched the birds, those in the fore with guns up. He watched Mrs. Exley, who was by far the most interesting thing in the woods that day.

She raised her gun smoothly, barrel glinting as the sun caught it, danced along its polished surface. She fired, and the first bird plummeted to earth. St. Audley took one of the other two and the third fled to safety in the trees.

An acrid cloud of smoke drifted over the field, the mingled scents of sulfur and saltpeter enveloping Ivo momentarily, overwhelming the damp, loamy scent of the woods. The dogs quickly retrieved the birds and the keeper tucked the limp, feathered bodies into his game bag.

Yesterday, it had been fishing. Today, it was grouse hunting. Tomorrow, they'd been promised a run with the Quorn. Lord Glendower's estate and the surrounding country offered a multitude of pursuits for a gentleman—or lady—with sporting proclivities.

No matter what they did, Mrs. Exley studiously avoided him. It wasn't overt, but she was masterful at it. After their encounter on the terrace, he wasn't going to get a second chance. At least not if she had anything to say about it. He should be grateful. Relieved. But he wasn't.

She stopped to reload. Several long curls fell forward over her shoulder only to be pushed impatiently back again. Ivo drifted toward her, captured by the way the dappled light played across her busy hands, highlighted her cheekbones, flirted with her lips.

"Lord Glendower wasn't joking when he complimented your shooting."

"And why would he do that?" She closed the frizzen over the pan softly, with no clumsy click. The powder flask was returned to the chatelaine she wore at her waist. She rested the gun carefully in the crook of her arm, sure and easy, as comfortable with the weapon as most women were with a babe. Finished, she turned to give him her full attention, blinking several times, obviously irritated and pointedly waiting for an answer.

Ivo beat back the urge to simply kiss her then and there. If she didn't shoot him, one of her friends was likely to do so, but, Lord, how he'd like to do something to shake the reserve out of her. To make her react. With anger. Surprise. Desire. He almost didn't care which. Anything would be better than that silent condescension.

"Gentlemen *are* known to brag about their womenfolk."

"As well as their horses and their dogs." Her voice was brittle. Dismissive.

She stared him down for a moment, her mouth set in a firm, disapproving line, her color high, cheeks flushed pink exactly the way they would be after making love. The image of her pink and tousled stopped him in his tracks and made his mind go blank. Everything subsumed beneath a vision of flesh damp with exertion, blushing with desire.

When he didn't respond, she stepped away from him, hurrying to catch up with the rest of the hunting party. Cursing under his breath, Ivo followed. Why did he flirt with her? Teasing her—at least in the manner he was used to employing with women— was obviously a very bad idea. Flattery utterly failed to charm her. She didn't want to be charmed by him, and he ought to be able to take a hint.

When Glendower announced an end to the hunt, Ivo fell in behind Mrs. Exley, wandering slowly, watching the sway of her hips as she strode along, oblivious. The pad holding her skirts out bounced slightly with each step—rhythmic, suggestive, impossible to look away from. They reached a fork in the road and most of the party turned off toward the village and the inn. Mrs. Exley watched them go, then turned to follow the small group led by her father-in-law toward the house.

Her eyes widened as she saw him. He could see her consider turning about again and marching off after her friends. He could almost hear the wheels turning in her head. He bowed slightly and swept one hand before him, inviting her to join him.

She raised her chin and stared him down for a moment before taking a single step toward him and setting off down the path. Ivo fell in beside her as she passed. He wasn't going to so much as touch her. He wasn't going to offer his arm, or to take her gun.

"Did you happen to meet Mrs. Hart while you were in Italy?"

Ivo glanced down. Mrs. Hart, was it? An infamous lady-bird, sent as something of a present to the ambassador of Naples by his nephew, her former protector. Ivo's mouth quirked in an involuntary smile. "I believe everyone has met Mrs. Hart. It's quite impossible not to have done so."

She bit her lip, but her dimple was in evidence, giving her away. She knew full well she shouldn't have asked him such a question. Courtesans were not a suitable topic, but then, he wasn't sure there was such a thing as a suitable topic between the two of them. Death and desire. Scandal and ruin. That's what they shared.

"And, before you ask, yes, she's very beautiful. And, yes, the entire Italian court is charmed. And, no, I wasn't among the gaggle of young blades vying for her attention."

"Gaggle?" she choked out, half laughing, but keeping her attention firmly in front of them, giving him only her profile and that mischievous dimple.

"What else would you call a large group of lovesick Italians? A herd?"

Mrs. Exley burst into full-throated laughter, the sound making his chest suddenly tight. The path they were following through the woods meandered, curving

around a magnificent oak. Glendower and the men
with him disappeared in the twists and turns.

"Somehow I don't think either geese or hoofed
animals are quite the right choice."

"A pack?"

"At least that sounds predatory." She suddenly
stopped and tugged at her skirts, ruthlessly ripping
them loose from the brambles at the side of the path.

"A hedge might be more appropriate," Ivo said,
glancing meaningfully at the offending plant. "Something dense and hard to avoid."

Something like himself, seemingly.

She laughed again, the sound startling a flock of
small brown wrens from the trees. Still chuckling,
they broke from the woods into a sunlit pasture. Ivo
blinked, trying to adjust to the sudden light. A herd
of Jerseys grazed lazily before them. A few lifted delicate, sculpted heads to watch them pass.

He paused as they came to the stone fence that
separated the park proper from the estate's grazing
land. The group that had been ahead of them was
nowhere to be seen. Only the two of them remained,
suddenly marooned on a quiet, pastoral island.

A cow lowed and another answered. A trill of bird-
song swept across the meadow. Otherwise, it was op-
pressively quiet. Except for the loud beating of his
heart, thumping in double-time as his blood rushed
and heated.

Ivo hopped lightly over the fence, weighing what
he might do, divining consequences.

They were alone.

A wise man would do nothing. He would walk away . . .

He turned and she handed her gun over. He carefully laid it to rest against the wall with his own, then
reached across to her.

They were alone . . . and she owed him.

Her eyes darted about, searching the pasture behind him. Ivo bit the inside of his cheek to keep from grinning, to keep from grabbing.

She put her hands in his, her grasp slightly hesitant. He shifted his weight, bracing himself. She scrambled over the fence, sure as a ewe on a rocky hillside, only to tumble into his arms as one leg got caught in layers of chemise and petticoats.

Ivo fell back a step as she fetched up against his chest, her eyes opening enormously. He caught her up tightly, holding her just off the ground as linen and camlet swirled out.

She stared up at him, barely breathing as he slowly lowered her to her feet. Gold flecked her eyes like the hammered surface of an ancient amulet. She didn't pull away, as he fully expected her to. She sagged against him, brought one gloved hand up to trace the scar on his cheek, kid-covered fingers disturbingly gentle.

He froze as her finger traced the narrow scar that cut down across his cheek. A shadow of beard, slightly rough on either side of the narrow sliver of scar tissue, pulled at the soft leather of her glove. He'd healed with no disfiguring pucker. Lucky.

The slight smile he'd been trying to hide slid from his face. Vanished beneath her caress. Her heart was hammering, pounding so loudly she almost couldn't think. The scent of bergamot and leather filled her nostrils. Made her want to inhale deeper. To bury her face in his neck.

This was a very bad idea.

She should have walked away. Should have run after Audley and Brimstone. But that irreverent thrill that went through her whenever she was near

Dauntry had overwhelmed her better judgment. The challenge he presented was impossible to resist. Sin incarnate. That was what he was.

He had powder streaks on his face. Little black dots dusting his right cheek, almost obscuring the natural beauty mark that lurked below the corner of his right eye.

When her finger completed its journey, she let her hand drop to rest on his chest, fingers splayed out. He inhaled audibly, as though he'd been holding his breath a long while, and brought his lips down to cover hers.

Hot. Urgent. Almost desperate. He tasted of the ale they'd all had before setting out, sweet and slightly earthy. His hands firmed about her waist. George went utterly still, savoring the moment, before her tongue darted out to meet his, curled inside his mouth to tease the soft edge of the inside of his lip, the slick hollow of his cheek. His stroked back, teeth clashing with hers.

She'd loved this. The feeling of a man's hands, the way he tasted, the impossible softness and heat of his mouth. The heady sense of power that came with the ability to control all that strength with nothing but the light caress of her hand, the seemingly submissive exposure of her throat.

Her nipples budded, hard and impatient against the stiff fabric of her stays. Blood pooled in her belly, a dull ache that throbbed in time with her heart. She nipped at his lip, urging him on, wanting more. Needing more. He slipped one hand down to cup her bottom, pulling her hips up hard against him, his fists tightly clutching her coat and skirts. Holding her firmly, the ridge of his erection manifest where it rode against her belly.

This was exactly as she'd been imagining it—God help her.

What was it they said about an Englishman who acted like an Italian? Something about his being a devil. Here was proof. A man who'd taken the fire of Italy into himself. And, at this moment, it burned for her. He burned for her.

His hand went to the front of her coat, slipped one button loose. George inhaled sharply, her whole body tight with anticipation. Queasy, shaking with need.

The distant sound of dogs barking intruded and sent her heart racing with panic. Dauntry pulled his head back with a slight jerk, like a horse startled by a rabbit dashing across the road. He blew his breath out in a long huff and rested his forehead against hers, keeping his arms loosely around her. His thumb traced slow circles against the small of her back. Comforting and arousing all at once.

She shivered, desire draining out of her core and flooding through her limbs, making her hands shake, her knees wobble. The magic moment they'd been suspended in popped like a soap bubble hitting the grass.

It was too easy to get lost in such a moment. Too easy to drown in sensation. Too painful to resurface.

She screwed her eyes shut, wanting to cry. To curl up and bawl. She shouldn't have let this happen. She had rules about flirtation and seduction. Rules she'd never violated. Not once. They were the only thing that kept her life orderly and safe, and kept her balanced just this side of social ruin.

The last sane corner of her mind railed at her to break his hold, but she couldn't get her body to comply. Her arms were around his neck, one hand locked in the curls of his queue. This was completely out of hand. Someone was bound to come along any minute.

After one more deep breath, he raised his head and took a step back from her. Her eyes opened. Her arms fell, trailing reluctantly across his shoulders, down his chest, then fell away completely as she sank down onto the wall, legs no longer able to support her. She took one shuddering breath, getting herself back under control.

"Well," she ventured.

Dauntry just stared at her, a slight flush making his scar stand out in bold relief. God, he really was beautiful. An impulse—to find out if the body hidden under layers of leather, wool, and linen was as perfect as that face—hammered hard through her, a relentless staccato of lust and curiosity. She could have him. Just the once . . . but not here. Not now.

George sat up a bit straighter. She could manage this. She could.

She forced herself up from the wall, picked up her gun, and strode off before he could say anything. Before he could touch her again. All she wanted to do was turn and curl into him. Bask in the warmth of his body, of his desire.

He'd kissed her. Not only had she let him, she'd welcomed it.

Welcomed it? She'd wallowed in it. Thrown herself into the moment like it was her last.

Only minutes ago she'd been secure in the knowledge that such a thing would never happen. She would never allow it to happen. That for all of Dauntry's palpable desire, she was in control.

Her resolve had crumbled as soon as his arms had closed around her.

No. It had been lost the moment he'd taken hold of her hands. Nothing but that small connection, glove to glove, and all her resolutions had melted away, nothing more than frost on an early spring morning.

Weak, wanton, and willful. Three things a woman should never be.

She'd always had trouble with the last, and occasionally with the second, but never with the first. At this moment she was dying to indulge all three. To lead him, not to the gun room where friends and family awaited, but to the grotto hidden deep in the garden. To the summer house, already shut up in preparation for the coming winter. To her room. To the enormous curtained bed with its enveloping layers of down and linen.

George touched one hand to her face, reliving the slight burr of his cheek against hers. It had been riveting in the moment. Wonderful.

She glanced back over her shoulder, her gaze meeting Dauntry's. He smiled, lazy and sure like a cat after a kill, but didn't rush to catch her. Should she find that troubling? Alarming even? She couldn't make up her mind. It all depended on what he wanted. On why he'd kissed her.

She wasn't about to ask him, not just now.

For now, it was enough that the she felt alive for the first time in years. Crackling to her toes with awareness and anticipation in a way that only frustrated desire and the promise of its fulfillment could achieve.

In pregnant silence, they crossed the last field before reaching the formal gardens and making their way to the gun room. Inside they found a large number of the guests already cleaning their guns.

George sat down and cleaned her own, rinsing the used powder out of the barrel and then disassembling the lock and oiling the whole mechanism. It was good to have something to do with her hands. Something simple. Physical. Real.

Had any of the others noticed her hands were shaking? That her breathing was still the smallest bit uneven? Had they noted that she and Dauntry had come in together? Brimstone was busy with his own gun and St. Audley was nowhere to be seen. They were the ones most likely to notice her overexcited state. Her oldest friends. Her champions since childhood. Her biggest obstacles.

When she finished reassembling the lock, she put the beautiful rifle away in its cabinet, lock-step beside its brethren. She leaned back against the paneled wall, bare hands pressed to the cold wood behind her, and studied the room. It smelled like home. Leather, bay rum, whisky, wood smoke, oil, and the faint hint of gunpowder mingling in the air. It felt like home. This was her place. Her kingdom. Far more so than the overheated drawing rooms of London.

Dauntry was still working on his own gun. Several unruly curls had slipped from his queue to fall forward, hiding his eyes. So beautiful—and if she was very, very careful, she could have him. Could allow herself the indulgence. Once.

Her rule kept things simple and under her control. One night of passion and then a clean, swift end. No question of being someone's mistress, or chance for any man to think he had the right to dictate to her or to rule her.

With an inaudible sigh, she forced herself to look away and went to excuse herself to her father-in-law.

If she tarried long enough for the others to finish up she wasn't exactly sure what would happen, but she was smart enough to know that something would. Being caught in flagrante delicto in the gun room was not something she aspired to.

Chapter 4

*Rumors run rife about the Earl of S—. Some say his
long sojourn abroad was due to his eloping with the
wife of a French butcher.*

Tête-à-Tête, 10 October 1788

As they assembled for the promised hunt on the fog-
shrouded lawn outside Quorn Hall, Ivo eyed Mrs.
Exley—George—with misgiving. When she'd mentioned she'd be joining the hunt, he'd pictured her
riding to the hall to farewell the men, or following
along to observe in a smart little carriage, not actually
riding to hounds. She, of course, had meant exactly
what she said.

It was ridiculous, the license she was allowed. Indulging her was one thing, but she was going to
break her fool neck. From the look of things, her
husband had never made the attempt to rein her in.
Ivo doubted it was possible to do so now.

He frowned, fiddling with his horse's reins. He
didn't have any right to dictate to her. A strong

desire to do so, but no right. And despite that kiss, she was unlikely to give him the right.

She was mounted on an enormous bald-faced gelding with startling blue eyes. It wasn't an attractive animal, but it was an impressive one, its sleek brown hide almost black in the morning gloom. The beast looked like far too much horse for a lady. Even one as intrepid as George.

The low mist swirled about the horses' legs, making disembodied jinns of the footmen who circled with trays and bottles. It gilded everything with a damp sheen. Ivo's coat, the reins, his face. Tiny droplets formed in his mount's mane, ran together to form larger ones which dripped steadily down onto the animal's shoulder.

George's gelding champed at the bit, spittle turning to foam where metal met sensitive lip. He shifted his weight from side to side, coat twitching with nervous energy. George barely seemed to notice her peril. She leaned forward slightly in the saddle and gave her mount a solid slap on the neck. The gelding tossed his head and settled, obedient to his mistress's silent command.

Ivo took a deep breath of cold, damp air. He let it out slowly, his eyes roaming over George. God, she was beautiful. Not the classic society beauty, but beautiful in the way a prizewinning race horse was, or in the manner of a finely wrought sword. Strong. Elegant.

Her habit hugged curves that only yesterday had been pressed against him. Wool lovingly cupped the swell of her breast, the long lines of her thighs. She held an ivory-handled crop in one hand, but she didn't seem to need it.

This morning she was once again safely hemmed

in by Brimstone and St. Audley, her two devoted bulldogs. Both of them eyed him as though he was trying
to snatch their favorite bone.

Which, in point of fact, he was.

He'd spent half the night thinking about it, sunk
in the kind of wicked imaginings that came so readily in the wee hours. Sleek, naked limbs, a cloud of
auburn hair, her soft cries echoing off the wainscot-
ing, or muffled by the bedclothes. The same images
that had haunted now tantalized.

The path from obsession to bedding wasn't any
wiser, but it was clearer. Like a series of stepping
stones revealed when a storm-swollen creek receded.
Mossy, slick, dangerous, but a way across all the same.
Maybe bedding her would be enough to cure him.
God knows she owed him something for what he'd
sacrificed.

Fucking him wouldn't turn back the hands of
time, mend the fences he'd broken with his grandfather, or make his mother forget the scandal he'd
almost caused, but it would be a beginning. A token.

Ivo accepted a stirrup cup from a milling footman
and tossed it back, smiling to himself as he saw
George do the same. He savored the burn of the
brandy as it slid down his throat. If he kissed her
she'd taste exactly the same. Sharp and fiery.

There was no explaining why she was so damnably
alluring. She simply was. There was something about
the way she held herself, her slightly husky voice, the
intelligence that burned behind her amber eyes.
Something fierce, defiant, and oddly masculine. Each
element on its own was nothing—but together?—
together they were everything.

He kept his eye on her as they approached the first
obstacle, a tall hedge that separated the road from an

open grazing field. The hounds had already scrambled through, a seething, baying swarm. George was riding at the fore, bent low over the neck of her mount, skirts trailing behind her. All around her riders peeled off, looking for a lower spot, a gate or other opening.

George aimed her mount right at the hedge.

Ivo's heart skittered, missing a beat, as her horse bunched its powerful hindquarters, muscles rippling under its glossy coat, and sailed over the fence. It hit the ground on the other side and galloped off without so much as a stumble, George still firmly in the saddle.

He wanted to haul her off her horse and beat her. He wanted to applaud.

Instead, he followed her over the hedge, putting himself into a two-point, correcting his balance to keep his seat. It would be just his luck to take a fall today and end up the butt of her two bulldogs' jokes.

He didn't like to think of himself as an overly proud man—not like his grandfather—but that would be more than flesh and blood could bear.

They didn't like him very much, her bulldogs. And they were not the least bit shy about making him understand that he was unwelcome. He didn't blame them. He knew what he wanted to do to her, with her, and he doubted they would approve. Whatever George was to the two of them—friend, lover, something in between—Ivo didn't care. It didn't make a bit of difference.

Ahead of him George and Bennett thundered across the field, followed closely by Brimstone and St. Audley. Ivo dropped his hands, giving his mount his head, and raced after them. The rest of the field trailed behind him, hooting and jeering as they urged their mounts on. They sailed over a particularly

sketchy rock wall, George giving a whoop of triumph
as she thundered on. Ivo shook his head. By all rights
she should have been flat on her back in the mud
long ago. Any other woman would have been.

As they rode across the field Lord Glendower called
to his daughter-in-law over the rock wall, taking her to
task. "You could have gone round, Georgianna," he
yelled.

Ivo found himself nodding in grim concurrence.
Not could have. She *should* have gone round. She
rode hard, too hard, took the highest jumps, the most
dangerous paths as though she had something to
prove.

Not in the common way.

That was how she'd been described when he'd first
met her. It was as true today as it had been then, but
for entirely different reasons.

George laughed off her father-in-law's chastise-
ment, calling back over her shoulder, "Pooh! You
know Hazard here would never fail me."

She glanced back over her shoulder, her eyes
meeting Dauntry's, inviting him to share her amuse-
ment. But he didn't seem to. No smile answered. Not
even a softening of the eyes. His mouth firmed, the
lower lip thinning in disapproval. George turned her
attention back to Hazard. She didn't require Dauntry's approval, but that look told her a world of
things he probably had no idea he'd revealed. If she
let him into her bed, gave him the vaguest rights to
her body, her time, her *person*, she'd open the door
to being ruled by his dictates.

She reined Hazard in as they approached a
thicket and the dogs disappeared into it, letting

their annoyance at having lost their quarry be loudly heard. The riders that were left gathered in a knot to watch and wait, steam rising off the horses. Everyone fidgeted in their saddles. Some adjusted their stirrup leathers, others retrieved flasks from pockets and passed them around. Their numbers had fallen off precipitously since they'd set off. Dozens had dwindled into a few.

Audley swung down from his mount and tapped George on the knee. She kicked her foot free of the stirrup and pulled her leg up so he could check the girth.

"All right and tight," he said, sliding his hand around her booted ankle and guiding her foot back into the stirrup.

George grinned. "Don't trust my groom?"

"Not at all. What I don't trust is that saddle of yours." He gave Hazard a pat on the rump and swung back into his own saddle. George sucked one cheek in between her teeth, bit down on it lightly, and watched him, still unsure exactly what he was up to. He and Brimstone had both been behaving strangely. Was the attraction between her and Dauntry so obvious?

A hand, unfashionably large, encased in York tan leather and possessing a large, white handkerchief, appeared before her. She glanced at the snowy white piece of linen, and then over at Dauntry. Laughter worked its way up her throat. She caught her lower lip between her teeth to stop it.

"Am I a mess?"

"I wouldn't go so far as—"

"Dreadful mess," Bennett cut in. "Got splatters all over your face, makes you look like you've got spots or something."

George glared at Bennett and accepted the handkerchief. She wiped her face, trying to ignore the fact that the neatly hemmed and monogrammed scrap of linen smelled of wool, tobacco, and bergamot. Of Dauntry. Her pulse sped. Her stomach gave a now familiar lurch as her senses strained toward him.

"Better?" she asked, batting her eyes at Bennett in imitation of the actresses at Drury Lane.

"Not so I can see. Now they're just sort of smeared." Bennett made a vague circular motion in front of his face with one hand.

She wiped again, scrubbing a bit harder. Why, she wasn't sure. It wasn't as if any of them looked any different, but she suddenly felt like the two-headed girl who'd been on display in London last year. It was unsettling. Out here it didn't matter how she looked. Or it never had in the past.

But today was different.

It was Dauntry looking at her with a slow boil behind his eyes. Brimstone treating her like a little girl, and St. Audley glowering like someone had snatched the last sticky bun out from under his nose. They were all treating her like a woman, and suddenly she felt out of place.

Damn them.

After one last swipe at her face she returned Dauntry's handkerchief. "Thank you, but I fear I'm beyond repair at the moment—"

She was interrupted by the sounding of the master's horn, calling the hounds back.

"They've lost him." She twisted in the saddle to look over her shoulder at the huntmaster. "Just as well. That's Sweeney Hall just over the rise, so we're not too far from the Turk's Head. And I, for one, am starving."

* * *

"So, Georgie, had your eye out for any aspiring wives for us?"

George raised one brow and stared St. Audley down as he took a seat beside her.

"You should know, Dauntry," the viscount continued, "that George here picks out all our wives. Or at least is called upon to give tacit approval before we're allowed to publish the banns."

"Audley." She gave her friend a stern, meaningful look, eager to defuse whatever confrontation he had in mind. "I'm not such a managing female as all that. You're thinking of Lady Morpeth. She's always swanning about with some little dab of a girl under her wing."

George took another bite of the excellent meat pie that had been served up by the Turk's Head and shook her head at her friend while she chewed and swallowed. Honestly. What was going on with Audley? He'd been shadowing her all day, and the hostility, cloaked in patently false friendliness, that was directed at Dauntry surprised her. She'd never seen the viscount behave like this. He'd even stood outside the door of the room the landlord had provided so she could wash her face. Clearly on guard.

"I tell one man that the chit he's just been dancing with is dumber than his spaniel, and I'm a managing matchmaker. Need I remind you that he did *ask* me what I thought of her? Just you wait," she added darkly. "When you fasten your attention on some hapless female, you'll be panting after me to tell you all about her. You know that women know all sorts of things about each other that you could never hope to hear about. Just as you all know things about men that women never hear about."

"Like what sorts of things?" Dauntry asked, his voice low, intent. George glanced over at him, a little flutter of awareness causing her stomach to turn over. She inhaled sharply and ignored it, even as her lips tingled with the memory of his.

Once. She repeated the word over and over in her head like a charm. Never more than once.

"Like that poor Mortley is in the basket again," she said, "though he's trying to keep it quiet. Hoping the Peabody chit will accept him before she gets wind of it. Or that Lawkes has had yet another *chère amie* decamp, leaving him with a scathing note attached, one hears, to a bawling brat. I think that makes three—brats, I mean—"

She was interrupted by Audley's roar of laughter.

"Where do you get your information?" the viscount demanded. "And I think Dauntry was really fishing for you to let us in on some of the secrets of your sex."

"Oh . . ." George smiled, trying to decide which bits of gossip to share. "You mean like that for all her prim and prissy ways, Miss Lydia Cross was caught in a *compromising* position with stupid but determined Ned Heath. Or that the notorious Mrs. Sheldon is taking an extended trip abroad, not because she's desolated by her husband's death, but because she's pregnant by her footman. Or Lord Jonathan Smythe, or the Prince of Wales. Which one is anyone's guess."

"Unfair, I say," the Earl of Morpeth began as he wandered back from the tap, a fresh mug of home brew in his hand.

"Unfair?" George cocked her head, amused.

"Unfair that I'm giving up my own sex, or that I'm doing so without you present?"

"Both, quite frankly," the earl answered. "It's unseemly for you to reveal the feminine mysteries to such unworthy persons as these," he added with mock severity, waving his hand at the younger men, flicking Brimstone with a bit of foam as he did so. Gabriel wiped his cheek with this sleeve and reached for his own glass.

George wrinkled her nose up at the earl, who tut-tutted in what George recognized as a fair imitation of his lady wife. He swallowed his pint in a single gulp, shoved his hat on, crushing the elegant arrangement of curls that made up his wig, and held out one hand imperiously.

"If you're finished enlightening the infantry, we should be on our way." He cocked his head toward the window. "It looks like rain."

Back outside, George couldn't but agree. Dark clouds were roiling on the horizon, coming on fast like the ranks of an approaching army. They even had their own drum and fife. A flash illuminated the sky in the far distance. Thunder rumbled. Away in the barn a dog barked, shrill and slightly hysterical.

In moments, everyone was mounted and cantering back toward the Court. Wind battered them, ripping hats from their heads, whipping George's hair into a tangled mass of knots. Occasional spatters of rain accosted them, enough to make the road dangerous, to numb fingers and toes, to occasionally penetrate the bower of the arching oaks which lined the three-mile drive to the house. As they rode beneath the trees, man and beast's breath fogging with each exhalation, George began to feel larger and more frequent drops.

Lightning crackled overhead, illuminating the cloud-induced gloom in a startling flash. A thunderclap exploded overhead. Behind her someone else's horse whinnied in protest. George flexed her frozen hands and blew the sodden feather that adorned her hat out of her eyes.

Dauntry was close on her right, spattered in mud, his coat already discolored at the shoulders, red turning the deeper color of dried blood as the rain soaked slowly downward.

As they clattered into the open stable yard, the heavens opened in an icy deluge. She shook her head, throwing wet hair back, her teeth beginning to chatter as the heavy rain soaked her to the skin. The yard was awash in running grooms, their shouts mingling with the sharp ring of metal shoes on stone and the deafening boom of thunder that George could feel vibrate through her whole body.

A groom took hold of Hazard's bridle, causing him to shy slightly. George kicked herself free from stirrup and horn and turned to find Dauntry standing silently beside her. Rain sheeted down, as though they stood below a waterfall. His hands rose, waiting.

Her chest seized as his hands closed around her waist. He lifted her from the saddle, guided her down to her feet. His strength—in his arms, in his body—was clearly on display. He didn't allow her to fall, prey to gravity, or even to slide. He was in perfect control. As though she weighed no more than a child.

Dauntry's eyes met hers, storm-dark, pupils indistinguishable. He blinked, dashing rain from his eyes. Droplets spilling from his lashes. She couldn't look away. Couldn't move.

Hazard bumped her as the groom led him away,

knocking her into Dauntry. With a crack of laughter she spun and ran for the house. She was halfway up the second flight of servants' stairs when Dauntry caught her. A hand latched onto her skirts, the sound of threads popping loud as the thunder outside. He took one last step, till he was even with her on the stairs, and held her pinned there.

George pressed herself back against the wall, overwhelmingly crowded in the narrow stairwell. Her wet skirts clung to her legs, weighing her down. Water flowed off them, rivulets becoming a stream as they joined and rushed down the stairs.

Dauntry was every bit as wet. His shirt and cravat were more than wilted. They drooped, revealing the strong column of his neck, the cluster of large freckles normally hidden there, like the secret birthmark of a fairytale prince.

George pushed back farther, denying the urge to lean in, set her lips to his bare throat. To leave her own brand there. Her own secret mark.

He let go of her skirts. Raised the hand that held her in place to brush the drooping feathers out of her eyes. He followed the line of her head, sliding his hand around to cup her nape. Held her securely, softly, as though she were fragile.

His lips captured hers in a kiss equally as gentle. Lips molding to hers. Hot tongue easing apart her cold lips, questing inside for a response. His hand curled into her hair and the other slid up her rib cage to cup her breast, his thumb finding her nipple through layers of clinging wool and binding stays. It slid back and forth, sending jolt after jolt of pure need to lodge in her belly, to make her thighs strain, and the secret place between her legs throb.

His head tilted as he slanted his mouth over hers.

She opened her own, tongue meeting his with all the fervor of desire denied, fobbed off, and ignored until it rises up like a swollen river and sweeps everything out of its way.

The sound of feet rushing up the lower stairs broke them apart. Brought her down with a lurch. George ducked under Dauntry's arm and fled up the stairs.

Could she really settle for having him only once? And if she couldn't, where would that leave her?

Safe in her room, she rang the bell for her maid and began to struggle out of her sopping clothes while she waited for the girl to appear. Wet wool pooled on the floor. Finally she stood in shift and stays, boots still on, unable to undress any further without assistance.

Her mastiff raised his head from where he lounged on her bed, his immense bulk taking up most of the available space.

"'lo, Caesar. How's my boy?"

His tail thumped, like a fist punching the bedding, but he didn't move to join her by the fire. Lazy beast.

George combed her fingers through her hair, pulling at tangles. Even after a drenching, her hair smelled of horse, and she knew she had a fresh layer of mud on her face.

She rubbed at a streak of mud on her hand, then chuckled as her maid arrived and she was stripped and bundled into a warm, quilted wrapper. Quite a pretty state for seduction, soaking wet and muddied to the brow. She put her hands out toward the fire and waited for the bath to be filled.

The hot water stung—nearly unbearable against frozen toes and fingers—as she climbed into the great marble tub in the adjoining room. It engulfed her in relaxing warmth as she sank below the waters, grateful for the current earl's renovations which allowed such easy luxury. There was simply something sensual, almost sexual, about being immersed in hot water, especially in a tub big enough for two.

George ran a soapy sponge over her breasts, down her belly. What was the worst that could have happened if she'd invited Dauntry to join her? If it were Dauntry's hand holding the sponge as it moved across her skin . . . George tossed the sponge away and sank below the water, rinsing her hair. That was not a safe fantasy.

She scrubbed the scent of horse out of her hair with jasmine soap and soaked until the water became tepid. Once out, her maid helped to dry her with towels warmed by the fire, then assisted her back into her wrapper. The slide of heavy silk felt wonderful against clean damp skin.

There was nothing planned for the rest of the day. The other guests were likely downstairs playing billiards, or attempting to cheat one another at cards.

Whatever they were up to, she wasn't in the mood for it. So she simply sat in her window seat while her hair dried, absently reading a novel, watching the gardeners prepare the flowerbeds for winter. Running that surprising kiss over and over in her head.

It had been a long time since a man had truly surprised her. And this one inspired a need no other man ever had. Not even her husband had been able to make her flush with desire with no more than a softening of the eyes. She winced at the disloyalty of the thought, true as it was.

Finally the dinner bell rang. She shook off her daydreams and got up to change, choosing a gown of bronze tobine with an extremely low neckline. Tonight she'd leave the fichu off. Nothing but a sea of skin from the fly fringe edging of the bodice that barely concealed her areolas.

It would do perfectly.

Once she'd changed and allowed her maid to re-arrange her now clean curls, she made her way down the hall to join the others.

She'd been placed in her usual suite of rooms on the first floor, at the end of the long gallery that housed the family portraits. On her way down the long hall she paused in front of the painting of Lyon and his older brother, Sydney, Viscount Layton, done when they were both in their teens. She'd teased them both unmercifully when their mother had proudly displayed it for the first time.

The brothers didn't look all that much alike, for which she was profoundly grateful. She didn't think she could stand to be constantly confronted with a living, breathing copy of Lyon. He might not have in-spired the same wanton heat that Dauntry did, but that didn't mean she hadn't loved him. He'd been the boy all her childhood fancies had rested upon. A love like that was special, not something to be found twice in a lifetime. Hell, most of the world failed to find it even the once.

Sydney was a harmonious blend of his parents: his father's sandy hair, his mother's brown eyes, his profile clearly bearing the rather aquiline stamp of his mother's family. Lyon, with his white-blond hair and his patrician nose, had been his paternal grandfather reborn.

George paused before old Simon Exley's portrait, too. He'd sat for it at the height of his strength and power. His wig tumbled magnificently over his shoul-ders, past lavish embroidery and a fortune in lace.

Here she could see the Lyon that could have been, *should* have been.

Tonight she simply stared up at the painting. A sudden constriction in her chest—a painful hollowness, like a bubble was forming inside her lungs—prevented her from drawing a full breath.

She wasn't supposed to have to contend with romances and intrigues at her age. She was six-and-twenty, for pity's sake! She was supposed to be living contentedly at Malvern Abbey with a bevy of rambunctious children and a doting, besotted husband. Instead, she was left with his doting family and a house in town constantly awash with rambunctious gentlemen and town beaux of every stamp.

She'd become one of the dowagers without ever having noticed. God, how had she come to this?

She frowned, pinching the bridge of her nose, blinking back tears. Disgusted with the morbid train of her thoughts, George turned away from the portraits and hurried down the hall.

With an ocean of wood, silver, and china between him and George, not to mention a large and extremely ugly epergne which almost entirely blocked his view of her, Ivo struggled to eat his dinner, to give the semblance of participating in the conversation taking place around him. Mostly he made do with monosyllabic replies and appropriately placed "Hmms."

The first two courses passed in a haze. Dish after dish consumed without tasting. Wine drunk without noticing. His cup emptying and refilling as if by magic.

He hated watching George being entertained by

her friends. In fact, he plain hated her friends. Especially that one. Brimstone. A golden-skinned, almond-eyed prince right out of a popular novel.

Bennett had said she never granted a man more nights in her bed than he could win with the roll of a die. But that didn't fit with her obvious closeness with Mr. Gabriel Angelstone, or with the Viscount St. Audley's overly possessive displays. They both acted as if they owned her.

She laughed, deep, throaty—a courtesan's laugh—drawing the entire table's attention to her. He narrowed his eyes, glancing quickly down the table before forcing his attention back to his dinner. He took a forkful of the roast pheasant and chewed it methodically. It might as well have been wood.

She'd come into the drawing room before dinner on Brimstone's arm, wearing the most outrageous dress he'd seen her in yet. Her entire chest and shoulders were exposed, her breasts pushed up to form a magnificent mounded display. It wasn't a dress. It was like a curio cabinet, designed specifically to call attention to the item on display. The spray of freckles on her left breast disappeared into the bodice like the dotted path on a treasure map, distracting him from the conversation taking place around him.

She'd stayed on Brimstone's arm until dinner had been announced, laughing loudly at whatever story he'd been regaling their small circle with. She hadn't come near him, hadn't so much as glanced his way that he could tell. It rankled.

As it was probably supposed to.

It made him want to do something outrageous. Something provoking. Something that would force her to acknowledge him and the fact that only hours before his hand had been cupping her breast, his thumb caressing her taut nipple, and she'd been kissing him for all she was worth.

Tomorrow the party would be over. George would return to London. He would return to Ashcombe Park, where he would attempt again to be the dutiful grandson. The worthy son.

Tomorrow he was going to have to put this nonsense behind him.

She stared up at him, brown-eyed like a cow and nearly as intelligent. Her mouth hung open, exposing straight teeth that were unfortunately stained and yellowed.

Philippe Lévis buttoned his breeches, choking down the bile that rose at the back of his throat. Why had he come along to her rooms? A tenner seemed an exorbitant amount to pay for that slack mouth.

He ran a hand over his waistcoat, smoothing the pile of the velvet. She'd disturbed it with her sweaty peasant's hands. Crushed it, wrinkled it into whorls.

His jaw clenched, teeth grinding. The room stank of dust, dirty linen, and sex. It overpowered him in waves.

Blissfully mute, she got up off her knees, the floorboards protesting as her weight shifted, and stepped away from him, swinging her hips like the whore she was. He stood, smoothed his waistcoat again. There was no fixing it. Heat flashed though him, far more rewarding than the sham of a release she'd just coaxed out of him.

His waistcoat would have to be steamed and brushed, which meant he'd have to go home and change before going out.

Damn her. The sloppy pig.

She stepped closer, ran one of her grubby hands up his chest, further abusing the velvet. The stench of cheap perfume swamped him, nearly making him gag.

He reached out, cupping her face between his hands. Her skin was clammy, sheened with sweat. She smiled, that soft, seductive smile all women used when they thought they had the upper hand, then frowned, confusion written all over her stupid face as he locked his hands around her throat and squeezed.

He was doing the gentlemen of London a favor.

If only this was the bitch responsible for his father's death, or his whore of a mother . . . but his mother was already dead and the cunt who'd killed his father was safe at her family's country estate.

The little peasant whore struggled as wildly as a wolf caught in a leg trap. Her hands pulled his hair, broken nails scratching his face. He held on, forced her back onto the bed where she plied her trade, and used his weight to hold her down until her hands went limp and the light faded from her eyes.

He climbed off her, pulled his handkerchief from the pocket of the coat he'd draped over the back of the chair, and carefully wiped his hands. Perhaps he'd not go home and change after all? A drink with friends and a bit of courtly flirtation seemed just the thing to cleanse his palate.

He took his time putting himself to rights. It wouldn't do to appear mussed, or to walk down the dank stairs that led to the street with undue haste. When his wig was perfectly arranged, his coat lying smoothly across his shoulders, and his hat tucked under his arm, he plucked a coin from his pocket and laid it on the rough table beside the bed.

He descended the steps with the quick, jaunty step of a well-satisfied customer, heels knocking smartly on the wooden stairs.

He had places to be. He had things to do. He had an appointment with vengeance.

Chapter 5

*Alas, we have been unable to learn the identity of Lord
S—'s supposed companion. But never despair, we will
continue the hunt . . .*

Tête-à-Tête, 12 October 1788

· It was a perfect autumn day. The sun was bright
and the air crisp, holding the clean scent that always
follows rain. The storm had blown itself out early and
the roads had already dried. Only a few puddles remained, dotting the long stretch of road that led to
town.

George took a deep breath, turned her mount out
of the brick and iron gates of Winsham Court, and
urged him into a canter.

Dauntry had taken his leave of them all the night
before. He'd worn an almost comical expression.
Regret, mingled with frustrated desire, and an un-
derlying sense of something she couldn't quite put
her finger on . . . anger? Disgust? Relief? He was

returning to Ashcombe Park and all the inherent responsibilities that awaited him there.

He'd been very clear about it after dinner, making sure she overheard. Whether his declaration had been for her benefit or his own she couldn't be sure. He'd sounded like he was trying to convince himself. But would desire or duty win out? Would he turn up on her doorstep?

Would he tamely acquiesce to her rule? Somehow she couldn't quite picture him agreeing, if only because he appeared to dislike being dictated to. Much as she did herself.

She missed having a man in her bed. Not enough to give up her independence, but suddenly the need was acute enough to consider the rather drastic step of breaking her rule and taking a lover in every sense of the word.

Dauntry had ripped away the blanket of numbness she'd carefully shrouded herself in, leaving her painfully awake to the world of sensual possibilities. It had been impossible to give in at Winsham Court, surrounded by her friends and family, but on the wider stage of London?

God, she hoped Dauntry didn't really mean to mire himself in the country.

With her maid and Caesar safely off the previous night in one of her father-in-law's smaller coaches, George was able to follow on horseback. She'd be made welcome at St. Neots with a private room, her own sheets, and a well-stocked cellar. Heaven. All reached without the damnable confinement of a coach.

Several hours later, George pulled her horse up short and smiled over her shoulder at Catton, her late husband's tiger. Behind him, the two armed grooms her father-in-law insisted upon also reined in.

In the middle of the road was a curricle. Absent one wheel, it lolled drunkenly to one side. In front stood a gentleman in a dark greatcoat fighting to keep his horses still while unraveling their traces.

Dauntry. The mere sight of him set her pulse racing. The hint of cheekbone visible above the high collar of his coat, the sureness of his hands as they calmed the horses. Hands that had touched her with every bit as much power and grace.

It felt like a sign, encountering him again so soon.

"I think we're about to play knight errant," she announced quietly, motioning for the grooms to follow her.

"I say, Dauntry," she called out, setting her mount in motion, "you *could* use some help, couldn't you?"

His head snapped up, a flush on his cheeks. George bit her lip to keep from smiling. He might forgive teasing, but outright laughter just might be too much for his pride to swallow. No man liked to be caught out in such a manner. And she had plans for this one. Tonight. One night. Alone on the road home, no chance of repetition. The circumstances were perfect.

"The wheel's come off," he replied, his tone deeply disgusted, "but I don't think either of the horses was hurt."

Catton leapt down, the skirts of his coat flying out. He carelessly dropped his mount's reins and hurried to assist with the daunting task of unhitching the horses and extracting them from the tangled web of harness and rein. While Dauntry held both horses by the bridle, Catton went over the team with quick, expert hands.

Even from several feet away George could hear Catton crooning to them, hands and voice soothing, reassuring. Letting them know it was all right to calm down.

The leader dropped his head, resting his beautifully dished forehead against Dauntry's chest. Dauntry's face softened momentarily, the tightness leaving his mouth. He let go of the bridle and moved his hand up to scratch the sensitive place behind the gelding's ear.

"They'll do very well, my lord," Catton announced, patting the second horse firmly on the rump, "though I think this one might have strained a hock. It'll bear watching."

George surveyed the scene from the saddle. She could get down and help, but she suspected her assistance would only provoke or embarrass him. It was probably irritating enough to be forced to accept the help of other men.

Once the horses were tied off at the side of the road, the two outriders dismounted and attempted to drag the curricle out of the road. They heaved up the wheel-less side of the carriage, the screech of protesting wood and metal making Talavera's ears swivel and flick. George stroked his neck, leather glove slicking over silken hide, and he settled.

With Dauntry and Catton pushing, the road was quickly cleared and the curricle deposited far enough off to the side to be out of harm's way. The carriage collapsed with a groan. A layer of mud and dust decorated its otherwise pristine finish.

"So what's to do now?" George asked.

"It's a good five miles farther to Oundale, but I think I can ride one of the carriage horses in."

"Nonsense. Tom and Henry can double up and

you can take one of their mounts. Even if they are broken to saddle, no one—and certainly not a man of your size—should be on them until you've had a chance to inspect them more thoroughly."

Dauntry accepted her solution with obvious relief, but he was still stiff with mortification. Tom waited for the other men to mount, then handed the reins of the leader to Catton, and those of its mate to Dauntry. The horses disposed of, he scrambled up behind Henry and the party set off for Oundale.

It was considerably later in the day than George had anticipated when they reached Oundale. Even now her maid was probably awaiting her, hot water roiling over the fire in preparation for her bath. Maeve wouldn't worry overmuch at her absence, however; she would merely think her mistress had delayed her departure from the Court another day or so, or had changed her mind and gone off to the races at Newmarket.

It wouldn't be the first time George had failed to turn up as planned.

Dauntry helped her down from her horse before the most reputable-looking of the town's three inns. His hands lingered on her waist for an extra beat, just long enough for her to feel the urge to lean into him. Before she could make such a show of herself he let go and turned to lead her inside.

She was relieved to find a decent hostelry at hand. The Gryphon had no aspirations to a tonnish clientele, but it was clean, with a private parlor unbespoken, and the warm, homey smell of fresh bread filling the taproom.

When the landlord bustled out, Dauntry carefully explained that he and his sister had had an accident, and they would be requiring two rooms for themselves, and one for their servants, as well as the private parlor and dinner, all of which the proprietor was only too happy to provide.

Sister, was it? George bit her lips to subdue her smile. Wife would have made everything so much simpler.

Her stomach tuned queasy. Perhaps he'd changed his mind.

Lord, how he'd wanted to say *wife*.

The thought tortured him as he made his way back from the blacksmith's. *My wife and I will be needing a room.* But at the actual moment, the eager publican smiling up at him, face shiny with sweat from the kitchen, it had been *sister*, and *two rooms* that had come out of his mouth.

As he neared the inn, he found George wandering up the street, a package wrapped in brown paper tucked under one arm. There was a hint of smug satisfaction in her expression.

"What on earth could you have found to tempt you in Oundale?"

"Not as many things as I should like, I assure you," she replied. "Tooth powder and brush, a comb, and a clean pair of stockings. That's all my little package contains. I should certainly be happier if it were a larger package with a nightdress and a set of slippers in it. But as my grandmother used to say, there's no use wishing for a lantern when you've got the moon. What does the blacksmith say about your curricle?"

Ivo stared at her, felled by the simple thought of her lack of a nightdress. She could sleep in her chemise, of course, but the idea of it was illicit and immediately erotic. Subtle as a Rowlandson print.

Why had he said *sister*?

He blew out a quick breath and forced himself to reply. "He's sent a boy out after the wheel and my trunk. I should be ready to go in a day or two at most, a large sum serving to inconvenience those who by rights should be ahead of me."

George laughed and tucked her free arm into his, carefree as a child. Ivo swallowed thickly and tried not to think about the warmth of her hand seeping through his sleeve, about the way her hip brushed his as they walked, about the jasmine scent of her hair.

He tried not to think at all. It was safer that way.

Dinner, when it was finally served, was simple country fare: mutton stew, full of carrots and parsnips, with soda bread and ale. For dessert, the landlord offered up a pear tart as he cleared the dishes and set the maid to stoking the fire.

When the pie was gone and their glasses full of the surprisingly good burgundy the landlord produced from his cellars, George pulled a slightly greasy deck of cards from the top drawer of the side table their dinner had been served upon, and suggested a game of écarté. She dealt the cards out, and collecting her hand, assumed such a devilish imitation of Bennett that Ivo went off in a peal of laughter.

"You are far too wicked a woman to be a sister of mine."

"I am the creature I was raised to be," she replied, cocking one brow up provocatively.

"Yes. I suppose you are."

He studied her in the candlelight. What was she, really? He still hadn't figured that out, and at that moment it seemed less important than ever. Whatever she was, he wanted her.

She was still wearing her riding attire, as was he, but she had removed her wisp of a cravat, and her shirt hung open at the neck, her slight dishabille somehow far more indecent than the low-cut dresses he'd seen her in nearly every night for the past week. The fitted bodice left little to his imagination. He shifted uncomfortably in the inn's hard chair, acutely aware of the sudden constriction of his breeches.

He lost hand after hand, only winning occasionally by sheer luck. Every breath she took was a distraction. The swell of her breasts rising like the waves of an incoming tide.

He couldn't keep his cards straight, couldn't form the strategy of his game. He just sat there, picturing her naked. Trying to come up with reasons that would keep them both at the Gryphon indefinitely: the sudden illness of her groom, a lame horse, a freakishly early snowstorm.

It was hard to remember that a world existed outside of this room. Nothing mattered except what was going on behind those amazing eyes of hers.

After winning yet another hand, George gave him a sleepy smile, collected the cards, and shuffled then back into a stack. "You must be exhausted," she said before polishing off her drink, "for your mind's not at all on the cards."

She tied the deck up with the string and paper they'd come in, then rose and crossed the room, returning the cards to the drawer they'd come from.

Ivo stood, somewhat clumsily. He was a trifle foxed, and trying not to appear too eager. He had to do this just right, or she'd bolt. One chance. That was what fate had given him.

He paused, one hand on the doorknob, and looked down at her. Her eyes were slightly unfocused. As he took a last step toward her, she smiled tremulously, and put one hand up to his chest to clutch his waistcoat. Her fingertips hooked over the edge to nestle between the thick silk of his waistcoat and the fine linen of his shirt.

His struggle to formulate a plan was wholly given up under that tiny encroachment. He let go of the knob and pulled her to him, groaning as she slid her other arm up around his neck, tilting her face up and offering him her lips.

Oh, yes. She was going to make it easy . . .

She flicked her tongue over his lips, parted her mouth to meet his returning thrust. Ivo caged her, turned her so her back was against the door, moved his hands slowly down until they gripped her hips. He deepened the kiss, tongue stroking, filling her mouth. He'd spent too many nights recently picturing this, and she was every bit as willing as he'd ever hoped or dreamed. Suddenly she was the siren without the rocky coast.

Breaking off their kiss, he slid one arm securely about her waist and turned the handle of the door. He wanted to be upstairs, in one of the large, sturdy beds. Now.

She didn't move when he tugged her toward him. He paused and looked down at her, captured again by the clear wing of her brows, the sculptural purity of her nose, the enticing bow of her top lip.

"Once," she said, that same lip blooming out, forming the word as though she were puckering for a kiss. "Just this one night."

Ivo let go of the handle and pressed her back against the door. "What?" He struggled to make sense of her statement. Surely she couldn't mean—

"One night, Dauntry. That's all I ever allow."

"No."

She stiffened slightly. Her eyes shuttered. She put one hand up to his chest and pushed him back a fraction of an inch.

"No?"

She looked honestly perplexed.

"No," he repeated, pressing close again, his erection riding against her belly. One night had been all he'd been after, what he'd thought it would take to appease his pride, but hearing her dictate it in that condescending manner angered him. "Six years, George. That's what I gave up for you. One night doesn't come close to compensating me for that."

"Compensating you?" Her eyes flashed, anger bubbling up, making the depths sparkle. "Tonight isn't—"

"Six nights. One night for every year." He cupped her jaw, ran his thumb along her cheek, savored the softness of her skin, the slight tremble of her whole body in response to the caress. He leant in, setting a hot, open-mouthed kiss to the delicate skin just below her ear. "You owe me at least that much."

"One."

"No." He bit her softly on the neck, teeth grazing flesh until she shivered, pressed closer.

"Three. I've never given anyone that."

"No." He rolled his head past hers, brushing her chin with his before tonguing her earlobe on the neglected side. She wilted back against the door, breath shuddering out of her.

"Six," she said weakly.

"Six." He kissed her hard, crushing her mouth beneath his. "Six nights, whenever and wherever I say, and you're not to offer any other man so much as a kiss until our bargain is complete."

"What makes you think I want you badly enough to agree?"

Ivo just smiled and kissed her again. She was down to nothing but sheer bravado. Her whole body had begun to tremble.

"Just tell me no, then." He pulled back slightly, just enough for the cold air of the room to rush between them, to dispel the warmth of his body against hers. "Send me off to sleep alone."

"Damn you," she said, her hand locked onto his lapel.

"Too late," he replied as he dragged open the door and half carried her up the stairs, too deeply in the moment to care who might be about to see them.

George paused as she opened the door to her room, locking eyes with him over her shoulder for just a moment, a challenging glint in her eyes. She was angry. Oh, yes, she was. But she was also every bit as excited as he was.

Angry wasn't a problem.

He shoved her into the room and fumbled behind his back for the lock. The fire was lit, lending a dull glow to the room. A single candle burned behind glass on the mantel.

The lock snicked audibly in the quiet room and she put one hand out to him, beckoning him to her. She grabbed hold of his hand, her grip strong and true, and pulled him toward the bed, never taking her eyes from his.

Her familiar wicked smile was back in place as she pushed him down onto the bed and leaned forward to kiss him. His favorite smile. The one that always seemed to imply some shared secret.

"Time to take your boots off," she whispered, sliding off him to kneel at the bedside.

Ivo lay back and stuck one foot out, riveted as she gripped his boot—one hand at the toe, one cupping the heel—and firmly tugged it off. She cocked one brow at him and he put his other foot out, laughing quietly as she wiped her prints off his boots with the skirt of her habit, ever the conscious Corinthian's lady.

When his boots were off, she unbuttoned his breeches at the knee, carefully removed his stockings, rolling the fine cotton down his calves and tugging it off over his toes. She ran one hand along his calf, fingers delving up under his breeches, sweeping lightly over the back of his knee. His cock throbbed, straining against his breeches. Her hand skimmed back down, circling his ankle, nails caressing bone and tendon.

Crouched there, she gave him an assessing look before she tossed his stockings over her shoulder and stood. Lifting her skirts slightly, she slid one knee onto the bed and swayed forward, climbing over him.

With her hands on his chest, she pushed him all the way down into the bedding, draped herself over him, one hand trailing almost absently down his chest, over the bulge so clearly evident beneath the fall of his breeches.

Ivo hissed as her hand cupped him, then moved up to grip his hip, thumb pressing down into the sensitive groove just below his hip bone.

Even as her hands explored, George continued kissing him, teasing him with her tongue, her lips, her breath, until he impatiently started tugging at her bodice. She smothered a laugh with one hand as he yanked, prodded, and poked, reminding him almost sternly that she was wearing all the clothes she had in the world, and if he ripped them she'd have to go about naked like Lady Godiva.

"That was rather the point," he growled, finally getting the last button undone. The room suddenly seemed too still, too quiet. She rolled off him and sat up before removing her coat. Ivo smiled suddenly, rising from the bed. He began pulling off his own clothes in a mad dash, only to realize that George hadn't continued to undress. She was just lounging there, almost fully clothed, watching him. The skirt of her habit had ridden up, revealing stocking-clad calves and one bare thigh that glowed in the dim light, pale as a marble statue. Her coat was splayed open, her sheer habit shirt revealing a pair of short stays—and her breasts. Her areolas just visible through the fabric in the dim light.

Ivo caught his breath, watching her watching him. Her languid pose was alluring. Erotic, even. And it wasn't an act; this was simply George. Bold as a queen, sure of herself, and she wanted him. Wanted him so badly she'd agreed to his earlier demands. Agreed to break her rule.

He slipped the buttons at the neck of his shirt, yanked it over his head, and threw it onto the floor before making a dive for her, wrestling and pulling until they were both breathless. He tossed her heavy skirt onto the floor. Struggled with her boots, sent them flying, deaf to the loud thump as they hit the floor.

He tugged at the tie to her short stays. "Damn." George muffled laughter with a pillow.

"You defy the rules in every other way," he protested with annoyance, trying to figure out how to unwrap the convoluted undergarment. "Why wear this?"

He got the tie undone, the long strings unwinding from around her rib cage. George slapped at his hands, reaching up and pulling the shoulders off, allowing the two pieces of the stays to fall away from her. She slid them down her arms and tossed them aside.

Ivo kept telling himself to go slow. To savor every moment. Regardless of what might transpire in the future, they'd never have another first night together and he wanted to remember every moment, wanted her to remember every moment.

He'd waited far too long to rush like a green boy.

But it just wasn't turning out to be that kind of night. He couldn't even remember exactly how he'd gotten out of his coat, or what had become of her habit shirt.

Once her stays were off, she pulled her thin chemise over her head and smiled invitingly up at him as she settled back into the pillows, naked and not at all shy about it.

He tried to steady his breathing, to inhale and exhale slowly though his nose, but that only made him acutely aware of the scent of George's perfume, musk and jasmine. Intoxicating.

She was even more beautiful than he'd ever imagined. Ever dreamed. Round and strong, with high full breasts and a coppery shadow between her thighs. She lay back and let him look as long as he liked, one hand idly playing with a curl at the nape of her neck. She had clearly defined muscles in her legs and arms and just the smallest swell of belly begging to be nuzzled.

She displayed all the classical softness, the womanly curves that he'd always found so alluring on a woman, but in a more refined form. His mistresses had always had always been Junoesque: lushly curved, soft. The lady before him appeared more like a Greek statue of Diana: young, athletic, endlessly challenging.

She reached out with one leg and hooked her foot behind him, pulling him down to her. Imperious. Demanding. A goddess in truth.

Ivo groaned and kissed her, one hand cupping her breast, palm filled with warm flesh. Making love to George had been his plan all along. Having George make love to him was something else entirely. It was the single most amazing thing he'd ever encountered. How had any man ever settled for a single night? How could anyone give this up?

"I think it's time for these to go." She deftly unbuttoned his breeches and slid them down, first with her hands, and then with her foot, hooking her big toe into the waistband and shoving them down. Ivo struggled to pull his feet out without breaking their kiss.

Her hand slipped down his belly and he gasped, letting his breath out with a hiss as her fingers lightly brushed his shaft, ran up and down its length, circled its head. Reverent, careful, but sure.

George let her hands roam, reveling in Dauntry's reactions to her softest caress. A nail traced lazily along his hip bone and he was shaking. He would go still, not even daring to breathe, each time she touched him.

Curious how far she could push him, she rolled him over gently onto his back, placed a string of kisses, blazing a trail. She placed one open-mouthed kiss to the spot on his neck that had so intrigued her, biting down lightly, savoring the way his head fell back farther as she did so and the way he said her name: half-gasp, half-growl.

Moving lower, she laved his nipples. Bit one hard enough to make him twitch. Ran her tongue down the grooves of his stomach.

He had more scars than the one he'd earned that night in Paris. A long silver scar ran across one pectoral and down along his ribs. Another cut across one thigh. Accidents in the *salle*? Bandits in the Pyrenees? Angry Italian husbands?

She wanted to know.

Wanted the details behind every nick and scratch. How had he passed the last six years? Had he been sorry to leave someone behind in Italy?

She wanted to know, and that disturbed her. He'd already got her to break her inviolate rule. To promise far more than she ever had before. He'd demanded, and she'd given in on every point. Wanton. How had he known she'd agree? That was the humiliating part: that he'd been so sure of her.

A shudder ran though him as she carefully moved his foreskin up and down his shaft, drawing it up over the head of his penis and then pushing it back down. Such a small action to provoke so large a reaction.

She studied his face, cataloging his reactions, taking note of what caused him to writhe and what brought him to quivering attention. He might have won the battle, but she was going to win the war. She was going to leave him a broken man. A wreck. Wretched and pining.

After a few moments of teasing she leaned forward and ran her tongue along the beautifully defined line of his hip. He clenched up, all the muscles in his stomach tightening. His cock twitched and thickened, demanding attention.

George smiled to herself and slid her body down between his legs, nestling into the bedding, and took him into her mouth. Men were so easy . . .

Chapter 6

Lord G——'s party has at last come to an end. We wait with bated breath to see which of the earl's many guests may have become Mrs. E——'s latest conquest.

Tête-à-Tête, 12 October 1788

Ivo swallowed convulsively as the room swam before his eyes. When it righted itself, he stared down at George, watching her mouth move over him, every nuance of lip, tongue, and teeth exquisite. Torturous. Divine.

He shut his eyes and tried to relax back into the pillows, wanting her never to stop, desperately wanting to feel her under him at the same time. This he'd certainly never forget. And she owed him five more nights . . .

When he could take no more, he reached down, locked one quivering hand in her hair, and dragged her up. Her face was alight with mischief and Ivo knew he himself was grinning like an idiot. Sex had never been fun. Not in this way. It had never been an entertaining romp.

He rolled her under him and crushed her mouth beneath his, skimming one hand down her side to her knee and then up between her legs.

She gave up a small sigh and eased her legs apart, opening fully to him as his fingers roamed about her curls. He parted her carefully, running callused fingers down into the warm valley until he found the sensitive peak hidden at its crest.

He circled his finger, teasing until she was shuddering, unable to hold still any longer. Used his chest and shoulder to hold her down. She didn't really want to get away. She was just startlingly responsive. Unbelievably willing. When she began to gasp for breath he removed his hand and slid quickly into the cradle created by her parted thighs.

He eased into her, watching her face, thrilling as she took a shuddering breath and tilted herself to accommodate him more fully. Slick heat enveloped him. Made him want to lose himself in her, to simply, selfishly fuck. Instead he moved slowly, grinding into her, riding until George wrapped her legs around him, sank her teeth into his shoulder, her nails into his back.

With a growl, he increased the pace of his thrusts, driving himself into her. She threw back her head. Pressed the heel of one hand into her mouth. He was so close to finishing it was all he could think of. A litany. *Not yet. Not yet. Not yet.*

George gave a strangled sob, shaking violently as she came, clenching around him again and again, the sensation dragging him toward his own release. She arched one last time and buried her face in the hollow of his neck.

Ivo thrust in as deeply as possible. Harder. Faster. Until his own climax took him. Pulled him down into near unconsciousness. He slumped heavily atop her, lost in the throbbing damp heat where they were joined.

Feeling her legs tremble against him, Ivo smiled into her shoulder. God, he loved that tremble, the unmistakable sign of a well-satisfied woman. He nuzzled the delicate skin where her ear met her neck and she made a contented little noise.

He rolled off her and pulled her roughly into his arms. "I've been picturing this for what seems like forever."

"Me, too," George confided, curling up against him. She pillowed her head on his chest, one finger lazily circling his nipple. "So I guess I *am* far too wicked a woman to be a sister of yours." She sat up slightly and kissed him again, lingeringly, then settled into his arms, shut her eyes, and seemed to immediately fall asleep.

Ivo couldn't imagine how she could drop off so quickly, but she did. He lay there for what seemed like hours, watching her, his head swimming with plans. Five more nights was simply not going to be enough.

Dauntry's head lifted from the pillow as George shut the door to the adjoining room. His hair slid over his shoulder in a tousled mess, curls twisting down into the shadow of the bedclothes. She shivered and hurried toward the bed, the icy floor making each step almost painful.

It was still dark outside, but the nearly full moon was blazing through the window, illuminating everything in shades of blue and gray. She grinned as Dauntry pulled back the covers and she slipped into the warm bed. Perhaps she should be embarrassed to be caught parading about in the nude, but what was the point? Dauntry had done far more intimate things to her than simply gaze upon her unclothed form.

She kissed him and snuggled into his side, laughing as he winced and pulled away from her cold feet. This was the kind of moment she missed more than anything, the small exchanges in the night, the closeness of simply sleeping with a man, the comfort of it. This sweet domesticity was far more dangerous to her rules than any mere bedding, no matter how skillful the lover.

"Gods, woman!"

George burrowed closer, sliding her hand up his thigh. "I just thought it would be wiser if no one walked in and found that you hadn't used your bed, brother dear."

He chuckled and rubbed his face into her hair, one warm hand pulling her closer. George slid her leg up over his hip possessively.

Ivo tossed George up into the saddle and glumly accepted that she was, in fact, leaving. She'd been remarkably cheerful and friendly all morning, and it made him oddly furious. He could feel a knot of resentment coiled in his belly, made worse by his knowledge that his reaction to her departure was ridiculous and unreasonable. She was expected. Her maid was probably already worried. She had to go.

When the inn's maid-of-all-work had knocked on the door, asking if she needed assistance getting dressed, George had shoved him out of her bed and into his own room, pressing herself to him for one last, hurried kiss before shutting the connecting door.

By the time he'd shaved, struggled into his coat, and finished tying his cravat he found that George had already gone down to the parlor and ordered their breakfast.

She looked clean and fresh. As though she'd had all her baggage and the service of a dozen personal maids.

He, on the other hand, looked pretty much as he felt: slightly crushed and disarranged. He didn't need the murky mirror in his room to tell him that. He'd nicked himself shaving—something he hadn't done in years—and not a single cravat had been willing to bend to his will.

She'd eaten her eggs and toast and chatted amiably throughout the meal, steering the conversation masterfully to politics and the latest power struggle between Tories and the Whigs. When she'd finished her tea, she'd risen, slapped her gloves in the palm of one hand, and called for Catton.

Her wizened retainer and Glendower's two grooms had appeared all too quickly for Ivo's liking, and Ivo had found himself standing alone in the inn's yard, watching her ride away before he'd realized that he didn't even know where she lived.

He hadn't expected her to depart so soon, without a word in reference to what had passed the night before. They'd made a very specific bargain, and he planned on holding her to it.

When she was out of sight he strode off to check on his carriage. He wasn't going to spend a moment longer in Oundale then he had to. He had things to do.

Things that required his presence in London immediately.

* * *

George smiled wistfully down at her hands and forced herself not to look back. If she looked back, she didn't know if she'd be able to keep going. She'd kept up a cheerful line of patter all through breakfast. It had irritated Dauntry no end, but it also prevented him from starting any serious conversations.

She wasn't up to one of those.

Not this morning. This morning she was still trying to cope with the ramifications of what she'd agreed to. The tension of their bargain, the promise of it, was almost overwhelming.

She blew her breath out in a huff and shut her eyes for a moment, putting her trust in her horse. Talavera rolled beneath her, muscle and bone stretched into a canter. She gave herself over to the sensation, to the experience, listening to the repetitive sound of hooves on dirt.

She opened her eyes.

Whatever Dauntry claimed, this wasn't about compensation. Or it wasn't only about that.

She'd awoken to find him watching her, a soft expression on his face. She knew that look.

She also knew the one he'd worn the rest of the morning. He'd had a mulish set to his mouth all through breakfast and she was conversant enough with the male sex to guess the source of this poorly disguised anger.

Especially if he'd convinced himself he was in love with her . . .

Infatuated? She'd grant him that. But there was a leap from that to a more serious emotion that they certainly hadn't crossed. But then, men rarely stopped to notice the difference. Or perhaps many of them were simply incapable of telling the difference.

George sighed and adjusted her grip on the reins, sliding the leather through her fingers.

In her experience, men had a way of leaving—or the world had a way of taking them away—and she wasn't going to open herself up to that again. Not after Lyon. Losing Lyon had been almost more than she could bear. Better to end things quickly. She'd promised Dauntry five more nights, and she'd give them to him. But that was all.

She shook her head and urged Talavera into a ground-eating gallop, putting both Dauntry and the temptation he represented behind her. It was better that she was going home. Better for both of them. Though, at the moment it certainly didn't feel that way.

If she stayed, if she allowed being with him to become an easy, nightly habit—even for a short time—it might become impossible to give up. He might become impossible to give up. The threat he already posed to her well-ordered world was bad enough.

Chapter 7

The Angelstone family's black sheep has returned with no ewe in tow. Apparently he has not been so lucky as to be invited into Mrs. E—'s bed.

Tête-à-Tête, 12 October 1788

Philippe froze as the stair creaked. He lifted his foot, gingerly transferred it to the step above the warped one, creeping closer to his goal.

The inn was silent with everyone asleep. Even the innkeeper's dog had settled before the fire, busy chasing rabbits in its dreams. An utterly useless beast, not worth the scraps to keep it alive.

His heart thumped in his chest. His hands began to shake. He'd pictured this night so many times . . . rehearsed it, hands locked about the throats of countless whores while their eyes pleaded then bulged, lips snarled and went slack, fingers clawed at him then stilled.

And, though the world was one dead whore the

better, it wasn't enough. The sensation of satisfaction wasn't even close to what he felt tonight.

The bitch responsible for his father's death was about to pay. Justice would be served. Six years late, cold as day-old piss, but justice all the same.

He'd stood outside the inn for hours, watching, waiting for her window to go dark, for the busy inn to subside into its nightly torpor. Every house, every inn, every palace had its own rhythm and its own pace, people coming and going like its life's blood.

Philippe let his breath out in a rush as he reached the hall. This was it. Since he'd come of age he'd been busy hunting her down. Worming his way into her good graces. Lulling her into believing he was just another of her admirers.

Lord knew she had enough of those. She was like a bitch in heat with a kennel full of hounds sniffing around her, all of them eager for a chance at her.

Just as his father had been.

His father had been a whoremongering gamester. A weak man. Easily led astray, but he'd been a gentleman all the same. A peer of France. The whore asleep up these stairs had lured him to his death and nothing had been done about it.

Nothing.

His mother had barely mourned before she'd remarried. Before she'd gone away to live in Nice with her commoner husband. She'd left Philippe behind to be raised by tutors, ruled by guardians and solicitors. She deserved to pay for dishonoring his father's memory just as the bitch upstairs should pay for his death . . . but she'd died only a few years after remarrying. Complications after delivering her new husband's heir.

The continued existence of women such as these was an abomination. An outrage. A festering injustice that burned as strongly within him today as it had in his fourteen-year-old chest. His father deserved better, and Philippe was going to see that he got it. He could do nothing more to his mother, but he'd see that the Englishwoman paid.

At the end of the hall, an unlocked door let him into a dark room. His quarry lay inside, asleep in the large bed that dominated the room.

Philippe shut the door behind him and crossed to the bed.

The fire in the hearth was nothing but ash. He could only make out the shape of her body beneath the bedclothes. The dark halo of her hair on the pillow. The soft sound of her breaths.

What a shame.

He wanted to see her face, for her to see his. He wanted her to know. Somehow, it wouldn't be complete if she didn't know why.

Maeve awoke with a start as the bed shifted.

She screwed her eyes closed, guilt sweeping over her. Her mistress had arrived after all, and not only had Maeve not been awake to greet her, but she'd been caught sleeping in the bed, not on the cot where she should have been.

She'd be lucky not to lose her position.

Face flaming, she pushed herself up, only to find herself shoved onto her back, pinned to the bed. A body moved over her, weight bearing her down into the crackling horsehair mattress. She bucked up, opened her mouth to scream, but no sound came out as hands locked around her throat, squeezed in, cutting off her breath.

She clawed at the hands, bucked her whole body,

twisting, trying to throw her attacker off, to catch a precious breath. The hands tightened, thumbs pushing in.

"You're a deceitful whore, Mrs. Exley. And your punishment is nigh."

Philippe took a deep breath and flexed his hands. They hurt. Every joint ached. She'd struggled longer then most. And once she'd stopped he'd still held on, unable to let go. He ran one of her curls between his fingers, wrapped it around his hand, and yanked it out. A memento . . . something to put inside the mourning ring his stepfather had sent him, to replace the lock of his mother's hair he'd burnt years ago. Something more fitting, a touchstone of his triumph.

He stood, tucked the curl into his pocket, and fumbled with the lamp on the table beside the bed. He tossed the glass guard down beside the body, yanked the wick free, and shook the oil reserve onto the mattress.

The pungent scent of whale oil filled the room, greasy and heavy, almost rancid. He held his breath for a moment, then breathed carefully though his mouth. Even then he could taste it.

Philippe pulled a tinderbox from his pocket, dropped the enclosed char cloth onto the bed, and struck the flint against steel, sending a shower of sparks onto the bed.

The char cloth blazed brightly for a moment, illuminating the dead woman's auburn hair, and then the bed went up in flames.

The sweetest feeling of bliss rushed though him. Stronger than lust, it quickened his whole body. Skin flushed, prick hard, he slipped from the room and out into the yard where his horse waited.

Chapter 8

*Lord St. A—continues to haunt Mrs. E—'s house.
Another eligible bachelor fallen under her spell.*

Tête-à-Tête, 15 October 1788

It was a full three days before Ivo reached London.
He was in a rare temper by the time he crossed the
threshold of his family's town house. Annoyance had
turned to disbelief. Disbelief to anger.

How could she have ridden away like that?

The more he thought about George's cavalier behavior, the more furious he became. And he'd
thought of little else during the past few days.

Once the wheel of his curricle was fixed, Ivo had
turned south, following the path so lately taken by
the object of his obsession.

He should be happy that George had left in a
friendly, amicable mood, but whenever reason sur-
faced, he ruthlessly shoved it down. Reason had nothing to do with his life. Not just at this moment,
anyway.

He'd spent the whole drive picturing her lying
naked in bed, her secret smile lighting up her face,
her hand reaching out to draw him down to her. It
was a maddening form of torture. The Sirens' songs
lured sailors to their deaths. George was their equal
but that was part of her allure.

She owed him five more nights, and he was damn
well going to collect . . . and then he was going to
convince her to give him six more, and so on, until
she accepted what he already knew: she was his.

The knocker was off the door, making the house
look abandoned and forlorn. He had to drive round
to the mews to find anyone. The metal-banded
wheels of his curricle rattled across the cobbles and
a startled groom hurried out, looking slightly aghast
at Ivo's unheralded appearance.

Ivo handed the reins over and leapt down from his
seat, grateful to be stretching his legs after long
hours minding the reins. He flapped the skirts of his
driving coat, shaking the dust of the road from it,
and turned out of the mews, heading back out to
Berkeley Square and down the short block that led
to Broton Street.

His family's town house was of respectable size,
though not so large or imposing as some of its neigh-
bors. The afternoon sun turned the creamy Bath
stone it was built of to gold, the darker veins seeming
to swirl within the stone blocks. His grandfather's
butler silently opened the front door before he
knocked. Apparently, word of his arrival had traveled
fast.

The man slid back out of his way, his face a mask
of well-practiced hauteur. Reeves would never stoop
to show surprise. Ivo handed over his driving coat
and hat and requested a bath upstairs.

While footmen trailed in and out with steaming buckets to be emptied into the large tub that had been carried out of his dressing room, Ivo stripped. He stood by in his shirt and breeches, fingering the bruise George had left on his shoulder.

Hours later, he lounged down to the library, wearing a banyan in place of his coat. It was of simple stenciled calico, without any of the magnificent frogs or colored lapels that adorned its more stylish brethren. Ivo was secretly amused at the pained look Hatch, the valet he'd inherited from his cousin, had given it as he shook it out and laid it on the bed.

He could see their first fight brewing.

Hatch was wasted on him, and they both knew it. The valet was used to serving an extremely fashionable young lord, a veritable tulip, and his new master had absolutely no desire to shine in that arena. Hence, he'd left him kicking his heels in town, rather than dragging him all over the countryside.

The last thing Ivo wanted was to be turned out in a fashionable blue-powdered wig, or encased in a spangled coat. Nor did he wish to mince in the red-heeled shoes of a dandy, or carry a muff. Hatch had practically wept at the sight of Ivo's muddy boots, and he'd carried away his shirt as if it were a dead rat left on the rug by the kitchen cat.

Ivo blew out a weary breath and settled down at the desk to read his mail. He quickly sorted the massive pile of invitations into past and upcoming and set them to one side. There were several letters from various friends that he would need to attend to right away, and an invitation to dine at his godmother's house the following night.

What Lady Beverly thought she was doing sending dinner invitations to people who were out of town Ivo hadn't the slightest idea, but it was nice to arrive to a warm welcome all the same. She'd always been a bit dotty.

He dashed off a note of acceptance and rang for the footman to carry it round, then quickly penned a short letter to his mother, excusing himself from Ashcombe Park for the next several weeks.

Several weeks during which he planned to bring George about to seeing things his way. Into accepting that this was more than a brief affair. She'd have to be convinced, though. Persuaded. Seduced.

God, how he was looking forward to it.

Ivo sealed the letter for his mother with a blob of red wax and set it aside. He sat back in his chair, enjoying the serenity of the library. The comforting smell of vellum, leather, and paper. The scent of the orange oil used to clean the desk and floor. The snap and sizzle of the coal in the grate.

He tried to picture where George was at this exact moment, but kept coming back to her naked, smiling at him from a tousled bed, long limbs gilded by firelight.

The following evening, Ivo walked up the steps of Lady Beverly's town house just before eight. He handed his coat, hat, and swordstick over to a footman and followed the butler to the drawing room only to find that her ladyship had yet to finish dressing.

Resigned to his fate, he spent an unamusing half-hour listening to her companion, Miss Spence, catalog all the most recent *on dits*. He nodded, pretending to listen, then brushed away the bits of powder that drifted from his wig to his sleeve. God, how he hated wigs. Normally he wouldn't have bothered wearing one, but Lady Bev liked to observe the formalities at her dinner table.

Miss Spence was some sort of distant relation of Lord Beverly's, and though she was not bright, and rarely entertaining, Lady Beverly had always staunchly claimed she couldn't do without her.

Ivo couldn't help but wish she'd at least make the attempt.

He sprang to his feet with particular warmth to greet his godmother's belated entrance. One more bit of mindless gossip and he was going to strangle Miss Spence. What did he care who the Prince of Wales was currently cuckolding, or whether Lady Jersey's sapphires were real?

"Get off, you young rascal," Lady Beverly said, slapping at him with one heavily bejeweled hand. "If I've told you once, I've told you a thousand times, it ain't polite to maul a lady that way." She put a hand out and smoothed her petticoats over her hoops like a hen settling her feathers.

He smiled and swooped in to kiss her again. "I know what you tell me, and I know what the ladies like, and the two don't seem to match up very often."

"Devil," she scolded, clearly pleased. She slipped her arm though his and marched him off to dinner. "Tell me all about what you've been up to, my boy. You don't come see your poor old Aunt Prue often enough anymore."

"I know," he assured her. "I'm an ungrateful child. I've been swamped with taking over for Courtenay: the drainage, crop rotation, different breeds of sheep. Not to mention the effort it takes to resist Grandfather's urging me to begin preparing to run for a seat in the Commons. It's been exhausting, really." He smiled down at his godmother as he helped her into her seat. "But I've recently decided that the perfection of English ladies just might make it all worthwhile."

Lady Beverly gave a sharp snort, and Ivo moved quickly to help Miss Spence with her chair. His godmother's companion sat down heavily, hair powder drifting about her like a flurry of snow. She began to sneeze and Lady Beverly said over her, "Last I heard you weren't making the acquaintance of any *ladies*. By all reports, you've done nothing but cavort with Italian hussies for the past few years."

Ivo pursed his lips and suppressed the urge to roll his eyes. Where did his godmother get her information? Hussies? He'd had one mistress the entire time he'd been there. And they had been entirely circumspect.

Well, they'd been circumspect for Italians. He blew his breath out in a little huff. "Mrs. Exley, whom I had the good fortune to meet at her father-in-law's recent shooting party, is most assuredly a lady."

"Oh, her," Miss Spence chimed in, pausing to sneeze again. "I always think of her as one of the men. There's really not much that's very ladylike about her."

Lady Beverly eyed him like a hawk and Ivo gritted his teeth. He shouldn't have mentioned George. "I found her very ladylike, though certainly not missish."

"Nothing to be missish about," his godmother said, fiddling with the placement of her fork. "Mrs. Exley's been making a spectacle of herself since she was plain Miss Glenelg. She was a hoyden during her season, threw herself away on Glendower's youngest son not a month into it—a delightful boy, but an heiress of her magnitude could have done better.

She could have had Lord Montagu if she'd deigned to notice him—and then she went quite wild when the young man died."

Ivo tossed back his wine and waited impatiently for the footman to refill it. An alcoholic stupor might be his only hope.

"Her godfather was just complaining about her antics," Miss Spence said, not a hint of malice in her tone for him to complain of. "The duke says she's quite lost to decorum—"

"Amelia," Lady Bev interrupted her, "Alençon said no such thing."

Miss Spence blinked, looking owlishly back and forth from his godmother to him. "But he did, Prudence. He said—"

"He said," Lady Bev said, her commanding voice overriding her companion, "that her rackety ways left her open to gossip."

"Yes, gossip that she's—"

"*Gossip*, nothing more, Amelia."

"Well, it's no wonder," Miss Spence insisted. Ivo reached for his once again full wineglass. "Running all over the country with that *foreigner*." She made a face, her lips wrinkling up like a prune. "Attending gentlemen's shooting parties. Riding *ventre à terre* in the park. Filling her house with—"

"I think we've wasted enough of our evening on the exploits of Mrs. Exley," Lady Beverly said as the first course was laid on the table. "I want to hear about Italy." She turned to Ivo as he was filling his plate with buttered peas. "What's the latest tittle-tattle? Has Hamilton really allowed Mrs. Hart to move into his house?"

Ivo smiled at his godmother and took a bite of the rare roast beef that had been set before him. At last they'd moved on to gossip that didn't potentially concern him.

Ivo arrived to pay a morning call at George's town house in Upper Brook Street just as a party of young blades was leaving. One of them tipped his hat, while they all looked him over as if he were a hunter for sale at Tattersalls.

He stared them down and they moved aside, the shortest of them brashly rattling his sword.

Like a dog growling to let you know he had teeth, Ivo thought. He did his best not to sneer openly. They were little more than boys, cocksure and eager to prove themselves. The one with the ready sword didn't even look old enough to shave.

It hadn't been hard to find out where George lived. He'd casually mentioned to Lady Beverly that he wanted to see her about a horse she might be selling and his godmother had jotted down the address for him. She'd smiled, sphinxlike, as she'd done so. He didn't trust Lady Bev when she smiled like that. It usually meant she was plotting.

He entered the front hall and handed his card to the desiccated butler, glancing about the entry with feigned boredom, hoping he didn't appear as eager as he felt. His stomach was tight, his whole body tingling with anticipation. To see her. Touch her. Taste her.

It had been four days since he'd done any of those things.

An eternity.

The small hall had dark wood paneling and a highly polished black and rose marble floor. A rather ponderous staircase led up to the first floor. Pocket doors that must let into a ground-floor drawing room were closed. Several narrow tables lined one wall, almost completely covered in flower-filled vases. Asleep, blocking the hall that led back into the house, was a large, brandy-colored mastiff. The dog didn't even crack an eye as Ivo entered.

Expecting to be left in the hall while the butler went to see if George was receiving callers, he was surprised when the man took his hat and led him nimbly up the stairs. He showed him into a densely occupied salon on the first floor.

George was seated on a large sea-green settee amid a veritable swarm of men. Lady Bev had warned him that he was likely to encounter other callers, but he hadn't expected to find her drawing room overrun. Now he understood the smirk that had accompanied his godmother's warning.

Four days since he'd kissed her, and judging by the number of guests currently filling the room, it was likely to turn into five. Their bargain was for when and where he liked, but he wasn't stupid enough to even attempt to drag her off with what looked like half the men in London as witnesses.

The window embrasure held several men whose large wigs and florid coats marked them as dandies. They were quizzing the ladies who passed below, loudly pointing out the ugliest hats in what appeared to be some sort of contest. A knot of gentlemen, including George's near-constant companion, the one who Miss Spence had so disapprovingly referred to as *that foreigner*, were gambling at a table set off to one side. Brimstone looked up as Ivo entered, and Ivo nodded, ignoring the cold expression in the man's eyes.

He stood in the doorway for a moment, then

stepped inside as George looked up from the young naval lieutenant seated beside her.

"Lord Somercote." George raised one brow inquiringly. He'd been so adamant about returning to Ashcombe Park, and here he was. It frightened her that her first response was an almost overwhelming desire to simply drag him upstairs and into bed.

Calm. Cool. Aloof. That was the proper response. The response that would keep her in control.

Instead of giving into her indecent and impossible impulse, she shooed away the young lieutenant who'd been flirting rather mawkishly with her. "Go and play with Westmoreland and Pound," she told him, shoving the confused fellow toward the dandies. "And put ten guineas for me on whatever headgear Sally Allbright in No. 10 comes out in today."

She turned her attention to Dauntry as he took the vacant seat beside her. "They're judging our unofficial Ugly Hat Derby. My neighbor is notorious for the atrocities she considers hats."

"Is there to be an Official Ugly Hat Derby?"

"All our derbies are strictly unofficial. No betting book here at the Top Heavy. Putting such things in writing is so very vulgar, don't you think?"

"The Top Heavy?"

George laughed outright, unable to help herself. "It's the boys' nickname for my house. I'll present you with the badge of membership later."

Dauntry settled back into the settee, like a king on his throne. He stretched out, one arm lying along the back, fingers almost touching her, his posture clearly proclaiming his intention of staying just where he was for as long as he cared to.

George glanced over at Brimstone. He was watching them over his cards, his expression remote. She narrowed her eyes at him and turned her full attention to Dauntry. She could smell the bergamot of his cologne, clear as if she were pressed up against him.

Her mouth watered, like a beggar invited in to join the feast. Her fingers itched to touch him.

"I found I had some rather tiresome loose ends to tidy up with my cousin's solicitor," he said. George repressed the urge to quiz him. He clearly wasn't about to admit that he'd followed her to town . . . how was he going to broach the subject of his remaining five nights?

"Ah," George replied, doing her best to sound every bit as cool, "business and duty call." She leaned forward and took a macaroon from one of the loaded plates of kickshaws on the table. Dauntry stared at her breasts and swallowed audibly. "I do hope your business won't keep you too tied up," she added, taking a bite, the flavor of almonds and sugar flooding her mouth.

She licked her lips, well aware that Dauntry was watching her. Of what that small, suggestive act did to a man.

"I don't think my business will take up all of my time. I was hoping to find Bennett here today." He glanced around the room. "I stopped by his lodging earlier, but he was out. I'm drowning in a flood of invitations. Obviously I recognize the worth of an invitation from the Devonshires, but how is Mrs. Stavely to be answered? Or Mrs. Burke?"

"Mrs. Burke is to be accepted," George replied. "She is the Duchess of Rutland's sister, and her parties are always noteworthy. Mrs. Stavely is to be politely refused; profound regrets sent with a small posy of violets, or other formal flowers, in the old style. She's a dear old relic, but her supper parties are dreadful affairs. Not a soul under seventy, and all the food cooked till soft."

George leaned forward as she spoke. His outflung fingers brushed her shoulder as if by accident, sending a jolt of desire through her, causing her nipples to tighten and her womb to throb. She took a deep breath.

Heaven help her, but she wanted him.

"If you'd like help sorting them all," she said, throwing caution to the wind, "I'd be happy to act as your social secretary until you get your town-legs. Go riding with me in the morning, and we'll sort them out afterward."

His assignation made, Ivo grudgingly acquiesced to the eager young lieutenant who had been waiting impatiently for a chance to return to George's side.

Puppy. It wasn't as if his adoration was going to get him anywhere.

While the lieutenant reclaimed his place on the settee, Ivo strolled over to the window and joined the men scanning the street below for women sporting particularly ghastly headgear.

While he watched, a door across the street opened and a woman almost dwarfed by a portrait bonnet trimmed with an enormous number of glass cherries and feathers walked down the steps and set off in the direction of Grosvenor Square.

"Cherries and feathers!" the dandy in the blue-spangled coat called out and the room erupted into laughter and bets.

"Don't forget, she's my entry. I claimed her sight unseen," George said from behind him.

The door opened as she spoke and Bennett wandered in, accompanied by her missing bulldog and her brother-in-law. All three of them were magnificently outfitted in suits of striped silk or lightly braided stuff and lavishly embellished waistcoats. Bennett swept his hat from his head, revealing an elaborately curled wig worn *au chasseur*.

"Georgie," he said, "do you mind if I steal Somercote here and take him off to Tattersalls? Nye is selling off Triton, and I think he should take a look at him."

"Absolutely. But if neither of you buys Triton let me know. I might talk to Nye about buying him myself. He's out of the same dam as Talavera."

Once they were out of the house Ivo turned to his friend, his brows raised, his mouth silently questioning.

"It's a madhouse, that's what," Bennett informed him, settling his hat firmly back on his head. "George has been playing hostess to that lot since she came out of mourning three years ago. At all hours the place is filled with men making do with George's instead of White's or Brooks's. Brimstone is forever complaining about it, but there's no gainsaying George on the matter, and it is, after all, her house."

Ivo curled his lip and nodded in sympathy. There'd be changes ahead if he had anything to say about it, and he had every intention of having that right.

Chapter 9

Who can be seen running up the steps of Mrs. E—'s house but the mysterious Lord S—. One is forced to wonder how many gentleman the lady can accommodate at once?

Tête-à-Tête, 18 October 1788

When Ivo arrived at George's early the next morning, invitations in hand, he discovered her ensconced over tea and scones in her boudoir with a handsome, battle-scarred colonel.

Her dog was pressed up against the man, drooling all over his once-white breeches with vapid dog devotion. The man looked up as Ivo was announced, and George turned to greet him with a joyous smile that went right through him.

"Somercote, I'm terribly sorry that I'm not yet quite ready, but Charles here just landed on my doorstep, and I'm plotting what to do with him." She motioned Ivo to a chair and asked if he'd like tea.

What he'd like was to strangle the relaxed colonel

who George familiarly referred to as *Charles*. Instead he accepted the offer of tea and tried to mask his irritation. Judging by the amused smile hovering on the other man's face, he wasn't succeeding.

She'd never used his first name. Not even in bed. It was Somercote in public, and Dauntry in more private moments. Suddenly he was overwhelmed with the need to hear her say *Ivo*. To fuck her until she couldn't stop herself sobbing his name. Shouting it loud enough to crack the plaster of the ceiling.

Her colonel had thick, dark blond hair that fell into his eyes and a disfiguring saber scar that ran from his hairline down over his right eye, ending at his jaw. He'd obviously been lucky to keep the eye. Just the sort of man most likely to appeal to a woman such as George. A battered hero.

"Colonel Staunton was a close friend of my husband," George said, her expression disturbingly soft. "He's just retired and arrived home." She smiled again and lightly pressed the colonel's hand. "I'm so glad you're home safe, Charles. After Lyon's death, and then Langley's, I don't think I could bear to lose another one of you."

The colonel smiled back warmly and squeezed George's hand in return. Ivo gritted his teeth and gulped down his tea, scalding his tongue in the process.

"I'm going to make him the rage of the season. You can stay with the Glendowers—they won't mind—between the countess and I, we'll have you ready in no time."

Her eyes were sparkling with plans, and Ivo noted with growing annoyance that the colonel almost absently retained her hand in a light clasp.

"We'll have a little dinner party—very select—invite all the really influential hostesses and—oh," she gave what in any other woman Ivo would have called an excited little squeal, "we'll have it at the Morpeths' house. Everyone will be clamoring to get you to their events before I'm done."

The colonel chuckled and replied that he was entirely at George's disposal. "But for now, I think I'll take myself off to find Layton or my friend Pomeroy. I'm in desperate need of clothes if I'm to fall in with your schemes, witch." He brushed a hand across his threadbare and patched breeches and pushed the mastiff off his foot. "And while I'm willing to be your slave in all things, I do think that they'll be better companions for what I need today."

"I don't think so at all," she replied. "I imagine I know quite as much about the Bond Street shops as they do. Besides, what you need most is a wife, and I'll be of infinitely more help with that."

The colonel wisely didn't respond to her, merely waving a careless hand in her direction and letting himself out of the room.

"Every year at Christmas that's the one thing Simone asks for: a new mother."

"Simone?" Ivo inquired, thrown off by the sudden introduction of stray colonels, wives, and mothers.

"His daughter," George replied as though Ivo were being dense. "Her mother died when she was three, and since Charles has no family to speak of, she's been in my care ever since. We'd best get going," she announced, switching subjects again, "or the park will be overrun and our chance for a good run lost."

She set aside her tea cup and rose, leading Ivo down the stairs, holding the skirt of her habit up out of her way, revealing a pair of very masculine top boots.

She sent a footman to have their horses brought

round, collected her hat and crop from her butler's fatherly care, and continued out onto the front steps to await their mounts' appearance.

She paused on the front steps, chewing slightly on her lower lip. "Charles is going to be a hard man to play matchmaker for. He's been in the army too long. My God, I sound every bit as bad as Audley said I am," she added with a chuckle.

She smiled as their horses were brought round from the mews and she allowed him to boost her up into the saddle. He let his hands linger on her waist, trailed them possessively down her thigh before stepping away and swinging up into his own saddle in one fluid motion.

"How about a quick run up Rotten Row? Then we can come back and see what can be done to sort out your life."

Ivo happily acquiesced to her suggestion, simply relieved that George didn't appear to picture herself in the role of wife to the dashing colonel. He fervently hoped it wouldn't occur to her, for it seemed all too obvious a solution to him.

As they turned the corner into Hyde Park, George's horse pushed eagerly forward. The earl had his mount's head tucked, holding it back even as it pranced in anticipation.

George glanced down the track. It was utterly deserted. Not so much as the distant tread of another rider to indicate that they weren't entirely alone. She flicked her gaze over Dauntry and smiled. Five nights. He was hers for five more nights.

His eyes met hers and his face softened, ready to smile. George dropped her hands and Mameluke exploded beneath her, a wild thing racing through the park, hooves churning up soil with every step.

An indignant protest and the sound of flying hooves pursued her. A gray head slid up beside her. The earl's glossy boot and solid thigh appeared. She glanced up and he smiled down at her, hatless, hair streaming out of his queue.

With a laugh he leaned forward and his big gray took the lead. Mameluke snapped at them as they passed and George reined him in, ignoring his protest.

Dauntry pulled his mount up short and glanced back over his shoulder, dark eyes boring into her. George's heart lurched and her hands shook, causing her mount to toss his head until she let the reins go slack.

He shouldn't be so beautiful. And she shouldn't let that beauty influence her as it did. She knew the feeling unfurling within her, and she didn't want any part of it. How was she going to keep herself whole when she was half in love with him already?

Chapter 10

Lord A— and Lord C— appear to be openly vying for the charms of a cartain Lady B—. Lord C—'s heir appears anything but cheerful at the prospect of a stepmother.

Tête-à-Tête, 18 October 1788

When they arrived back at her house, George led Dauntry to her library. He was still flushed from their ride, his hair a disheveled tangle. She closed the door behind them and held out her hand for his invitations.

He withdrew several large fascicles tied up with string from his coat pocket and handed them over with a flourish.

"Good Lord. You're very popular, aren't you?" she teased. Untying the first bunch, she skirted around the desk and took a seat behind it. He pulled his hair loose from the remains of his queue and finger-combed it back into a vague semblance of order. George let her breath out in a slow sigh and firmly began sorting his invitations into three piles.

"These," she stated, indicating the largest stack,

"you can simply ignore. It's sheer presumption for these people to have sent you invitations in the first place. You don't know any of them, and you don't want to: jumped-up mushrooms and cits, the lot of them. These," she indicated the next pile, "are worth considering, if they don't conflict with anything in this pile." She tapped the smallest stack with her index finger. "These are the invitations that everyone wrangles for."

She plucked one from the most important pile and held it up. "The Devonshire rout. Everyone will be attending. If you'd like, you can join my party and dine here beforehand."

George glanced up, smiling at his acceptance of her invitation, and Ivo found himself leaning forward to kiss her, as he'd been wanting to do every minute since he'd arrived. He'd come close to yanking her off her horse in the park and hauling her across his saddle. There'd been a moment there, when she'd paused and simply stared at him as if she were really seeing him for the first time.

Standing over her while she'd sorted his invitations, close enough to smell her perfume, was torture.

He captured her lips lightly with his own and was just beginning to deepen the kiss when the rattle of the door handle sounded through the room like a thunderclap. He hurriedly wrenched his head around and pretended to be studying the invitations spread out on the desk.

George's butler entered the room, followed by both her bulldogs. George rose to welcome them and Ivo noted with satisfaction that she was just a bit clumsy as she moved round the desk. She even had a faint blush on her cheeks. Such small proofs that she was not indifferent shouldn't have made him want to smile, but they went a long way to appeasing his pride.

They had still not discussed the events at Oundale, had carefully avoided all mention of the place, in fact. He didn't know who he wanted to punish more, himself for wanting her so badly, or George for her seeming indifference. And it was *seeming*. He was now sure of it. She'd been not the least bit hesitant about accepting his kiss a moment ago, or about returning it, for that matter.

"You give him a fob yet?" Brimstone inquired, the low rumble of his voice cutting through the room.

"No," George said, moving back to the desk and opening the top drawer. She plucked out something small and held it out to him in the palm of her hand. "I promised you this yesterday."

He glanced down at the object. It was a simple gold watch fob. He picked it up and turned it over in his hand. Where the seal should have been were the words *Strayed from the Top Heavy* engraved in a swirling script.

"My godfather gave me the original as a joke," she remarked with a shake of her head. "But I've made it a tradition. A gift that singles out my friends and admirers."

Ivo stared down at the fob. Friends and admirers, or lovers? He couldn't help but wonder. She herself had said she never granted any man more than one night. That could mean only one of two things: either she'd spent a lot of lonely nights since her husband had died, or she'd taken half of London to her bed.

He couldn't help selfishly hoping it was the first, but he honestly didn't care if it was the latter. It didn't matter. None of her former lovers was ever going to enjoy her charms again.

Ivo called frequently during the days leading up to the promised rout. Frustratingly, he never managed to get back into George's bed. By week's end, merely being admitted to her presence in no way satisfied him. Nor did it fulfill the tenets of their bargain. Being near her without being with her was slowly driving him mad.

When he arrived for dinner the night of the rout he found George's house near to overflowing. It might as well have been a fashionable gentlemen's club. With callers constantly coming and going, it was impossible to get her alone for more than a moment, a fact which was fast beginning to irk him far more than George's impish smile.

Smythe led him up past the main salon to the smaller boudoir on the third floor. There was a small group already gathered there, including Bennett and several other men he'd met at the shooting party. George was seated in the middle of them, curls powdered to a faint gray, attired in a perfectly indecent gown of yellow topaz silk embellished with a great quantity of passementerie. The bodice was cut so low he was sure he could see the top of her areolas peeking out of her décolletage. He kept telling himself he was imagining it—must be imagining it, not even George could be that outrageous—but, nonetheless, he couldn't stop himself from staring. Almost couldn't stop himself from reaching out and touching.

Seated beside her was a lovely blonde who appeared to be about his own age. She perfectly suited his ideal of womanhood: she was stately and voluptuous, with just enough decorum in her dress to impress the world with a clear idea of her status. Her hair was threaded with a scarlet ribbon that matched the red brocade of her gown, surmounted by three enormous white ostrich plumes. She was introduced as Lady Morpeth. Ivo bowed over her hand with a schoolboy grin.

When he straightened and released the countess's hand, George said, "I'm sorry there isn't more female companionship tonight, but frankly, I just don't know all that many women who are willing to brave my house."

"You mean you don't know very many men who are willing to share these four walls with their wives," Brimstone said with a smirk.

"If some of you would just get married," Lady Morpeth chided, "Georgianna and I wouldn't always be a circle of two."

Bennett jumped into the fray to assure Lady Morpeth that if only he could find a woman with half her beauty and a smidgen of her wit he'd marry her tomorrow.

"Fustian," she responded, clearly flattered. "I don't know how many simply wonderful girls I've thrown into your path, only to have them cry on my shoulder afterward."

"Girls, my dear Lady Morpeth. *Girls*," Brimstone said. "It's damn distressing to be constantly forced to spend all one's time with girls so fresh from the schoolroom that they've not a clue about the world. No conversation. No opinions. No wit. They're children, and what's worse, they're boring."

"Boring?" Lady Morpeth sounded put out and perturbed. "I assure you that Miss Franklin was not boring. She was very well informed and quite beautiful. But you didn't take to her any better than the rest."

"Well informed?" Bennett sputtered. "That girl, while extraordinarily pretty, is about as bright as my boot, and about as well informed as my six-year-old nephew."

Lady Morpeth smoldered visibly. Before she could respond, the door swung open and Smythe arrived to announce dinner, saving Bennett and Brimstone from her wrath.

George went down to supper on Morpeth's arm, leaving his wife to Ivo. On their way down the stairs, Lady Morpeth professed in a loud stage whisper that she possessed an addiction to faro.

"Rupert knew I had gambling in my blood when he married me," she informed him. "So it's a good thing I also have luck, or I'd have put us both in the basket by now."

From in front of them the earl called back to his wife, warning her to quit bragging.

Ivo laughed. George glanced back at him with a peculiar expression on her face. It wasn't jealousy, but it was awfully close to possessiveness.

Satisfaction and desire welled up, filled his chest, pushed out into his limbs.

He had her.

They traveled to the Devonshires' in two carriages, the ladies riding in one with Lord Morpeth and Brimstone. Ivo crammed into the second with the rest of the men, elbows and knees pushing against each other. By the time they arrived, the hostess had already stopped personally receiving guests, but was easily spotted standing across the crowded ballroom, surrounded by her court of Whig grandees. The Morpeths stepped off to greet their hosts, and Brimstone quickly swept George out onto the dance floor to join in a riotous Scottish reel.

Ivo found himself wandering about with Bennett and George's brother-in-law, Viscount Layton. All three of them carefully avoided the circle of turbaned mothers accompanied by the remnants of past seasons' debutantes. Every once in a while, he would catch a glimpse of George as she flitted by in the arms of yet another man. And each time he had to grit his teeth to keep from storming out into the sea of couples and tearing her away from whatever bounder she was with. Eventually Layton deserted them to flirt with a dashing young matron who'd caught his eye while Ivo and Bennett drifted out of the ballroom for a few rubbers of whist.

When he reemerged several hundred pounds the richer he found George flirting with an elderly roué. The old man was dressed in the first stare of fashion. He was still ruggedly handsome, despite the lines of dissipation that marked his face. Jealously welled up in Ivo as he patted George on the arm and she laughed at whatever sally he had just made, casting him a coquettish glance out of the corner of her eye.

Ivo glared disapprovingly at the scene before him until George spotted him and beckoned him over.

"Somercote," she called, attracting the attention of a large segment of the guests, some of whom tittered loudly as they watched the scene unfold, "come over here and meet my master of horse."

"Alençon," George's elderly admirer ventured, languidly extending his hand, a fortune in lace cascading from his wrist, a large emerald ring adorning one finger. "Purveyor of ponies, and ardent admirer of anything and everything our George deigns to fancy."

Ivo smiled in spite of himself as he shook the ancient duke's hand. He was behaving like an ass, jealous of men old enough to be her grandfather. The duke looked him over, sizing him up. Taking him in from the very expensive wig atop his head to the sapphire buckles on his black silk pumps.

"Ivo Dauntry, Earl of Somercote. And I imagine you've quite a bit of competition there. All the world appears to admire Mrs. Exley."

"Certainly the male half, anyway," the duke conceded. He sighed and touched his fingers lightly to George's cheek. "Take this child out and dance with her, my lord. Don't know what the world's coming to when beauties like this are left to rot with old men like me. If I were thirty years younger—twenty even!—I'd not allow a one of you near her. It'd be pistols at dawn for sure."

"Flatterer," George remonstrated, standing on tiptoe to kiss the duke's cheek before allowing Ivo to lead her out onto the floor.

The musicians struck up a quadrille and Ivo led her through the intricate steps of the dance.

"Are you having a good time?" George asked innocuously, as the steps of the dance brought them together and their hands joined momentarily.

"I am now." Ivo turned away, moving as the dance required.

"Now who's offering Spanish coin?" she asked with a flirtatious twinkle.

"Not I." Ivo caught the slightest hint of her perfume as they passed. The faint scent of jasmine resurrected a panoply of memories, furthering his enjoyment of the envy he saw on so many other men's faces. They might imagine, but he knew. And he intended to keep it that way.

"Did I mention that your dress is indecent?" Dauntry smiled at her with as close to a saturnine expression as George had ever seen. "Alluring, charming, and incredibly indecent."

"No, you didn't." George felt her smile growing even wider. "But I'm glad you approve."

Dauntry leered back at her. As the music ebbed, he maneuvered her off the dance floor and out one of the long open doors and onto the terrace.

She tilted her head so she could see his expression, but made no protest as he led her down the marble stairs and out into the artfully lit formal garden. Other silent couples were slipping off into darkened corners, or returning, slightly rumpled, shaking out their skirts, shooting their cuffs, patting their hair back into place.

Scandalous, really, the things that took place at balls. George bit her lip, concentrating on keeping her balance on the uneven gravel path. Pebbles rolled and slid, her heel skidded out from under her. She kept upright by clinging to Dauntry's arm, hard and impossibly strong beneath the velvet sleeve of his coat.

She was thoroughly intent on enjoying her own foray into impropriety. Events such as this really were more fun when one was flirting in earnest.

Lord knew she'd never thought to become any man's mistress . . . at least, not until now, not until Dauntry. Why he should prove different from the others she didn't know. She'd thought about it long and hard, studied it from all angles, trying to pin it down, to categorize it. She hadn't come to any conclusion at all.

He simply *was* different.

Along the far right wall of the garden they found a secluded bench, well screened by a bower of evergreens. Dauntry paused, blew out the lamp that had been hung just outside, and pulled her into the dark recess. His hand skimmed up her side, slipped easily into her bodice, lifted her breast enough to free the nipple.

He cupped her bare breast and ran his thumb across the exposed skin. "Wearing powder, aren't you?" he whispered, close enough that his breath caressed her skin.

"Yes—"

He bit her ear. She gasped, unable to continue her sentence or even think.

Her nipple budded against the warm center of his palm as his fingers slid enticingly across her flesh. Her head fell back and she began to yield. After a week of flirtation she was almost surprised to finally be in his arms. Surprised and immensely grateful. If only they were somewhere more conducive to seduction than a garden.

The sudden sound of feet coming down the gravel path and a high-pitched, feminine giggle broke them apart. Dauntry pushed her deeper into the arbor, blocking any view of her with his back and shoulders. When the merry couple's footsteps had receded into the dark, he pulled back slightly. In the dark she could just make out the wicked grin he was wearing.

A moment later he was straddling the marble bench that took up most of the space inside the arbor and she was straddling him. Her hands gripped his shoulders, searching for purchase. Her feet dangled alarmingly. One shoe slipped off as she tried to find the ground.

"Eh-eh-eh," Dauntry chided, hands sliding from her waist to her hips, holding her immobile. He dipped his head and caught her nipple between his teeth, pulled on it, drew it into his mouth. Heat enveloped her. Pulsed through her. He sucked harder, rolling the flat of his tongue over the ruched tip of her breast. Bit down hard enough for her to feel all of his teeth, distinctly.

"Stop it," she hissed. He was going to leave a bruise.

He took his mouth away from her breast, leaving her nipple tender and damp. It tightened painfully as the cool night air rushed over it.

"Ever made love at a ball?" His hands moved down her thighs, swept her petticoats up and to the side with a loud rustle of silk. She shivered, unable to help herself.

"Ever wanted a man so much you didn't need kisses? Petting? Preparation?"

She throbbed even as he spoke. Wanton. Hungry. Ready. "No . . ."

His hands fumbled between them. He gripped her hips, lifted her, brought her back down so that the head of his cock rode the already slick folds of her sex, lodged at the entrance of her body.

"No, you never have?"

Her weight bore her down.

"Or, no, you never will?"

The thick head pushed in, parted her, and the shaft followed, filling her. Her hands locked on his shoulders, fingers digging in.

He thrust up, the muscles of his thighs and back powerful enough to raise them both. She sank down another tantalizing inch, unable to control her descent. Unable to do anything but bite her lip and pray she didn't cry out.

His hands slid back around to grip her bottom, kidskin soft and warm against her skin. She tried to grip with her knees, to gain some small bit of control. He chuckled, low and evil, and leaned back, rocking her, drawing her down.

The bullion trim and metallic embroidery that decorated his suit scraped the tender flesh of her inner thighs. The hilt of his dress sword dug coldly into the back of her right leg.

She arched as he hit the mouth of her womb, running painfully aground. "Not there," she gasped.

"No, not there," Dauntry agreed, straightening, lifting her, bringing her back down at a different angle. "There."

Her body met his. He groaned, bringing his arms up and around her, wrapping his hands around the tops of her shoulders. Pulled down on her as he thrust up, entering her as fully as possible.

George gave up trying to control the situation and began to rock in time with his shallow thrusts. She was close. So close. Her feet and hands were tingling. She couldn't catch her breath. So close . . . She tucked her head to his shoulder to keep from screaming.

Dauntry pulled her down hard and she felt the pulse of his climax deep inside her. His cock twitched. Once. Twice. And went still.

She made an incoherent whimpering sound of protest. She'd been so close.

"Didn't finish?"

He sounded pleased, the bastard.

"You weren't supposed to. That one was for me." He settled back, leaning away from her, his cock still hard inside her. "I've got all night to make it up to you." He kissed her breast and tugged at her bodice and stays until she slid decorously back inside them. "Promise."

She rocked forward, taking every last bit of him into her, wanting to bite him, slap him, punish him. Wanting him to keep his promise that very moment, not at some distant point in the future.

"I'll make our excuses," she said. "Meet me on the front steps." She kissed him softly, just a brief meeting of lips, then bit his full lower lip hard enough to make him wince. She let go feeling wicked, wanton, and oddly powerful.

Dauntry lifted her off him and swung her to one side.

She fished about in the dark for her shoe. Found it, shoved her foot back in. She took a moment to shake out her gown, straighten her bodice, and let the hammering of her heart subside, then she slipped out of the arbor and hurried up the path.

My God.

Gravel crunched underfoot, loud as cannons in her ears. Giggles erupted out of dark corners. Moans and gasps joined them in a decadent chorus.

Dauntry had just tupped her in the gardens of Devonshire House and she'd enjoyed every moment of it, so much she half wished to turn about and ask him to do it again.

The first notes of a country dance washed over her as she stepped onto the veranda, lively and playful. She smiled and glanced out into the seemingly deserted garden before hurrying inside to find her friends and make her excuses.

It took several minutes for Ivo to bring his raging body back under control. He certainly couldn't go anywhere in the condition he was in. He sat in the arbor, breathing deeply, mentally tallying the cost of dredging the pond at Ashcombe Park, until he'd calmed down enough to lose his erection.

He stood and buttoned his breeches, smiling into the darkness. He couldn't remember the last time he'd done something so outrageous. So indulgent. So delightfully selfish. And she'd enjoyed it. Amazing.

After smoothing the skirts of his coat, he hurried after George, slipping through the hall, skipping the ballroom entirely. He wasn't about to force his way through the throng inside, or risk bumping into one of their friends. He had a promise to keep, and he meant to spend the rest of the night keeping it. Repeatedly.

When he'd collected his coat and hat, he hurried down the steps to find George already waiting for him, her secret smile glinting in her eyes.

"I've told Lady Morpeth that you're escorting me home." She slid her arm through his and tugged him down the block toward her coach. "The boys are used to taking a hack home, or out to one of their clubs. They may have already left for all I know."

Ivo climbed into the carriage behind her. The footman shut the door and Ivo pulled George into his lap. Before they had even rolled away from the curb he had her tumbled back across his legs and the seat. He removed one glove with his teeth and sent his now naked hand questing up under her skirts.

"Will your house be full as usual?"

"Possibly . . ."

She gasped as he slid a finger into her, ran his thumb over her still engorged clitoris.

"The boys sometimes regroup there after a ball before setting off for their clubs or their mistresses' beds."

He slid a second finger in and she began to pant and

to rock, her body reaching for the release so recently denied her.

"It's not unusual for us all to end the evening with a drink."

She gasped and her legs began their telltale quiver.

"But if I choose to have that drink in my boudoir rather than the drawing room, who's to gainsay me?"

"No one," Ivo ground out. "Not if he values his life."

The carriage came to a sudden halt and George leaned in to nip his already abused lower lip before she slid hurriedly out of his grasp and flung her skirts down in a semblance of propriety. The door opened and the footman lowered the steps. Ivo leapt down and helped George down the steps.

In the golden glow of the lamps she was enchanting. Tousled and wanton. Her pupils were huge, her nostrils flared, like a filly ready to bolt.

Ivo followed her into the house and up the stairs, breathing slowly and regularly as he held himself back from jollying with her on the stairs. It would be so easy to stop her, bend her over, and fling up her skirts . . . Instead he contented himself by watching the sway of her hips as she moved ahead of him.

As they rounded the corner on the first floor and made to go up to George's private floor, the drawing-room door opened and Brimstone silently looked them up and down.

"George," he said, "we were hoping you'd come home early tonight." He held the door open, clearly waiting for them to enter. He met Ivo's gaze over George's shoulder, his expression curiously bland.

Ivo gritted his teeth and followed George into the nearly full room. There was absolutely no graceful way out of it. One couldn't say, for example, *Pray excuse us, but we were just on our way to the lady's bedroom for a late night romp.*

Well, one could, but only if he were ready to be pounded to a pulp and thrown down the stairs.

Inside he saw most of George's regular admirers. They were lounging about the room as if it were their own, cravats missing, brandy glasses in hand, wigs set aside.

George moved to her regular seat like a sleep-walker, as though she were unable to stop herself. The other half of the settee was currently occupied by Colonel Staunton, looking cool and all too handsome for Ivo's peace of mind.

"I had a letter today from Simone," the colonel was saying. "It was very full of Aunt George and the plans you've both been making for Christmas. I'm going down to see her in a few days, and we'd both be very pleased if you'd consent to join us."

George desperately tried to follow the colonel's conversation while damping down her disappointment. Dauntry's trick in the garden had left her in a state of acute distress. She wanted—needed—him to fulfill his promise. The ache of unfulfilled desire was actually painful. No matter how she sat, swollen flesh seemed to rub and throb, demanding attention.

Normally this was exactly what she did after leaving a ball: come home and play hostess, receive callers until the wee hours, and then drop into bed as the sun came up. Tonight she just felt trapped. Charles was asking her questions that she felt too scattered to answer properly, and Dauntry was sitting rigidly across from her, his jaw clenched so tight she kept expecting to hear teeth shatter. The colonel continued to map out his plan for going to see his daughter and George vaguely heard herself agreeing to accompany him. All the while her mind was simply swirling as she tried to come up with some way of getting the boys out of her house as quickly as possible.

She yawned and Charles patted her hand and told her she should go to bed. Her heart leapt, but none of them rose to leave. In fact Brimstone was busy topping off glasses.

A loud party of bucks could be heard coming up the stairs. It would be fruitless to try and leave. It was a risk she was willing to take, but slipping away now would simply incite too much talk. Rumors she could handle. Witnesses were something else.

The new arrivals came in, led by one of her most ardent admirers, the Comte de Valy. George cast Dauntry a pleading glance.

He grimaced back at her, clearly put out.

The comte claimed her hand and bent over it with a Continental flourish. *"Bonsoir, ma chérie. Vous semblez le beau ce soir, en tant que toujours."*

Dauntry rose and crossed the room. He poured himself a rather large glass of brandy. He was probably going to need it. She felt an urge to get thoroughly ape-drunk herself.

How much brandy would it take to damp down the throbbing between her legs? The excited tightness of her nipples?

Dauntry slung himself into the window embrasure and slugged back his drink. The young comte continued to prattle at her as more and more men arrived, refugees from every ball, drum, and rout in London.

George kept greeting them as they filtered in and out, trying to claim that she was exhausted, to chase

them out. But her subtle hints never took root. They
were all too used to having the run of her house
whether she was home or not.

Bennett finally arrived and sent her off to bed with
a firm command and a promise to convey his friend
home. She watched him bundle a nearly uncon-
scious Dauntry out of the room and sighed. This was
not the night she'd had planned. Not the evening
Dauntry had promised her. Not even close.

Chapter 11

Reports of wild goings-on in the Devonshire gardens have tongues wagging all over Town. Sadly, Mrs. E— figures in far too many of the tales for them all to be true . . .

Tête-à-Tête, 24 October 1788

Ivo woke to the din of the coal man making his weekly delivery. His head pounded with every beat of his heart, with every rattle from the street, every call of an orange girl and cry of a carter. He slowly rolled over, trying not to move his head too quickly, ran his tongue around his cottony mouth.

God, he felt awful.

He blinked in the dim light. He was in his own bed, in his own nightshirt. He suddenly had a vague recollection of Bennett taking him in hand and conveying him home.

He stared up at the ceiling and ran though all the things that were wrong with the world, starting with his pounding head and the unpleasant taste in his mouth and ending with waking up alone, the treachery of mankind in general, and his miserable obsession with the one woman in London it was impossible to be alone with.

He'd wasted his second night . . .

He spent the next hour mentally undressing her. Picturing exactly how the silk of her dress felt. How it sounded. How it felt as its weight spilled over his arms when he pushed it aside. He'd relived and embellished their previous encounter. Plotted variations on the theme. It was an entertaining topic to contemplate, but it hardly helped to alleviate his irritation. And it was far from satisfying.

She had a reputation as something of a temptress. He'd had an earful over the past week. An entirely undeserved reputation, he was now sure. Being George's lover took more than mere desire, it took planning and generalship of the highest order. If she'd been experienced at sneaking lovers into her private apartments, she'd have been better at it by now.

His irritation began to ease. She hadn't entertained anywhere near the number of lovers that rumor held her to have had. Last night in the Devonshires' garden had told him that much. To have never indulged in *amore al fresco*? That was innocence indeed.

Eventually he clambered out of bed and rang for his valet. Even the dim clang of the bell made his head swim. He slipped back under the covers and burrowed in. Some indeterminate amount of time later Hatch silently entered the room and took in his condition with a single raised eyebrow.

Ivo managed to mumble, "Coffee. Toast. Please."

His excellent valet did not so much as reply. He simply nodded his assent and whisked himself out of the room.

Bless him.

Ivo sagged back into his pillows, draped an arm over his eyes, and waited. The scent of coffee and buttered toast wafted into the room, announcing Hatch's return.

"Oh, thank God," Ivo uttered in reverent tones, wrapping his hands around the hot coffee cup. He was thankfully imbibing coffee and pondering the newfound joy of a large, efficient staff when the door burst open and his grandfather strode into the room.

His grandfather's tread made the whole room seem to shake and shimmer. Ivo's left eye throbbed and began to twitch. He set his coffee aside and pressed one hand over his eye. This was just what he needed.

"What in the blazes have you been doing?" the old man bellowed, his normally impassive face beet red, his wig slightly askew. "Do you have any idea how upset your mother is? How big an insult you've dealt your intended bride?"

"My what?" Ivo sat bolt upright. The room swam, then came sickeningly into focus.

"I'm not about to discuss this with you while you're lolling about in your bed like some degenerate. I'll see you in the library in exactly fifteen minutes."

The marquis stormed out of the room as loudly as he'd entered it, heels resounding through the house like a drum going into battle, calling orders loudly enough to make Ivo wish he were deaf. Or dead. Dead would be so much more peaceful.

Hatch appeared from his dressing room as if nothing had just happened, a plain coat of brown superfine draped over one arm. "If I'm to shave you before you meet with his lordship, you'll need to rise immediately, my lord."

Ivo threw off the bedclothes and climbed out of

the warm comfort of his bed. The dregs of brandy in his stomach lurched, trying to come back up.

Could his day get any worse?

"Your mother and Miss Bagshott are willing to overlook this lapse of judgment. This *mauvais goût* of yours." Silence stretched while his grandfather stared him down, dark eyes narrowed with irritation under his wild, bristling brows. "I'm not." The marquis spread his hands out on his desk, every inch the stern disciplinarian. Ruler of his own small kingdom.

Ivo clenched his teeth and counted to ten. The muscle in his jaw popped. How many times was he going to have to tell his grandfather that he was not willing to fill his cousin's shoes to the point of marrying Courtenay's childhood sweetheart?

"Your mother wished me to let you go your own way, make your own choice, but . . ." The old man sputtered to an end, unable to find the words, a vein popping out in his forehead. "But I won't allow you to throw your life away a second time on *that woman.*"

Ivo pressed his lips together to keep from yelling. Allowing this to become a shouting contest wouldn't help. Gossip had obviously wound its way into the heart of Suffolk. His mother had undoubtedly succumbed to a case of the vapors, resulting in his grandfather appearing like an avenging archangel to drag him home by the scruff.

He was a grown man, for heaven's sake. Not a boy to be schooled, or a dog to be called to heel.

The marquis opened the magazine that lay on the desk between them with an overly loud rustle, turned it, and slid it toward him with an elegant flick of his wrist.

Ivo stared down at the Tête-à-Tête feature of *Town and Country*.

> *Our newest earl, so recently returned to these shores from warmer, less discreet climes, has made a beeline to the side—and one can only assume the bed—of the amphibious Mrs. E——. Considering how often they've been seen together one has to wonder if she's thrown away that fabled die of hers and granted him carte blanche.*

Ivo's vision swam behind a red blur.

His grandfather raged on. Ivo let the tirade wash over him. How many times had he done this over the years? Arguing was pointless. The marquis was used to having his own way. Better to let him blow himself out.

"They'll be here tomorrow, and then you'll do whatever it takes to sweep this mess under the rug."

"What?" Ivo blinked. He'd clearly missed something.

"Your mother. Miss Bagshott. And Miss Bagshott's mother. They will be here tomorrow. You'll squire them about town, take them to the theatre, to Astley's, shopping. You'll make a proper show of courting her. Then, in a few months when the gossip has died down, you'll do your duty and you'll marry."

Ivo sucked in both cheeks. Jumping over the desk and throttling his grandfather wouldn't make his life any easier, tempting as the prospect was.

Marry Miss Bagshott?

He'd see her in hell first.

George brooded in her boudoir all morning, listening to the coal fire pop in the grate. She drank too much tea and paced about the room in her dressing gown. Never before had she thought of her boys as an imposition. Something of a bore on occasion, but never an imposition. But last night had been awful. There had simply been no way to get them to leave.

Caesar pressed his head against her thigh and looked up at her longingly. She patted his huge head, rubbing the loose skin back and forth over his skull. He seemed especially dear to her after the fire that had claimed her maid's life. If Maeve's dislike of the dog hadn't extended to shutting him in the stables for the night, she'd have lost him too.

It had been horrible to arrive home only to find out that Maeve, as well as several other guests, had died in a fire that had swept through the Dove and Snail. Maeve had been with her since Georgianna had left the nursery, a calm, steady presence.

She wiped at her eyes with her hand. Maybe she'd feel better after taking Caesar out for a walk. He shouldn't suffer because of her foul mood.

They both needed air and action.

She took him on a long ramble through the still quiet shopping district of Old Bond Street and down to St. James Park. She had learned early on that the cows in Green Park were too much of a temptation for the dog. Horses, he seemed to sense, were not to be molested, but with cows all bets were off.

He was enough of a terror to the nursery maids taking their small charges out for a gentle morning airing. Inevitably, one of the children would come racing up to Caesar, who was only too happy to play. The child would wind up covered in slobber and dirt. More than once George had exited the park amid the shrieks of an irate maid to "Take that great beast away!" while the children, oblivious to their

elder's distress, followed behind, begging George to
return with Caesar the next day.

Today the park was filled with maids and their
charges—tinkling laughs and high-pitched screeches
echoed across the lawn—but none of Caesar's special friends were present. George walked briskly
around the lake while her dog gamboled along
beside her. He woofled menacingly at a stray cur who
dared to bark at him, sniffed, and marked his terri-
tory. She called him back when he ran toward the
water, smiling as he hung his head and returned to
heel. Once away from the water, she snapped her fingers and he ran off ahead, tail wagging furiously.

She'd finally made the momentous decision to
embark upon an affair. A liaison. And she couldn't
seem to manage to steal so much as an hour with Dauntry without being interrupted. There had to be a way.

Perhaps she'd confess all to Helen Perripoint.
Helen never seemed to have problems carrying on
her amours. She should have paid more attention to
Helen's advice over the years. There was obviously
more to this than simply having a ready supply of
Élixir de Venus at hand to prevent conception.

Walking back through Mayfair with Caesar happily
trudging alongside her, George cut past Carlton
House, and turned up St. James Street. Proper
women were not supposed to be seen on St. James
Street, not even in a carriage, but George had always
blithely ignored that dictum. No one was likely to
think worse of her for appearing there than they already did. The Top Heavy had already put her
beyond the pale for the more fussy elements of the
ton. And since only other women—none of whom
would be present to witness her impropriety—were
likely to be offended, George didn't bother to worry

about it. It was by far the quickest route, so why shouldn't she use it?

As she turned the corner to Upper Brook Street and home, Caesar bounded off ahead of her to greet Dauntry, who was descending the front steps of her house. He bent and commanded the dog to sit, then stood absently petting him, waiting for her to reach them. George held out one hand and smiled ruefully at him.

"How are you faring today?" God, she wished they hadn't been interrupted last night. She could still feel the hollow ache. Desire denied, cut off in its prime.

He took her hand, placed a quick kiss just where her glove ended at the wrist. She flushed, lust rekindling in an instant.

"I've the devil of a head." The low growl of his voice cut right through her, vibrated inside her chest.

Her smile slid up at his confession. She squeezed his hand. She'd been there more than once herself. "Would you care to turn about and come in? I'm leaving tomorrow for Malvern Abbey, so this is our last chance to see one another for a week or so."

Dauntry followed her up the front steps. Quick. Eager. Caesar trotted up after them, then took off toward the bowels of the house.

"Smythe, I'm not at home today," she said, as they entered and made for the stairs. "Not to anyone."

Her butler nodded and shut the door behind them with silent efficiency.

George hurried past the currently deserted drawing room, up the carpeted stairs that led to her boudoir. Her mouth was dry, her stomach queasy. He'd made her a promise last night . . . she wanted him to keep it.

Once inside her rooms, Dauntry shut the door behind them. The small gilt clock on the mantel chimed eleven. George stripped off her gloves and hat, tossed them down on the marble-topped table beneath the Fragonard. She gazed at the laughing girl swinging high while a smiling boy lurked in the bushes, watching. Tried to ignore the way the scent of bergamot invaded her senses, made every bit of her strain toward him.

Their bargain preoccupied her mind. She felt dumb and breathless.

He'd made her a promise last night.

His own gloves landed beside hers. Tan leather fingers mingled with blue. Loving. Indecent. His hat followed, settling beside hers as though it belonged there.

Hands slid around her waist. The heat of his body permeated the layers of her gown. His mouth, hot and wet, came down on the naked skin of her neck, trailed down her shoulder, the slightest hint of teeth making her catch her breath.

How did he know exactly where to touch her? Exactly how to touch her? That she liked to be bitten?

She gripped the edge of the table, marble chilly beneath her hands. Dauntry slowly unhooked the front of her gown, one hook after another. His hands were sure. Deliberate. He spread it wide, eased it off her shoulders. The heavy moiré silk hit the floor with an audible rustle.

George held her breath as Dauntry kissed the exposed skin just above her shoulder blade while he tugged loose the hooks that held her petticoats. Deft fingers untied the pad that held out her skirts. One hand slid around the front of her stays, settled over the soft flesh of her belly.

Her breath escaped in a rush.

He leaned against her. Large. Heavy. Intimidating

in a way that was oddly exciting. He caught her earlobe between his teeth, traced the sensitive shell of
her ear with his tongue.

"Here suits me fine." Teeth grazed her neck. "But the
couch—or, better yet, the bed—might be preferable."

George swallowed thickly. "The bed." Oh, God.
Please, the bed. "There." She pointed to the connecting door, unable to say any more.

Dauntry's fingers snaked into the lace of her stays,
tugged her backward, tipped her off balance. He swung
her up into his arms, juggled her as he opened the
door to her room and carried her in. Two steps and she
went flying, landing in the middle of her bed with
enough force that the bed gave a screeching protest.

She fought her way up out of the layers of bedding, floundering up onto her elbows, only to fall
back when Dauntry wrapped one hand about her
ankle and hauled her toward him.

"Dauntry, wha—"

"Ivo."

He tugged her all the way to the edge, legs dangling over the sides, knees indecorously spread. He
knelt at the side of the bed, hands pushing her legs
apart, shoving her shift up.

"Say it."

George stared at him. What the devil?

"Ivo. Say it. You call that damn colonel Charles,
and Brimstone is Gabe as often as not." He froze.
Fingers digging into her calves. "Say it."

George grinned, biting her lip as she did so. Sometimes jealousy was an amazingly attractive feature.

"Ivo," she said deliberately, a chuckle welling up
inside her, "what the devil are you doing?"

"Keeping my promise, strumpet." His mouth slid
up her leg, from the silk stocking covering her knee

to the bare flesh above it. He bit down on the tendon at the top of her thigh and she squealed. Embarrassing as it was, there was no other word for it.

Before she could protest his tongue was slithering up the valley between her thighs, parting, probing. His hand come up to rest against her belly, pushed her onto her back as his mouth locked over the sensitive peak now exposed to his predations.

George's fingers wound into his hair, nails stroking his skull, palm coming to rest on his crown. A moment later she tugged, trying to dislodge him.

Ivo smiled to himself and sucked harder, flicking his tongue over her faster, pressing in against already overly sensitive flesh.

How was it that he hadn't tasted her yet? He'd spent an entire night in her bed and never once gotten his mouth on her like this.

She pulled harder, a fistful of hair steadily wrenching upward.

She could pull his hair out if she liked. He wasn't about to stop. Not now. She was panting. Her feet pressing against him. She got one up and pushed hard against his shoulder.

Ivo shrugged it off, wrapped his hands around her hips, and held her down. She was making a series of inarticulate protests which he suddenly realized were his name. "I-Iv-Iv-oh. I-I-Iv . . . oh!"

His stomach clenched while his cock swelled inside his breeches, impatient to get loose. He slid two fingers inside her, locked his mouth over her, and took her over the edge.

Legs wrapped around his shoulders, squeezed with impressive strength, trembled with her release. When she let go, Ivo stood, thumbed open the fall of his breeches, and flipped her over with one hand.

She twisted like a cat, amber eyes meeting his. Ivo slid his hands over her exposed bottom, gripped her hips, and leaned in until the head of his cock found the entrance to her body.

George's eyes widened. Her hands fisted in the sheets.

Without preamble he thrust in, pelvis meeting derrière as she took him all, encased him in hot slick flesh. She arched up, rising to meet him, silk-clad feet scrabbling for purchase on the polished wooden floor.

He found his rhythm. Fast. Hard. Lost himself in the simple sensation of body meeting body. There was nothing simpler. Nothing purer. Nothing truer than the understanding two people could establish in the solitude of a bed.

When George had been reduced to a writhing wanton Ivo stopped. He didn't want her to finish. Not just yet.

He leaned forward, used his weight to hold her in place, and quickly pulled loose the knot holding her stays shut. He yanked out the lace and ran his hands up her torso. There was nothing but a layer of fine linen between them.

George twisted, the fine muscles of her back sweetly alive under his hands. She moaned as he pushed his thumbs up the line of her spine, arched and rolled. He let her pull away, roll over, shed her stays and shift.

Naked, she curled up in the middle of her bed. A thing of beauty. " Do you intend to remove your coat and boots, or is the point to spend the afternoon taking me like a pirate?"

Ivo laughed, peeled off his coat, and turned to sit on the bed while he wrestled with his boots. Much as the picture she painted appealed, that hadn't been his intent.

Chapter 12

Whatever the truth of Lord S—'s life abroad, he is clearly not pining for any lady he may have chanced to leave behind.

Tête-à-Tête, 25 October 1788

Philippe ground his teeth as Mrs. Exley's carriage rolled away from the curb. The wheels rattled on the cobbles, gratingly loud. A costermonger hawked her oranges, a young shepherd ambled past, his small flock of sheep trotting gamely before him.

The bitch was supposed to be dead, not setting off to cavort in the country with yet another of her lovers. He cracked his knuckles one at a time, enjoying the sound and the momentary hollow feeling of each joint as it snapped. He leaned back against the cold stone of the building, sucked in through his teeth, and spat.

It was bad enough to discover he'd killed the wrong woman, had, in fact, wasted his time strangling a servant. But in the past few days he'd seen that damn bitch squired about on the arm of no less than five different men.

She was going to pay. He'd see that she paid. And he was going to enjoy it. Every delicious, overdue moment.

When she arrived back in town, George found Brimstone, attired in full evening kit, kicking his heels in her boudoir. He was sprawled in a chair, voraciously eating shortbread while reading a gothic novel she herself had abandoned halfway through. Ghosts and imprisoned heirs had littered its pages.

A dusting of powder dulled his hair to gray. Heavily ribbed silk encased long limbs. Paste glinted from his buttons and his buckles.

She'd left the colonel at her country house to become reacquainted with his daughter, with a firm promise that the two of them would make the journey to Winsham Court in a few weeks to join the earl's family for their Christmas celebrations.

All she wanted tonight was to send a footman round to Dauntry's residence with a note inviting him to a late supper. She'd been actively scheming toward that end all day while trapped in her carriage. Planning exactly what she'd do to him once she had him alone . . .

Gabriel's presence clearly made that impossible. She blew her breath out in resignation. The anticipatory lust she'd been firing with daydreams turned to ash.

"There you are," Gabriel said, not bothering to get up. "This is a ghastly book." He tossed the offending volume away and sat up, his feet hitting the floor with a crack.

"I'm sure it is, but it's also all the rage right now. The ladies love these gothic romances. It gives me something to make small talk about with them when we retire after dinner."

"Well, I'm not here to read your dreadful book," he announced, reaching for the last piece of shortbread. "I've come to escort you to the theatre. The dowager is in a great frenzy over some play or other, and so Alençon is taking her. And nothing will do for them but that I bring you along. A royal command, you might say. So hurry up, my dearling, and get cleaned up."

"I'll hurry, but only because it's Grandmamma. Besides, no one is ever on time for the theatre." George crossed the room to pull the bell rope to call for assistance and hurried into her bedroom to wash and change her gown.

"His Grace said to be there on time," Brimstone called after her. "Lady Glendower actually wants to see the play."

George shucked her carriage gown, washed her arms and face with the warm water the maid brought, and selected a gown of bronze silk, trimmed with narrow rows of mink. She dusted her face and décolletage with powder and allowed the maid to help rearrange and powder her hair.

Tugging on her gloves, she reentered her boudoir. "Ready," she announced, shaking her head as Gabriel rose, dusting crumbs from his coat and breeches.

The curtain was still down as Gabe led her through the door of Drury Lane. The gallery was filled with roving gentlemen making their way from box to box, fetching refreshments for the ladies in their charge, or merely drifting about to see who was present.

Overly warm air, reeking of sweat and hair powder, pressed in, making George take a hurried breath through her mouth as they plunged through the crowd.

The duke and the dowager countess were already seated in the Glendower box, the countess eagerly spying on her acquaintances through her opera glasses. Candlelight reflected back from the lenses of a hundred other pairs as their fellow attendees did the same.

"Georgianna, sweetheart," the countess exclaimed as they entered, "I'm so glad that scamp got you here."

George kissed the old woman warmly and greeted the duke with a sly smile. "Your Grace, I am shocked to find you concealed here, quite alone, with my kinswoman."

"Very good, my dear," the duke drawled, silently clapping his hands. "You play the outraged matron to a tee. I wonder, wherever did you learn that?"

"You, Alençon, are a despicable beast," interpolated the dowager with a wink for George. "My granddaughter may choose to be shocked at your behavior if she wishes."

"Our behavior, my dear Sophia, our behavior." The duke languidly straightened the lace peeking from the cuffs of his cut velvet coat.

The dowager harrumphed and sent Brimstone scurrying off to fetch refreshments. "And none of that lemonade stuff either. Can't stand the stuff."

George sat chatting with her husband's grandmother and the duke until Gabriel returned just as the curtain came up. They did their best to attend to the play over the raucous behavior of the bucks in the gallery below, but one of the more fashionable impures seated in a nearby box was slowly tossing roses to the men gathered below her, causing a near riot.

"It's a damn fine thing I know this play," the countess announced with one of her disdainful snorts. "Because I can't hear a thing over those louts." And with that, she leaned out over the edge and emptied her glass onto the crowd below.

A howl of protest erupted, followed by what was clearly a fight breaking out. The dowager settled into her chair with the air of a satisfied hen.

On stage, Kemble chewed through his monologues as though he were addressing the troops before a forlorn hope. George drank his performance in. *Hamlet* had always been her favorite of Shakespeare's plays, and no matter how it was performed, she always enjoyed it.

The melancholy Dane. The doomed madwoman who loved him. The friends who betrayed him, and who were in their turn betrayed. It was a fascinating story.

When the curtain went down for the intermission, George sallied forth from her box with Alençon, strolling through the crowd to visit friends. They found Lady Morpeth heartily bored by the evening's performance, but looking forward to the farce.

"I never could stomach all the ins and outs and thees and thous. It's simply too much work." The countess hid a yawn behind her hand while her little black pageboy fanned her.

George laughed at her friend and went so far as to agree that Shakespeare could certainly be hard to follow, especially when whole scenes had been cut to shorten the running time.

"You mean it's actually longer?" Victoria shot her husband a glare when he had the temerity to laugh.

"Yes," he said, the faintest of smiles curling his lips, "but it makes sense."

"I sincerely doubt that, Rupert, but I shall allow you and George to like it all the same."

George thanked her friend for her magnanimity and excused herself, allowing Alençon to lead her on to the Duchess of Devonshire's box. On the way, he gave a sudden shout of surprise and pulled George to a halt.

"Lady Bev's here," he whispered, leading her toward a box into which an elderly woman in a deep purple sack gown had just disappeared. "Amelia Spence would no more come to see *Hamlet* on her own than she'd move to Morocco to queen it over the Bedouin hordes."

"Are you making poor Lady Beverly another of your flirts?" George demanded, as the duke led her onward to the box in question. "I must warn you, sir, I shall be forced to tell Grandmamma that you are a rake."

"Your grandmother, like almost every other woman alive, prefers a rake, my dear. And Prue has been one of my flirts far longer than Sophia."

George grinned. The old roué was absolutely correct. Dark, dangerous, and likely to lead a lady astray? Those were attractive qualities indeed.

Inside Lady Beverly's box they found the Earl of Carr ensconced amongst the ladies, his lavishly embroidered coat resplendent even among all the feminine finery. Lady Beverly was smiling at the earl, while Miss Spence looked on Friday-faced, her gray fringe all but hiding her eyes.

At the front of the box stood a young woman about George's age. Two middle-aged matrons sat beside one, one dressed in a fashionable gown of striped silk, the other in a gown every bit as out of date as Miss Spence's sack gown.

All three women turned their attention to George as Lady Beverly greeted her appearance with a happy smile, relief clear in her eyes. George pressed her lips together to keep from grinning. Entertaining country cousins had never been among Lady Bev's favorite activities.

"Get out," Carr cried as the duke entered behind her, throwing up one hand, as if to ward off an evil vision. George glanced back over her shoulder to catch Alençon smiling, showing his teeth in a slightly menacing manner. The duke pushed forward and claimed Lady Beverly's hand, bending over it with a dramatic flourish.

"I warn you, Alençon, no shoving in, or I shall take this one from you." Carr beckoned George over to the seat beside him.

"Boys!" George eyed them reprovingly, while Lady Beverly laughed, fluttering her fan like a girl making her debut.

"For heaven's sake, Georgianna, don't discourage them. I've nearly forgotten what it's like to be fought over."

"Now, that is a clanker if I've ever heard one." George nodded to Miss Spence. "I seem to recall more than one story of a duel being fought over you. It makes me terribly jealous."

"Do you like men to fight over you? Like dogs with a stolen bone?" The young woman standing at the front of the box raised her chin. The cap covering her curls fluttered. Her voice was oddly hard and loud enough to carry to the boxes on either side of them. "I would think that something to be avoided by any lady of taste or principles."

George blinked, mouth falling slightly agape before she closed it with a snap. She felt a twinge of guilt. A duel had been fought over her, and the results had been anything but pleasant. A rush of anger burned the guilt away.

She flicked her gaze appraisingly up and down the unknown woman, taking in her less than modish gown and the gaudy garnet set that adorned her neck and ears. The woman stared right back, hardly even blinking. George knew dislike when she saw it. This unknown woman burned with it. Why?

"Perhaps so," Lady Beverly chimed in hastily. "But one can hardly deny the romance of it all. Though now that the men are more apt to attack one another with guns than swords, it all seems a little sordid. Georgianna, this is Lady Dauntry, Miss Bagshott, and her mother, Lady Bagshott. Ladies, let me make you known to one of the true sights of London, Mrs. Exley, our famous Lady Corinthian."

George flicked her glance over the lady in striped silk again. So, this was Dauntry's mother? She had a rounded, mother hen look to her. She smiled tentatively, a worried crinkle marring her brow.

"Mrs. Dauntry. Lady Bagshott. Miss Bagshott." George forced a smile, refusing to acknowledge the Bagshott ladies' frosty reception. She would not fall into the trap of playing the game. Overt dislike wasn't an uncommon reaction from the country gentry.

They watched their own with a hard eye for any

possible misstep or transgression, and they sought to impose their mores equally upon the rest of humanity. Their small-mindedness gave her the headache.

She was well aware that she was more likely to be held up as an example of what to avoid rather than a model to be emulated by women such as these. What on earth was Lady Bev doing with such dowdy guests? It wasn't at all like her.

Before anyone could reply the curtain parted and Dauntry entered, followed by his grandfather, their hands filled with champagne flutes.

"Here you go, Aunt Prue . . ." Dauntry began gaily enough, turning to distribute the glasses. He stopped in mid-sentence, mid-step. As his eyes met hers his face paled, then flushed, a slow bloom creeping up from his collar. Behind him the marquis stiffened, his eyes scorching her from across the box.

George's whole body flamed in recognition. Lust raced through her, licking every secret, intimate part of her all at once.

"Mrs. Exley," Ivo managed to get out, allowing Carr to relieve him of the flutes and distribute them to the ladies in their charge. "I thought you still in the country."

He glanced about, gorge rising. His night was going from bad to worse. The air crackled with anger. The emotion radiated off his grandfather like heat off coals and positively oozed off the Bagshott ladies. His mother looked like she was about to faint.

Miss Bagshott was staring off into space, lips pressed so tightly together they disappeared entirely. Her mother looked equally offended, her color high even under the veil of heavy cosmetics. The beauty mark she'd placed at the corner of her mouth disappeared into the wrinkle of her frown.

There was not a doubt in Ivo's mind that they knew exactly who George was, and what their relationship was rumored to be. His godmother's mischievous expression didn't reassure him a jot, and it could only serve to further infuriate the marquis.

He held his own flute out to George, consigning his nearest relations to perdition. In a perfect world, he could just drag her out into the hall and find a private place behind a potted fern . . . Sadly, his world was far from perfect.

The ladies' perfumes mingled in the air, but George's overrode them all. Jasmine filled his nostrils, swirling through his head, heady as brandy on a warm night.

"I didn't know we'd have visitors. I should have thought . . ."

George took the glass, her expression closed, almost haughty. She sipped, her eyes never meeting his. In fact, he was almost sure she and his grandfather were staring each other down like two beasts fighting over a kill. She took another sip and his grandfather moved past him to hand glasses to the Bagshotts.

"I hope you found the colonel's daughter well?" Ivo grasped at straws as everything around him seemed to slow down. His cravat became tighter and tighter by the second, as though someone were twisting it, strangling him. Sweat poured down his back, making his shirt stick to his skin.

It had been impossible to escape this outing. He had been endeavoring to behave as formally as possible during the past week. To give the Bagshotts and his family nothing to latch on to. But the old man had arranged this evening behind his back, explicitly including his name when the invitation was issued.

Everything had been going off rather well until George had suddenly appeared.

"She's very well, thank you," George replied, sounding nonchalant and slightly jaded. He'd heard that tone before, and it boded ill for whomever she directed it at. "I'll tell the colonel you asked; I'm sure he'll be pleased. But for now, do come in and finish the introductions. I had no idea you knew Lady Beverly. She was just introducing me to her guests."

George smiled in a brittle way, eyes cold enough to give them all a case of frostbite. Ivo swallowed, deep foreboding flooding through him, making his heart thump unevenly. Her sword was drawn, the point circled, ready to parry and then attack.

"Let me do the honors correctly, Mrs. Exley." His grandfather's voice cut through the chatter that filled the theatre. "Miss Bagshott is betrothed to my grandson. She's come up to town with her mother and Somercote's mother to buy her trousseau."

George's expression hardened. Ivo's stomach tried to turn itself inside out.

"Then I really must welcome you to London, Miss Bagshott. I trust we shall be seeing quite a lot of you."

"I doubt that, Mrs. Exley. I don't find that I have much of a taste for *your* circle, or their amusements."

Silence reigned for the length of five heartbeats. Ivo was sure of that fact. He counted them. Miss Spence's high-pitched titter broke it, releasing them all.

"Then that shall surely be our loss, Miss Bagshott; we shall miss you at Almack's." George tossed back the rest of the champagne in her flute and held the empty glass out to him. Her hand was steady, the small slice of forearm visible between glove and *engageantes* called to him. Ivo took the glass, horrified by the farce taking place around him. It was like sinking into a peat bog—A slow, strangling death.

"Alençon," she turned to the duke, smiling, a cat with all her claws extended, "aren't we due in the Duchess of Devonshire's box before the curtain goes back up?"

"Quite right, my dear." The duke rose, sketched a shallow bow to the assembled ladies, and led George off without a backward glance.

"Eleanor," Lady Bagshott hissed. "That was foolish in the extreme. To make an enemy of such a woman—"

Ivo took a deep breath, waiting for the fireworks to erupt. It needed only this. He was a hairsbreadth away from pitching his grandfather over the railing.

"I don't care." Miss Bagshott's hands fluttered, smoothing her skirts over her hoops as though that would fix everything.

"Well, you certainly ought to," Lady Beverly interjected.

His grandfather stood there fuming, like Zeus displeased, ready to singe them all if they so much as said a word.

"The gossip columns have had more then enough to say about Mrs. E and the dashing new Earl of S. It is all t-too-too mortifying. How dare she come here? Speak to me like that? Look at me like-like-like I'm some bug crawled out from under a rock. Take me home!"

Leaving his mother to enjoy what was left of her evening, Ivo escorted the Bagshotts out of his godmother's box. The marquis stalked down the hall before them, back ramrod straight, wig seeming to bristle. They passed George on the duke's arm. Ivo grimaced. His eyes met hers briefly, begging her to understand what had just transpired.

She stared back with shuttered eyes. Beautiful. Perfect. Remote as marble.

The ride back to Grillion's was not enlivened by anything that could remotely be considered conversation. Eleanor sat huddled in one corner, face turned away, while her mother gave her a regular bear garden jaw, and the marquis raged at them all in turns.

Ivo leaned back into the squabs and counted the minutes until the evening was over.

One of London's eerie yellow fogs had descended, shrouding the city in a heavy, muffling cloak. Ivo had been riding up and down the same deserted stretch of Rotten Row for nearly an hour. The sun had barely risen, a pale hint of light leaking over the rooftops of Mayfair, little more than a flambeau in the fog.

This might be his only chance. George sometimes rode there in the wee hours of the morning. He had no doubt that he'd be refused admittance should he dare to attempt to call on her at home.

Eventually, the distinct jangle of harness sounded in the distance. The soft rhythm of hooves on sand—two horses, trotting. At first all he could make out was an orange spot bobbing toward him through the fog, then George slowly emerged, her persimmon habit glowing like a lantern.

When she spotted him, clearly waiting for her, she drew up short, allowing her groom to catch up with her. Her mount's breath coalesced with the fog. It stamped impatiently, shaking its head. George eyed him as though he were a day-old eel pie.

She was obviously not inclined to accord him the private moment he so desired.

Ivo blew out a resigned breath. The lady was put out; no doubt about it. There would be no teasing his way back into her good graces. He'd have to wait her out, but all the same, it would chafe too much not to even attempt to clear himself.

"George, about last night, Miss Bagshott's behavior—"

"Was atrocious." She straightened in the saddle, chin tilted up in an almost unnatural position. "But not unprovoked. The papers and gossips have found plenty of fodder in us, my lord." Her mount crow-hopped, expressing his rider's agitation.

He was in trouble.

If they'd reverted so far that she was coldly addressing him as "my lord," she was determined to make this far harder than he'd imagined, than he'd hoped. He'd rather she railed at him. Cursed him. Hit him with her crop, even. Anger could be fought, defended against, turned on its head. Anger would give him a way in.

"I'll not repeat Miss Bagshott's socialism, but you should warn her that it would be wiser not to pull caps with me a second time." She nodded dismissal and rode off into the fog at a smart trot. Catton turned about in his saddle as he rode past, giving Ivo a warning glance before disappearing in her wake.

Ivo sucked in a frustrated sigh and turned his horse back toward Mayfair. There was no point in pursuing George, not in the current mood she was in.

Things were bad when the servants warned you off.

He had every hope of clearing things up. Of explaining. Regardless of his grandfather's claims and his mother's wishes, he had never been engaged to Miss Bagshott. And he never would be.

And, as her parting words as he'd assisted her out of his grandfather's carriage had been something to the effect of never having been so humiliated, and being sure that she could place her dependence on his not thrusting his presence upon her ever again, there was clearly no expectation in that quarter of a forthcoming offer.

He was sorry that expectations had been raised, but he hadn't been the one to raise them. As for George, she owed him four more nights, and if he had to use her promise to blackmail her into listening to him, then so be it.

Chapter 13

Mrs. E— appears to have conquered yet another lordling, if reports of wild rides in Hyde Park and late-night revels in her home are to be believed . . . and believe them we do.

Tête-à-Tête, 4 November 1788

George flexed her hand around her crop, savoring the weight of it. A gallop that had brought out a foaming sweat on her mount had done nothing to calm her. She was still shaking with the urge to beat Dauntry senseless and give him another scar to remember her by.

Running lightly up the steps of the Morpeths' town house, she found herself still fuming. An afternoon surrounded by men was about as appealing as overcooked turbot. And the idea of being anywhere Dauntry might be able to find her was insupportable. Victoria's salon offered a safe haven. Possibly the only one in London.

The humiliation of the sensation of heartbreak

that had welled up inside her when his grandfather had introduced his future bride was still fresh. It shouldn't have mattered, and that's what stung the most.

He'd teased her into breaking her most sacrosanct rule, and this was the price she paid for it.

Damn him.

And damn her for letting this happen. She knew better.

She was greeted at the door by her godson, Hayden, who slid across the marble hall as though it were ice, his cries of "Aunt George!" causing their long-suffering butler to wince, squeezing one eye shut as though it would somehow make the boy quieter.

George braced herself for the inevitable collision. Hay threw his arms around her, hugging her tightly.

The Morpeths' youngest son was still in the nursery, while the eldest was at Eton, but nine-year-old Hayden had yet to be sent away to school. Next year . . .

"Hello, Hay." Something about Hayden just forced one to adore him. She hugged him back, then brushed his hair back into place with her fingers.

He smiled up at her, pale gray eyes full of mischief. He hugged her again for good measure before releasing her. "I wanted to ask you something particularly. Before Mother arrives."

"And what might that be, imp?" She repressed the urge to respond with a conspiratorial smile. The last thing Hay needed was encouragement.

"Julius's godfather is taking him to see a review of the troops in Hyde Park when he comes home," he began, staring up at her earnestly, his small frame aquiver.

"And you want me to take you, too?" It was all too

easy to picture the trouble he was likely to get them both into at such an event.

"No! I want you take me to Astley's! They have zebras now," he threw in as his clincher.

Zebras. An inducement indeed. "And wherever did you hear about this new addition?"

"Oh, Ned Arden was telling me all about it yesterday."

"Well then, that seals it. We *must* go. It would be insupportable for such a slow top as Ned Arden to steal a march on us."

Hayden gave her a beatific smile and assured her that he'd been sure she'd understand the necessity of the thing once it was properly explained to her.

"We could take Aubrey, too," he added, generously including his baby brother in the treat. George smiled, and conceded that they could indeed take Aubrey. She was still chuckling when she entered the drawing room, Hayden having run off to find his father, who had promised to take him out for a fencing lesson that morning.

He was such a charming little monster. Zebras, indeed.

Victoria, upon George's entering the drawing room, inquired immediately what her son had wheedled out of her. "For I know that look," she said, "all of Hayden's victims wear it."

George could do nothing but laugh for a moment. Victoria was really far too knowing. Though with three extremely lively boys and a husband that encouraged their most outrageous antics, she clearly needed to be.

"Hay just wants to go to Astley's," she assured her friend, taking a seat next to her, petticoats spilling over the settee. "I think we'll take Aubrey along as well, if you'll entrust two of your offspring to me at once."

"Are you sure?" Victoria inquired. "After what happened last time?"

"But last time it was to see a traveling circus, and how was I to know Morpeth gives Hay such exorbitant amounts of pocket money? And really, can you blame him? It was—after all—an equestrian monkey." George's lips quivered, but she managed not to laugh.

"That's all very well for you," Victoria retorted acerbically, eyes snapping with wrath. "You didn't have the little beast rip apart two of your best hats, bite quite the best cook you'd ever employed, and then crown his iniquities by urinating upon the poor Prince of Wales during a morning call."

"It didn't."

"I assure you, it did," Victoria insisted, sternly repressing a smile. "You should have seen his distress. A new coat, too."

"So that's why Hay's pet was sent into exile. But you needn't worry. I doubt even Hay could induce Mr. Astley to sell him a zebra."

"A zebra?" Victoria echoed warily.

"Yes, a zebra. That's what makes an outing to Astley's imperative. Or possibly, the imperative arises from the fact that your neighbor's son has been bragging about having seen the zebras already."

An outing with the children suited George's needs perfectly at the moment. It would keep her out of her house, and make it impossible for Dauntry to corner her. The busier she kept herself, and the less she was home, the better.

Eventually this feeling would pass. The urge to kill

him would fade. The desire she felt for him would disappear. Eventually . . .

So, it was with determination that she set off with them two nights later, accompanied by both Alençon and Aubrey's godfather, Bennett. Bennett had given her a sympathetic look when he'd joined her in the Morpeths' drawing room, but he'd held his tongue. If he'd pleaded his friend's case she wasn't sure what she might have done, but odds were it wouldn't have been suitable in front of the children.

Upon entering Astley's Royal Amphitheatre, they were met by the proprietor himself, Mr. Philip Astley, and ushered to a prime box. The duke clapped his old friend on the shoulder in greeting, and was assured by him that he would be back at the end of the evening's entertainment to lead them backstage for a special treat. Alençon winked at George as he took his seat, and they all settled in for the show.

The night began with a much reduced *Romeo and Juliet* performed entirely by poodles that had Bennett in stitches. By the end of the performance he—along with a large number of others—was howling right along with the dogs.

Across the dog-filled arena, a sudden movement caught George's eye as the dogs were herded out to be replaced by a troop of ponies that danced the gavotte. While the ponies circled and pranced, George stared blindly past them at the Marquis of Tregaron entertaining the Bagshotts.

The curtain at the back of the box moved aside and George wrenched her gaze away. She didn't need to see Dauntry playing the doting bridegroom. Her stomach—not to mention her temper—wouldn't be able to handle it.

Down in the arena trick riders, little more than

boys themselves, were leaping on and off cantering horses, standing on their backs while they galloped round the ring, doing backflips off them to thundering applause. Beside her Hay shook with excitement, while his little brother stood in his seat, only Bennett's restraining hand locked onto his coat keeping the boy from tumbling over the railing.

The promised zebras finally arrived, accompanied by female trick riders, their forms scandalously displayed in extremely brief costumes. The boys' eyes widened, and the adult men leered. Throughout the theatre, gentlemen sat up and took notice, perhaps for the first time all evening.

A titter rose up from the gallery below, and the sound seemed to twist around her throat. George took a deep breath, inhaling the mingled scents of horse, sawdust, and the unwashed masses.

They weren't laughing at her, but it felt as though they were. She clenched her hands in her lap and refused to give in to the urge to glance back across the arena, to look for Dauntry.

The show culminated in a mock Roman chariot race with teams of dogs harnessed to miniature chariots driven by monkeys. They careened around the track, completely out of control, until there was a tremendous crash that caused the grooms to rush out into the arena en masse.

The spectators erupted into partisan shouts as the grooms struggled to rein in the chaos in the arena. Bets were furiously laid, children shrieked a high-pitched accompaniment to the monkeys. Bennett kept a hand locked on Aubrey's coat.

When the chariots had disappeared—two of them being ignominiously dragged from the arena still attached to madly barking dogs and scolding monkeys—the crowd began to clear. George kept her attention solidly on Hayden and Aubrey. The younger boy had begun to wilt in his chair. He rubbed at his eyes with his fist and yawned.

George gathered him up, pulling him into her lap. He burrowed into her, rubbing his face against her like a puppy.

Mr. Astley returned to invite them to join him for a tour. The boys were allowed to pet the zebras, while Bennett and Alençon flirted with their riders. Hayden flashed her a cheeky smile. No doubt his nemesis, Ned Arden, would be hearing all about this on the morrow.

Chapter 14

The Marquis of T— is reported to have stormed out of
a recent performance of Hamlet. *Can it be that there*
is something rotten in more places than Denmark?

Tête-à-Tête, 11 December 1788

A footman let down the steps of George's well-sprung traveling coach, the thunk as each step unfolded loud in the quiet morning street. He handed George up into the coach and helped her new maid, Ellen, in after her. Caesar leapt in after them and immediately disposed his bulk across the entire back-facing seat.

Ellen smiled indulgently and squeezed in beside him, allowing the dog to rest his head in her lap.

It had been raining, sometimes snowing, on and off overnight. The molten sky seemed to threaten a renewed attack. There was a loud, echoing boom as her final trunk was strapped to the boot and the coach lurched into motion.

George tucked the fur carriage rug more tightly

about her and set her feet on the hot brick that had been provided. Across from her, the dog began to snore.

George let down the folding table from the side of the coach and played patience while they rolled through the intermittent storm. When she finally grew tired of the game she put the cards away and began reading Raspe's *Baron Munchausen's Narrative of His Marvellous Travels and Campaigns in Russia*. Ellen worked slowly at her tambour frame, steadily making progress on a white-work fichu.

The light thrown out by the candles burning behind glass was barely enough to read by. George couldn't imagine doing needlework. But then George couldn't imagine doing needlework under the best of circumstances.

The sound of a shot cracked the night.

The coach rocked to a sudden halt, sending George sliding across the seat.

Caesar snorted and raised his head, ears cocked up attentively. Ellen's eyes were wide, clearly visible even in the dark coach. George tensed beneath the thick fur of the carriage rug, hands and feet going cold, every nerve alive.

Outside there was shouting—her coachman's voice, sharply overridden by another.

They were being held up.

There was no other possibility.

In the sudden quiet, George could hear the jangling of the harness as the horses fretted. The creak of wood and metal as the coach shifted. The thump of feet hitting the ground. Clearly James had been ordered down from the box. Where was Thomas? Had they shot him, or had that simply been a warning shot?

Heart fluttering up into her throat, George released the panel behind her head and removed the

double-barreled pistol hidden inside. Why hadn't
she brought outriders? Lord Exley was going to be
furious if she lived to confess her foolishness. Brimstone would flay her alive. She'd never be allowed
to travel without an escort again.

The shadow of a man moved past the small window,
a deeper point of darkness in the inky night. The muddy
roads had made for slow going. They should have reached
the Three Greyhounds—and safety—hours ago.

George motioned Ellen to get behind her. The girl
climbed past Caesar, one hand pressed over her
mouth. She gave a muffled sob as George shoved her
into the corner.

Caesar crouched on the floor, hackles raised, muscles tensed beneath his fur, two hundred pounds of
sinew and bone poised for destruction.

George cocked one side of the gun and waited,
kneeling on the seat, out of the dog's way.

The man who opened that door was in for a nasty
surprise. Two, really. George could almost feel sorry
for him. And if she, and all her servants, survived,
she might even be inclined to pity . . . to mercy.

But not at this exact moment. Now was not the
time.

An eternity passed before the handle turned and
the door was thrown open. George held her shot as
Caesar sprang, his weight bearing the startled highwayman down.

The man screamed, scrabbling to escape. Curses
filled the night, skittering about like bats erupting
from a cave at dusk. The dog's baritone snarls, nasty
and brutish, made George's hair stand on end.

Another shot rang out and the window of the
coach shattered, showering the far seat with glass.
Ellen screamed, breaking into loud, hiccupping sobs.

Anger bubbled up, cutting off reason and fear. George leapt down, took aim, and fired. Powder flashed and the resulting explosion bloomed in the darkness. The nearest highwayman gave a muffled cry and fell from his saddle.

The familiar scent of sulfur perfumed the air, deadly and almost frightening for the first time in her life. George filled her lungs, drinking it in, reaching within herself for the courage of Boudicca.

The first man was pinned beneath Caesar, either dead or limp with terror. George couldn't have cared less which. He deserved whatever happened to him. Wrath welled up within her, filling her to her fingertips. It warmed her, reassuring as an army at her back.

The third highwayman sat upon his horse, still as a statue, seeming to stare right through her. Daring her to shoot him.

George cocked the remaining hammer, the sound alarmingly loud in the dead quiet of the night. The highwayman flung his spent pistol to the ground, spun his horse round, and sped into the night, great-coat flapping behind him.

George swallowed hard as her knees gave out and she sank to the ground. Mud flooded her skirts, soaking through the fabric until she was wet to the skin.

Merde.

Not only was the bitch a better shot than any woman had a right to be, but the bumbling peasants he'd hired had so fouled things up that she was now the only one of them armed.

Philippe flung his spent pistol to the ground and yanked hard on the reins, bringing his mount about. The nag swung its head toward his knee, teeth bared.

Philippe kicked it in the face as hard as he could. It turned away, ears flattened to its skull, but it did as it was told.

God, how he hated riding. The manifold discomforts. Saddles that rubbed. Exposure to the elements. The stink of horse working its way into your clothes. Into your skin. And he hated this particular horse more than most, bony, ill-tempered beast that it was. Even its gaits were uncomfortable.

He'd spent a small fortune arranging this. And what had it gotten him?

Nothing.

At best? Two dead henchmen, each with fifty pounds in his pocket. At worst? Two wounded men who, while they didn't know his name, did know that this had been no mere robbery.

A branch whipped across his face, cutting the skin. Philippe cursed and bent lower in the saddle, flailing at his mount with his crop.

What were the odds that either she or one of her legion of lovers wouldn't put this together with her maid's death and come to the correct conclusion?

It was all that damn dog's fault. How could he have known that she'd drag that monster along with her? That had been the tipping point. When the dog had taken Black Charlie down as though he'd been a stag, there'd been no hope of recovery after that.

Merde. Merde. Merde.

George curled into a ball, tucked into the bed the innkeeper's wife had warmed with a copper pan filled with glowing coals. She shut her eyes and willed herself to sleep.

Caesar's tail thumped softly on the bed and George

reached out to pet him, running her hand down his shoulder and side, taking comfort in the solid feel of the dog there beside her. There weren't enough roasts, feather beds, and roaring fires in the world for him.

Ellen had finally stopped crying after they'd reached the inn. The innkeeper had sent one of his grooms off for the doctor, who'd come and stitched up Thomas's arm where the attacker's first shot had left a deep furrow, filled with bits of shredded livery that had had to be carefully picked out.

She was as clean as a pitcher of hot water and a sponge could get her, which meant she wasn't nearly as clean as she'd like to be. She wanted to wash the whole night away, climb into a large tub of steaming water and scrub until her skin was raw. But there had been no chance of a bath at the late hour they'd arrived at the Three Greyhounds.

They'd promised her one in the morning. After which she'd need to meet with the local constable to explain the two dead bodies they'd arrived with, slung over a single swaybacked mare.

Her shot had been as true as she could ever have hoped, and Caesar had proved why the Romans called mastiffs the dogs of war. Whoever the man who'd opened the coach door had been, he hadn't had a chance.

It had been a robbery. Nothing more. Just a robbery.

Highwaymen were a common hazard.

But George couldn't shake the ominous feeling that had come over her when she'd faced down the third man. There had been something wrong. Something very wrong about the way he'd been looking at her.

Chapter 15

*Lord S— now appears to be the party most worthy of
our pity. A man without bride or mistress. Turned
away by both his family and the butler of No. 5.*

Tête-à-Tête, 14 December 1788

"Georgianna!" Lady Glendower practically ran
across the great expanse of marble floor, her hair in
wild disorder, cap askew. "We've been worried about
you, darling. You were due two days ago."

"The roads are a quagmire," George replied, hugging her. The honeysuckle scent her mother-in-law
favored enveloped her, welcoming her home. "And
I had a few misadventures that I'll tell you about
later."

The countess gave her a searching look, fine brows
drawn together over the bridge of her nose. "There's
a fire all made up, and Mrs. Stubbs is already heating
some wine."

George shed her pelisse and hat and stood huddled
by the fire, warming her frozen fingers, listening with

half an ear to Lady Glendower gush about the preparations, the early arrivals, and the profound chaos that had taken over her house.

"I can't even get into my dressing room," she declared with a note of triumph. "It's filled to the ceiling with presents. Poor Martha has to contort herself terribly to retrieve so much as a shoe."

"You're always like this." George moved away from the fire as one of the logs snapped, sending a shower of sparks and cinders toward her. "I can't remember a Christmas that wasn't something of a romp. Just wait until the children all arrive. Perhaps we can convince Hay to ride his pony through the Great Hall again? Or maybe Sydney can oversee a hurling match in the courtyard? I don't think anyone's been brave enough to do that since Lyon shattered part of the roof."

"Perhaps just this once we could get through the season without sending Glendower into fits."

"But what fun would that be?" Gabriel appeared in the doorway and lounged over to sink down onto a settee placed facing the hearth. He extended one hand and drew George down beside him. "Griggs had your bags taken up to your room. And little Simone Staunton is clamoring to see you. Why so subdued, love?"

George flinched. Trust Gabriel to notice she wasn't herself. "I'll tell you later. After dinner." He looked at her very much as her mother-in-law had, mobile brows frowning. "Honestly. I'll tell you everything, just let me change and eat first."

"I don't like the sound of *everything*." He took one of her hands and chafed it between his.

"And you won't like it any better after dinner, but leave it till then all the same." George leaned in, resting her head on his shoulder, taking comfort in the familiar solidity. The shadow of stubble that shadowed his jaw. The sheer physicality of the way he touched her. He was sure of his welcome.

The one person she could always count on.

After she'd drunk the hot wine sent up by Mrs. Stubbs, Lady Glendower sent them both off to their rooms to dress for dinner. As she shooed them off she suddenly brightened. "Perhaps Simone would like to join the adults for dinner? None of the other children have arrived yet, and I hate to think of her eating all alone."

George smiled at her mother-in-law and shook her head. "And you say I indulge Hayden. You're shameless with that child."

"Well, I never had any daughters of my own, and you were one of the boys through and through. So I'm making do." The countess linked her arm with George's and walked with her up the stairs, their petticoats fighting for dominance with every step. "I quite enjoy her visits, and I most sincerely hope you've made it clear to the colonel that he's not so much reclaiming a daughter as joining the family."

"I think he's quite clear on that point," George assured her, parting from her as they reached the door to her room. "Quite frankly, I think he's too shy to deny you anything you asked him. The poor man has absolutely no idea how to deal with women. And mothering of any sort completely routs him. You'll have him wrapped around your little finger in no time."

George quickly washed and changed into a simple gown of striped tobine. She collected Simone from the nursery and escorted her down to the family dining room.

Simone skipped happily along, obviously excited by her invitation to join the adults. She was wearing the pearl necklet her father had brought her, and she spent the entire meal showing it off to anyone who would look.

When the meal was over, the ladies excused themselves and left the men to their port. George rose and left with them, wanting to spend the first night cozily with the countess and the dowager. As she exited the room, Gabriel raised one brow. George scrunched up her nose at him.

Provoking man!

She followed the other ladies down the hall to the blue salon, where a roaring fire and wine awaited them. The gentlemen joined them shortly, tonight being really almost a family affair, and George found herself repressing a laugh as Simone gravitated immediately to Gabriel and set about practicing her girlish wiles upon him. He bore it all in good stride, but sagged back into the couch with relief when Miss Nutley came to collect her.

"Now that the infantry has left us, I think it high time you explained exactly what detained you."

Chapter 16

*All the world has deserted Town for country hearth
and home . . . the truly interesting question is for whose
hearth and home?*

Tête-à-Tête, 14 December 1788

Ivo folded up the collar of his greatcoat and adjusted his muffler. The mist had begun to turn to
snow. Flakes melted against his skin, sending icy
rivulets down his neck. Bennett swung up into the
saddle and brought his mount under control with a
firm grip on the reins.

Ivo's mount danced across the cobbles, iron-shod
hooves ringing loudly against the stone. He gripped
the saddle with his thighs, flexed his calves, pushing
his heels down. His godmother, whom they were escorting, was already safely ensconced within her carriage, dry and eager to be on her way.

They'd be lucky if the roads weren't impassible.

Resigned to a long, wet day, he signaled to the
coachman. With a snap of the reins and a sharp whis-

tle, the coach lumbered forward, its wheels clacking loudly as the coach rolled down the street.

He and Bennett rode just in front of the coach, neither of them talking as they concentrated on controlling their grain-high mounts. Ivo's horse shied about, prancing, nimbly cross-stepping in its exuberance.

Ivo grimaced behind his collar and stepped up the pace as they reached the edge of the city. Snow flew past him in flurries. It stuck to his coat, melted, and soaked into the exposed leather of his breeches. His toes were already numb.

He'd eagerly accepted an invitation from George's brother-in-law to join them all for the Christmas holidays. He'd been looking forward to the weeks of close confinement with George, until his godmother and Alençon had dashed his hopes of a quick reunion over breakfast.

They'd been discussing the yearly Glendower house party, explaining who would be there, reminiscing about past events and scandals, when Lady Bev had let slip how delighted she and the dowager countess were with Colonel Staunton. Alençon leapt in with the fact that he and Carr were convinced they just might make a match of it.

When Ivo had uttered "Who?" in horrified tones, Alençon had replied, "George and the colonel, of course," causing Ivo to choke on his tea.

It wasn't bad enough that he had to fight his way past her adoring hordes. That her bulldogs circled and snapped at his heels. Now everyone was scenting bridals, and the groom they'd settled on was someone else.

Two days after George's arrival, the house had begun to fill. George strolled downstairs on Charles's arm, trying not to laugh as he regaled her with a detailed description of his most recent foray to Bond Street. Charles simply wasn't inclined to put as much thought and effort into his wardrobe as seemed to be required.

"I don't want to become a damned caper merchant. I just want to buy a coat. Bloody tailors make it out to be a life or death decision. As if it matters if I choose superfine or Bath coating, velvet or damask."

George lost the battle, mirth bubbling over as they reached the bottom of the stairs. An exhausted-looking Lady Beverly stood in the hall, flanked by two men in dripping greatcoats. Griggs assisted Lady Bev with her cloak, while several footmen stood ready to take the gentlemen's coats and hats.

The nearest man tossed his hat aside and shrugged out of his coat, revealing Bennett. He smiled widely at George when he spotted her.

The other man had his back to them as he gave the footmen directions for their luggage. Dauntry. She didn't need to see his face to know it was him. The way he stood. The way he moved. The simple act of handing over his coat. Every motion spoke to her.

Ah, the perfidy of friends and family. George's throat tightened. Her stomach turned over, pressing against the stiff enclosure of her stays.

The twinkle in the old woman's eyes was more than enough to tell her everything she needed to know. She'd brought the earl along with designs in mind.

Damn her and her matchmaker's soul.

Ivo stood rooted to the ground, staring at her.

Her eyes met his. Desire whipped through her, hard and undeniable. Equally impossible.

He was impossible.

"Lady Bev, come with me at once." George dropped Charles's arm and hurried over Lady Beverly. "You must be chilled to the bone. And the two of you had best change immediately. I'll have Griggs send up arrack."

Ivo settled his coat over his shoulders as he hurried down the stairs, Bennett a few steps ahead of him. She'd been clinging to Staunton's arm, smiling up at him.

His gut churned.

She was his. What was he going to have to do to make her realize that? His. Not Staunton's. Not her damn foreign dogs'. Not anyone's but his.

They were greeted in the drawing room with a round of ribbing for their late arrival and summarily borne off to the billiard room. Ivo cast one resentful glance back at George before allowing himself to be drawn out of the room.

She didn't even seem to notice he was there. Damn frosty woman. He grimaced as he spun his cue idly. There was no point in pushing ahead before knowing the lay of the land.

Every fiber of his being itched to storm back into the drawing room and force her to listen to reason. To him.

He had a fortnight, after all.

Surely that would be long enough to bring her round?

George bit into a warm scone, savoring the tang of butter, the sweetness of currants. She added a splash of milk to her empty teacup and poured herself a second cup of tea, emptying the pot.

Fragrant steam curled upward, the hint of bergamot reminding her unwelcomingly of Dauntry.

She'd spent the whole night lying awake, wanting to creep down the hall to his room. It was humiliating how badly she wanted him. How much she missed him.

Calm. Cool. Collected. Those were the things she was supposed to be. A heartless bitch, even. Above such petty emotions as lust and loneliness.

The door opened with a rattle and her brother-in-law and Gabriel burst in, unruly as a pack of foxhounds who'd caught the scent. Sydney loudly demanded if she could remember where they had left the curling stones.

"We haven't had those out in years." She drank the dregs of her tea, grimacing when she discovered it had grown cold while she'd been daydreaming. "I think they're in a spare tack box out in the barn."

"The green one," Sydney agreed, looking hungrily at a plate loaded with eggs and a thick slice of beef. "I'd totally forgotten about that. When we were children, we kept them in the bottom of the toy chest in the nursery. I looked there this morning—nothing."

George thought for a moment. "We used them every winter, and as I remember, we were quite territorial about them."

Gabriel grabbed several wedges of toast and loaded them up with a dripping abundance of marmalade, explaining between bites that the boys had asked to go skating later, and he and Sydney had had the brilliant idea to teach them all to curl. "I don't think we've passed that bit of our childhood on."

"Excellent proposition." George tried to refresh her cup for a third time, forgetting that the pot was empty. "This is the first time in years the pond has frozen solid and I say we take advantage of it."

When they finally got to the pond it was after noon. The ice was already whizzing with the village children playing tag on homemade skates of bone and wood. Their brightly colored caps stood out starkly against their muted coats and the white snow. The vicar's wife was obviously still a prodigious knitter.

The gathered children greeted Sydney with a cheer and were shyly introduced to the visitors. The Morpeths' three boys and Simone were already known to most of the locals, having spent large parts of their young lives running through the village. They had been joined for the day by all the other visiting children and most of the younger adults.

George supervised the children putting on their skates while Sydney assisted the three young Misses Tilehurst with theirs. Gabriel, Dauntry, and Charles were left to haul the curling stones out of the gig and carefully lug the heavy stones out onto the ice.

Dauntry looked thoroughly confused and confounded by the stones. He'd insisted on coming along, his attention wholly, intently, on her.

Why couldn't he accept his *congé*?

George had made sure she'd been surrounded by the children in the sleigh. No room for any of the men. Dauntry had no idea how effective a chaperone a swarm of children could be.

He was about to find out. Poor bastard.

George strapped on her own skates and joined Gabriel and Sydney on the ice where they were attempting to explain curling to the gathered children. She skated in lazy figure eights around them, interjecting explanations and clarifications.

The fur tippet around her throat tickled her cheek. The breeze raised a flurry of snowflakes from the bank.

Dauntry was down at the other end of the pond, skating in swift, sure circles around Charles, who was experimentally pushing the stones across the ice, a look of pure determination on his face.

George forced herself to quit watching him and turned her attention back to the children.

"Perhaps we should simply show them?" she suggested, cutting off another long-winded explanation. Sydney called all the children over to watch a practice match, then set them all to it.

They spent the rest of the afternoon learning the peculiar natures of the various stones: which ones slid to the right or the left, which picked up speed as they went, which didn't. George and Sydney refereed, leaving Brimstone and Dauntry free to supervise the play at the other end.

George kept waiting for the simmering dislike between the two men to explode into something more. Dauntry was stiff with irritation, Gabriel's face was set in a blank mask that she knew hid disdain and an urge to plant his fist in Dauntry's too pretty face.

When everyone finally grew tired of curling, Sydney organized a huge game of tag. Everyone racing about the ice to the best of their abilities, the high-pitched shrieks of the children cutting through the air.

Hayden zipped past in pursuit of the youngest Tilehurst girl. Caught her, sent her flailing across the ice and into George.

George fell back into the snowbank at the pond's

edge, sending up a shower of snow. Hayden's excited laughter and Gabriel's voice calling her name drowned out everything else as she floundered in the snow.

Closer than anyone else, Ivo grabbed his chance. George just lay there, laughing. Her petticoats were hiked up, showing most of her legs from the knees down. Elaborate orange and green clocks crawled up her stockings, led his gaze where it already wanted to go.

Lust and irritation in equal measures pulsed through him.

He held out his hand, half afraid she wouldn't accept his help. She put her hand in his, fingers brushing his palm as her hand curled around his. Her gaze met his, a flicker of unmistakable desire in it.

Ivo braced the edge of his skates so he wouldn't fall or slide and hauled her up. She found her footing and smiled up at him, curls slipping out at her temples, a disorderly riot framing her face.

Snow dusted her hair, crystalline powder that caught the light, reflected and refracted it so that she glowed.

That was the first smile he'd had from her in what seemed like forever. It cut straight through him. Gutted him.

No woman could smile like that at a man and not forgive him.

Chapter 17

A little bird tells us that Lord S— has followed Mrs. E—. Will he be welcomed as the fox welcomes the hound, with tooth and claw?

Tête-à-Tête, 17 December 1788

After dinner, Ivo retreated to the billiard room, only to be followed by George a scant half-hour later. She went straight to the Duke of Alençon, her jasmine scent flooding through the room, making him dizzy. Making it impossible to ignore her.

The duke was seated by the fire, brandy in hand, feet stretched out onto a footstool. Ivo shifted his weight and rested the cue on the toe of his shoe, watching her. Desire flooded through him in a rush, leaving him lightheaded.

She motioned toward the duke's feet and he obligingly swung them down, allowing her to use the footstool as a seat. She sank down in a sea of silk, her back to the billiard table, the fine bones of her neck begging to be stroked.

The flames lit her hair, light gleaming through the curls, obscuring the edges. Ivo tried to concentrate on the game, while Bennett quizzed him with his eyes. Ivo grimaced, and sank his shot.

His throat was dry, his hands cold. What should have been the simplest thing in the world seemed impossible. He wanted her, quixotic, infuriating woman that she was. Wanted her badly enough that he was on the verge of making a fool of himself.

At that exact moment, he'd have given his entire fortune to have been able to cross the room and caress the fire-warmed skin of her neck, tickle her nape, smell her hair. To have the right to do so. Her shoulders, covered only by a flimsy fichu, sloped elegantly away from that enticing neck.

The duke chuckled and Ivo forced his attention back to the billiard table. He couldn't seem to keep his eyes off her for even a few minutes. And the duke seemed only too aware of the direction of his thoughts.

The old man had the decided air of a pampered hound parading his bone before a starving cur. The surety that his right was unassailable.

George hadn't so much as glanced at him since she'd come in, though he could tell her whole body was tense. The line of her back was stiff, her hands arranged in her lap in a pose of demure rest that he knew to be unnatural for her.

He could only hope it was a reaction to him—the strain of the effort not to respond to her own desires. Four nights . . . that's what she still owed him. He knew it and she knew it.

The question was, how did he go about collecting?

Alençon smiled at her, his lazy king-of-all-he-surveyed smile, and held out his now empty glass. George took it without a word. No doubt her godfather was enjoying himself hugely, watching her and Dauntry circle like a mare and a stallion set loose in the same paddock.

She filled the duke's glass, heavy amber liquid flowing from decanter to glass, fumes rising to tease her senses. Sydney wandered over, leaned against the commode. "Your imp has demanded sleigh driving lessons. And I thought perhaps you'd like to assist. In fact, I'm going to insist upon it."

George laughed at the picture of Sydney trapped all day teaching Hay—and likely all the other children— to drive. They'd have him ripping his wig to shreds before the horse had broken a sweat.

"I'm yours to command. Let me deliver Alençon his brandy and we can go somewhere quieter to plot."

She returned the duke's glass to him while Sydney waited, then she allowed him to lead her off to the drawing room for tea. It had been time for her to leave anyway. Past time. Dauntry was practically vibrating and she couldn't take it anymore. Every inch of her body came alive when he was near with the need to be touched and the desire to touch him in return . . .

She couldn't fathom what he thought he was doing, making such a show of himself. Gabriel and Alençon kept making sly comments. Lady Bev had been far more direct, as was her wont, simply begging George to show her poor godson a little mercy, pointing out that he was, after all, only a man, and one could expect only so much of them.

How was she supposed to cope with such innuendo? Such expectations? Especially in the face of his grandfather's pronouncement?

* * *

After their driving lesson the children ran off to the house, Sydney in tow, in pursuit of Mrs. Stubbs's promised chocolate and biscuits. George lingered in the barn, making sure their gallant little mare got a bit of extra attention after her exertions.

She ran her hand down Velvet's neck, smoothing the slick hide over the hard muscle that lay beneath, then ran her fingers through the curling strands of mane. She pushed the mare's curious lips away from her bodice, whiskers prickly against the palm of her hand.

She held the apple she'd filched from the kitchen while the horse bit into it, slobber coating her hand. She turned it, careful to keep her fingers out of the way so Velvet could take another bite.

She was still in the stall fussing over the mare when she heard Bennett pointing out the strong points on a team her father-in-law had recently purchased.

"Sturdy legs, wide chests, large heads. The whole team bred and broke by General Iverson. He's got the old horse magic the Irish go on about. Never starts out a team too soon. Never ruins their mouths. I've never driven an Iverson team that wasn't superb. He's been crossing his Cleveland Bays with a huge black he imported from Friesland, and the result are these beauties here. If you're really interested in a good, stout team I'd be happy to give you his direction."

"I'd appreciate that." Dauntry's voice sounded loudly in the peaceable silence of the barn. Every sense stretched out to where the two men stood. Awareness caused the hair on her arms to raise.

"I've no intention of setting up strings on all the major roads, but I do think I'd like to have changes in place between London and Ashcombe Park. Can't stand the bony nags and break-downs the posting inns pawn off on you."

George finished feeding the last of the apple to Velvet, trying to quiet the sudden shaking of her hands. There didn't seem to be enough air in the barn, and what there was smelled of dung and straw and warm horse. When the apple was gone she slipped the headstall over her shoulder and emptied the grain bucket into the trough.

Dauntry really hadn't yet adjusted to his new station. No posting house was likely to give such poor mounts to Morpeth, or her father-in-law, or even to herself. If you weren't known, they'd give you the worst they thought they could get away with. He really was going to have to learn how to come the earl in public, distasteful as he might find it.

She gave the mare one last slap on the rump and exited the stall, being careful to latch it securely behind her. Velvet was a consummate escape artist, and once loose, was the devil to catch. The sly thing had spent more than a month loose in the home woods over the summer before being caught.

Without glancing toward the end of the barn where Dauntry was, she strolled slowly down to the tack room. Inside were trees filled with a varied collection of saddles: gentlemen's saddles, ladies' sidesaddles, children's saddles of every description and size, even a couple of beat-up cavalry saddles. The walls were lined with tack boxes, hung with grain pails and pegs holding a vast array of headstalls, lead ropes, bridles and bits.

The tack room smelled of horse sweat, saddle soap, dust, and hay. A homey, comforting smell. The stable had always been the place she went to think, to calm down, to simply *be*.

She shook her head, wishing she could settle the roiling uncertainty within her, reaching up to hang the headstall with its mates with unsteady hands.

Footsteps, loud and heavy, sounded on the wooden plank floor behind her. She took a deep breath, let it out with a huff, overly conscious of the other presence that filled the tack room.

She turned to find Dauntry directly behind her, eyes intent. He was just standing there, staring at her. If he'd been another sort of man she'd have said *heart in his eyes*. But it wasn't his heart, it was simply lust. Pure unadulterated lust. And she could feel its response well up inside her.

She cocked her head and stared back at him appraisingly, refusing to give ground.

He took one step closer, booted foot pushing between her own. Another, that forced her back against the wall. His lips covered hers with a sureness that caught her off guard. With her head trapped amongst the headstalls, her feet tangled among the dangling lead ropes, she didn't have anywhere to go.

Dauntry leaned in, hands going to either side of her waist, deepening the kiss. His tongue stroked hers enticingly, inviting her to play. Damn the man, but she missed him. Humiliating as that was.

Then, just as suddenly as he'd pounced, he ended the kiss, leaning forward farther, forehead resting against the wall beside her, body holding her in place. He was breathing heavily, each exhalation shuddering out of him.

"What do you think you're doing?" George pushed her arms up between them so that her hands rested on his chest.

"Our bargain hasn't been fulfilled." His lips were right against her ear, breath scalding her skin. His hands tightened, thumbs pressing into her ribs, squeezing her stays in tight.

Her knees nearly buckled.

"It's as *fulfilled* as it's going to be." She thrust her hands out, pushing past him, swallowing down the urge to slap him, to ball up her hand into a fist and break his nose.

Our bargain hasn't been fulfilled.

What an ass he was.

Ivo cursed under his breath and threw one hand out to catch her, then thought better of it. Her fingers were flexing in agitation. If he touched her now, she'd gouge out his eyes.

He sank down onto a convenient tack box.

That wasn't at all what he'd planned. Wasn't what was supposed to have happened.

When he'd seen George sauntering down to the barn, he'd excused himself and followed her, thinking it was the best chance he was going to have to speak to her alone. Perhaps the only chance.

She spent most of her time with the children, or with that damned colonel, and now he'd gone and made everything worse, clutching at her like some soldier on holiday.

He really had meant just to talk to her, to clear up the misunderstanding his grandfather had created. Instead he'd pushed her up against a wall and mauled her.

Damn it all!

He pinched the bridge of his nose, trying to ward off the headache he could feel coming on.

Damn. Damn. Damn.

* * *

George stormed back into the house and up to her room. What the hell did he think he was doing? Damn him! He'd shaken up her life badly enough, and now he had the gall to show up and demand she live up to a bargain he'd forced her into under duress.

A bargain which dishonored them both.

She'd never taken a lover who was married or promised elsewhere, and she never would. Not knowingly.

She tossed her hat and redingote onto the bed and flung herself into the window seat, staring out across the south lawn, watching the slowly falling snow. The muffled countryside was beautiful. Quiet and deserted.

She pulled the pins from her hair and shook it out, rubbing the tingles from her scalp as her hair settled around her shoulders.

The problem was, she'd kissed him back. That, just for a moment, was all she could think about. And whether or not it would have been safe to push him down onto a tack box and climb on top of him.

Annoyed with herself, with Dauntry, with life in general, she pulled a blanket from the bed, and spent the afternoon curled up under it reading. She didn't go down for luncheon, or answer her door when a knock sounded, loud and peremptory.

She wasn't interested in seeing anyone right now. Not Gabriel, not Alençon, not her father-in-law, and certainly not Dauntry.

All she wanted was a quiet afternoon, undisturbed. And if for large parts of the day the book remained open to the same page while she stared out the window and tried to think about something other than her unfulfilled bargain, well, only she was aware that that was how she had employed her afternoon. If anyone asked she'd simply say she was catching up on her correspondence.

She was still in her carriage dress, curled up in the window seat, cold but unwilling to move, when her maid arrived to help her dress for dinner. Ellen didn't say a word, but George could tell she was concerned by the way she fussed and fidgeted, laying out her gown with agitated motions.

George forced herself up and waved away the gown, choosing an informal caraco and petticoats instead. She hurried across the house to the wing that contained the countess's rooms, her every step muffled by a never-ending series of carpets, overseen by the eyes of ancestors dating back to the reign of Henry VII.

She caught her mother-in-law just as the countess was leaving her room. "I'm going to eat with the children tonight, if you don't mind. Apparently there's some sort of trouble brewing between the younger ones. Hay was telling me all about it this morning, and I think it might be best if one of us gave a look in."

Lady Glendower gave her a curious look but didn't inquire if she had some other motivation for avoiding the rest of the guests. "You're still planning on going to Leicester with Bennett tomorrow?"

"Yes, Mama. Bennett and I shall execute all your orders to the letter."

When George entered the nursery, Hayden was nowhere to be seen. The absence of the most volatile of the nursery's ranks sent a chill through her. Hay was capable of the most startling and amazing things if left to his own devices.

Miss Nutley's wan smile left George with little doubt that things had spiraled out of control. Simone's governess was one of the most capable women George had ever encountered. If she was looking harassed, things were every bit as bad as Hay had said they were.

The middle Tilehurst girl, Caroline, was openly resentful of her eldest sister's inclusion with the adults, and with her own interment with the children. She bossed them around, flouted Miss Nutley's gentle rule, and took out her displeasure on them all.

"I've come to dine with the children, and to solicit their help with the upcoming Christmas festivities."

Excited chatter broke out among the children. Miss Nutley's smile softened, her eyes clearly communicating her understanding of the visit.

As they were taking their seats for dinner, Hayden slipped in, face alight with mischief. George groaned silently. He'd clearly committed some act of devilment, and was quite pleased with himself.

He took in George's presence with a slight gulp, and a look of wide-eyed innocence. His most guilty expression. George recognized it immediately. A smile twisted up one corner of her mouth. That was the problem: Hay at his most outrageous was also Hay at his most charming and adorable.

As he slid into his seat, Hay shot a glance to his older brother and then to Simone, who giggled. Whatever he'd done, they'd all been in on it.

Dinner progressed amicably enough. All the children were caught up in George's entertainment schemes for the annual Christmas fête. Even Caroline seemed mollified by having her ideas listened to, her opinions solicited.

The Glendowers' annual Christmas fête and public day was one of the biggest events on the local social calendar. All of the local gentry would be present, as well as the villagers and the tenants of the Glendowers' estate. There would be food, music, and games.

The earl would host various sporting contests for the gentlemen. The countess and dowager countess would sponsor some sort of cooking contest: apple pie, gingerbread, plum pudding. It changed every year. The main ingredients would already have been delivered to all the participating households. Judges' slots would be awarded to the gentlemen as prizes and by lottery.

At the end of the day, the Glendowers would hand out presents to the assembled guests. Expensive baubles for the gentry, more practical things for the villagers and tenants. George had spent the last few afternoons closeted with her father-in-law going over the lists: who had a baby in the last year; who had married; who had died. Most of the gifts had already been purchased, and a steady stream of wagons had been arriving for weeks. There was a small list of things that were still outstanding, and Bennett had volunteered to take George into Leicester on the morrow to collect them.

But first she had to find out what the children were up to.

All through the meal, Julius, Simone, and Hayden kept smiling covertly at one another. Smirking, really. Whatever it was he'd done, it had to be something terrible.

George thought about it as she ate. She'd better send a maid to check Caroline's room. Especially the bed. Two summers ago, the boys had filled their tutor's bed with leeches, and had found the enter-

prise most rewarding, as it had achieved their ulti-
mate goal: the man's immediate resignation.

When the meal was over, George took a seat by the
fire, and carefully made lists of the children's sugges-
tions for games and prizes.

Lord Glendower arrived not long after they had
finished. Several footmen followed him, each carrying a large urn of assorted marbles. The last footman
had a bag filled with the small drawstring bags the
maids had been sewing all year.

While the children were busy helping Lord Glendower divvy up the marbles, making sure to put a
good selection in each bag, the nursery maid crept
back into the room and went straight to George's
side. She was laughing silently as she leaned forward
and whispered, "He gave her an apple-pie bed, made
with stable sweepings."

"He didn't?"

"Oh yes, ma'am, but it's all been cleared away, and
the bed remade clean. Not but that she didn't de-
serve something, ma'am, the way she treats the little
mites."

Knowing full well that if the maids were defending
something that caused them extra work, the behavior
that had caused it must be extraordinary, George
thanked the girl, and eyed the children assessingly.
She called Julius over from where he was bagging the
marbles Aubrey chose and motioned for him to take
a seat.

"So, do you want to tell me what Hayden's been up
to?"

Julius blinked, then leapt into the breach, "She de-
serves it, Aunt George. Really. You know I don't usually support Hay's pranks, but she's a monster."

"Well, the maids have already cleaned the bed, and

I think we'll keep it between us. No need to get you all in trouble, when I'm sure you were provoked. But no more tricks. We'll find a better way of dealing with Miss Caroline. She's just feeling left out. Her sister is downstairs, and Simone got to eat with the adults, too. Don't worry, I'll take care of it. And if she doesn't improve, you're to tell me before Hay attacks again."

Julius smiled, looking suddenly like a miniature copy of his father. "Thank you, Aunt George." Then he slipped away, returning to where Aubrey was still seated, happily playing with the marbles.

Maybe some special job at the fête could be found for Caroline?

George hated to reward the girl for her behavior, but someone clearly needed to pay some attention to her. Her sister's first season was the only topic of concern for their aunt at the moment. And Caroline, like everyone else, was excluded from the triumvirate that was Julius, Hayden, and Simone. Taking it out on the smaller ones wasn't a good way of expressing her frustration, but George could understand it. And if all George's attempts didn't work, then Hayden could be loosed again.

Chapter 18

Can it be that the Angelstone Turk has returned to the hunt? The lovely Mrs. L— certainly appears to have passed into the keeping of a certain Scottish lord . . .

Tête-à-Tête, 19 December 1788

George pulled on her gloves, flexing her fingers to work them into the tight confines of the tan leather. She glanced about the hall, counting heads: Hay and Simone were whispering, Julius was riding herd on Aubrey, and Miss Tilehurst had control of her two sisters.

All of the children were accompanying her to Leicester, with the stated purpose of buying gifts for their parents. In reality, George wanted to get them out of the nursery before Caroline drove Hay to further retaliation.

It was a bright, beautiful day. Last night's snow had coated the roads deeply, so they'd elected to take the large sleigh. George double-checked that the children were all dressed warmly enough, hats and gloves on, coats buttoned up tightly, mufflers tied round their necks, then shooed them all out before her.

The sleigh was waiting out in the drive. Up on the box was Dauntry, reins in hand, the capes of his greatcoat draping his shoulders, making them appear even wider then they normally did.

George blinked, less than pleased. Her stomach gave a now familiar lurch. Her nipples budded, pressing against her stays with rough insistence. Her body's strong response only set her teeth on edge.

Why this man? England was filled with attractive rogues she could bed, and she wanted none of them.

She glanced around while the children clambered into the sleigh. Bennett was nowhere to be found. Annoyance flashed through her, overriding the bloom of lust.

Dauntry smiled at her, a lazy, self-satisfied smile. An invitation to sin. George kept her face carefully neutral and stepped up into the sleigh.

As she settled the children, tucking them under the blankets, making sure the warm bricks were near their feet, she eyed the earl with repressed hostility.

"Just where is Bennett?"

She took a seat between Julius and Simone in the forward-facing seat.

"Still in bed. Got a terrible cough. I'm sure he'll be better tonight, though."

"I'm sure he will," George agreed with asperity, glaring at his back. His queue snaked darkly down his back, the end curling as though he'd twisted it.

Simply perfect. A whole day trapped in close quarters with the earl, courtesy of Bennett, and probably Lady Bev as well. She was going to do something vile to Bennett when they got back. Flay him alive and strip the flesh from his bones. Better yet? Write a scathing report to Helen Perripoint, the lady he was currently attempting to bed.

While she fumed, Dauntry twisted in his seat, turning to ask Hay if he'd like to drive part of the way. "You can all take turns," he suggested to the other budding whips as Hay clambered up onto the seat beside him and stuck his tongue out at his elder brother.

Hayden drove most of the way, Dauntry supervising him carefully, guiding him through the differences between driving the small one-horse sleigh they'd had out the day before and the larger two-horse sleigh they were in today.

As they approached the outskirts of town, Dauntry took the reins back and carefully steered them to the White Hart. They passed under the archway that led to the yard and the ostlers came running. One went to the horses' heads and Dauntry leapt down from the box, boots landing with the distinct sound of wet snow underfoot. George jumped down before he could come to her assistance, and turned to help the children. She herded them inside while the earl dealt with the ostlers.

A note sent over the previous day had reserved a private parlor, and they all hurried in to warm up. The children huddled close to the fire, cheeks pink with cold.

The landlord appeared with hot chocolate and the children fell upon him as if they were starving. When the cups were drained George walked them out to the street, gave them each a five-pound note, and sent them out to shop.

Hayden and Simone took off like wild animals, pelting down the street toward the familiar shops.

Julius, with his youngest brother in tow, headed off behind them, followed closely by the Tilehurst girls.

As the children disappeared down the street, Ivo turned an apprehensive eye toward George. "Isn't this rather like turning the Goths loose in Rome?"

"Much. Though they won't have a year to sack the city, only a few hours, so we'll have to hope for the best." She pulled out her list, snapped it open in a businesslike way, and studied it for a moment. "Mr. Brittle's shop first," she announced with decision.

Ivo trailed along beside her, not quite brave enough to offer her his arm. She'd radiated her displeasure the entire drive. Even now she was stiff with annoyance.

For the moment, it was enough to just to be able to watch her. To be near her.

She had on her favorite Russian fur hat, with a deep pumpkin redingote with matching fur reveres and cuffs. One arm was thrust all the way through an enormous bearskin muff, the hand that protruded clutched her long list.

She strode purposefully down the street, stopping here and there to greet fellow shoppers. Most of the townspeople seemed to recognize her, to have a friendly greeting for her, or a message for her in-laws.

He followed her into a small shop filled with boxes, bins, and jars of various candies. The scent of sugar and peppermint overwhelmed everything else.

The proprietor greeted her like an old friend. He bustled forward, wiping his hands on his apron. "Mrs. Exley, we were wondering when we'd see you."

The old man chatted with George, took the list she had prepared, and promised to have it all boxed up and sent over to the White Hart. That done, George sallied forth to her next destination, her demeanor frosty at best. She placed what seemed like enormous orders to Ivo at the butcher, the grocer, and the cheesemonger.

She dragged him into an apothecary shop to purchase vast quantities of Denmark Lotion, Dr. Johnson's Restorative Pig Jelly, headache powder, and a dozen other things Ivo had never heard of. She double-checked the earl's earlier order with a toy merchant and added a few things of her own, mostly brightly colored tops and jackstraws. The jolly little shop owner packed the dangerous implements in with the other toys while Ivo repressed a shudder. He could clearly imagine the terror the boys could inspire armed thusly.

At the mercers', she picked out lengths of cloth, checking off names on a long list. She bought spools of silk ribbon and thread, dozens of small ribbon rosettes in assorted colors, cards and cards of pins and needles, and several pairs of scissors.

Ivo leaned over her shoulder and peered down at her list.

"Exactly what is all this for?"

He was unable to picture any need George, or the other ladies at the Court, could possibly have for large amounts of serviceable stuff and linsey-woolsey. George certainly didn't sew her own clothes, and a more insipid decoration than the rosettes she'd pounced on with such glee he couldn't even begin to imagine.

"Some of it is for the servants. Some for the tenants. Everyone gets a present, something frivolous. Hair ribbons, books, pipe tobacco. All of the tenants also get a crate of foodstuffs. Treats they couldn't normally afford as well as more practical gifts: a good pan, cloth to make up new clothes, new shoes, knitting needles and yarn. Glendower's practically feudal about his people, keeps an account book concerning them like any other responsibility. The gifts for the tenants and servants elsewhere were sent off weeks ago. This is just a little last-minute stocking up."

George checked her list again and took off down the street, leaving Ivo staring dumbly after her. She disappeared into a large bookshop and lending library. By the time he caught up, she already had a stack forming on the counter and the shop assistant hustling about helping her collect things.

Ivo stood silently at the counter, studying the growing pile of plain paper-bound books. George continued to add to the stack until it threatened to spill onto the floor.

"If you have a few copies of any of the fashion magazines I'll take those as well."

The owner tied up all the books and magazines in brown paper and sent his assistant staggering off to the inn, arms loaded down with packages.

George turned to him, surveying her list with a critical eye. "Not much left. I have to pick up a few items the countess ordered from Madame Dupree's, stop by Greely's and pick up Griggs's present, and then I think we're done."

Ivo stared at her in silent amazement. He'd never imagined paying attention to this level of detail. His grandfather certainly didn't. The marquis didn't even known the names of most of his servants, let alone his tenants. The maids were all Mary, the coachman was John, and the stable hands were all simply called *boy*.

Ivo had managed to learn their real names over the past few months, but he'd never thought to go to these lengths. It wasn't that his grandfather was a bad man, he was simply feudal in an entirely different sense: undisputed ruler of his own small kingdom.

Ivo much preferred Lord Glendower's sensibilities.

George would make more than a dream lover . . . she'd been in training her whole life to make a lord the perfect wife. If he could only bring her round he could have them both: the lady in the drawing room and the whore in the bedroom.

What more could any man wish for?

At Greely's clock and watch shop, George explained what she needed to Greeley Senior and inspected the selection he pulled out for her.

Every inch of wall space was covered in clocks, the tabletops a sea of them as well: gilt, ormolu, wood, all of them ticking until the sound was comforting, like the roar of the ocean.

"What do you think, Dauntry?" she asked, having whittled the contenders down to three. "Open-faced, or closed so he gets that satisfying snap when he shuts it?"

"Snap," Dauntry ruled.

George nodded, sure the old martinet would appreciate the extra flair opening and shutting the watch would offer.

"It's settled, then. I'll take this one." She pointed to a small one with a tortoiseshell case. "And a nice heavy chain, and a good fob."

Mr. Greely pulled out a suitable chain and offered her a velvet-lined tray with a selection of fobs. George looked them over carefully, and finally chose a detailed, miniature sphinx.

"That completes our errands. Shall we go and find the children?"

She stepped out of the shop, squinting as the full light of the afternoon sun hit her. Dauntry bumped into her as she stopped abruptly. She glanced over her shoulder.

The corners of Dauntry's lips curled up, one hand went to the small of her back, steadying her.

"George—"

"We're in the middle of the street, my lord." She took a step away from him, shook out the skirts of her pelisse. She knew that tone. The sound of a man about to make a confession. "You can have your say in the privacy of the parlor, if you must."

Fortunately, when they arrived at the White Hart the Tilehurst girls were waiting for them, all of them sitting in the parlor, reviewing their purchases. The earl gave her a put-upon look to which she refused to succumb.

Julius and Aubrey arrived as George was taking off her coat, Julius loaded down with a varied assortment of packages. They'd gotten their father a very long black carriage whip, and several packages of replacement whip ends, as well as an ingenious brass handwarmer meant to be filled with sacks of heated sand. Julius unwrapped a beautiful silk and mother-of-pearl fan for their mother, explaining that he and Aubrey had had to pool their money for it, but that it was worth it. George agreed, heartily endorsing their choice. It was just the sort of pretty bauble that Victoria would love, and the plain silk could be painted with any number of fanciful designs.

Lunch was already on the table, and the meal half eaten before Hayden and Simone came scrambling in. They set their packages down on a small side table and came over to join everyone else.

"Sorry we're late, Aunt George," Hay said, sliding

into an empty seat and helping himself to some sliced beef and a few carrots and parsnips. "It took us longer than we thought to find everything."

"That's what I assumed." George took a sip of her wine and eyed them thoughtfully. They didn't look excited—or dirty—enough to have been out causing any real mayhem. Perhaps they'd actually behaved themselves? While the children finished their meals, George wandered back out to the taproom to supervise the inkeep's son loading the gig she'd hired to carry all their purchases back to the Court.

"Thank you, Thomas. I can always count on you."

The boy beamed, almost blushing, and ducked his head. She leaned against the wall, watching the gig fill with crates, boxes, and parcels tied up in brown paper.

Her shoulder blades twitched and she glanced across the yard. She hated the sensation of being watched. She liked the lick of fear that flickered through her even less. Before all this nonsense with the highwaymen it would never have occurred to her that the sensation boded ill, but today she couldn't escape it. Couldn't ignore it.

Her own half-formed fears after being attacked by the highwaymen, combined with Brimstone's concern when she'd confided in him, suddenly welled up. Panic flooded through her. Choked her.

She whirled about and all but ran back into the inn.

Dauntry met her just inside, the children trailing behind him, loud and excited, full of chocolate and sticky buns.

George took a deep breath. She was being ridiculous. She was in Leicester, for Heaven's sake. Safe and sound. The streets were hardly likely to be teeming with criminals.

Dauntry called for the sleigh while she bundled the children back into their coats. The innkeeper passed her, carrying hot bricks for their feet, and she ushered the children out behind him.

Dauntry was already on the box, breath fogging in the crisp, cold air. Julius scrambled up beside him while she and the rest of the children settled under the blankets once more.

She spent the drive back watching Dauntry guide Julius's hands on the reins, trying to shake the panicked feeling of being watched. Wondering what it was he had wanted to say.

"Tighten up on the reins, you've let the left one go slack."

Morpeth's heir blushed hotly and did as he was told, sliding the left rein between his fingers until he once again had the team riding their bits.

Behind them, the children were singing, loudly and off key. Every once in a while the song would falter and George's soft tenor would be revealed until the children picked the song up again.

Just being near her tied him up in a knot of sexual frustration. It was disturbing. Exhilarating. Or it was when something could be done to satisfy it . . .

Their return to the Court coincided with that of George's second bulldog. The viscount was just climbing down from his coach as Julius reined in their team.

Ivo frowned as St. Audley helped George and the children from the sleigh. Young Thomas rattled past, driving round to the servants' entrance, where he could unload the gig.

"I'm so glad you've joined us," George said, sliding

her arm around her dog's. "There have been far too many political discussions, if they may be so politely termed, and not nearly enough real conversation. I'm counting on you to correct that."

The viscount laughed, sounding pleased with his welcome. As well he should be, the bastard.

"Frivolity at your command, my dear."

Ivo gritted his teeth and took the reins from Julius. When the boy had hopped down from the box, he gave them a sharp snap and lurched off toward the stables. Once he rounded the house, stable boys came running.

He handed the team over with relief and hurried inside, as eager for a fire and a brandy as the horses were for their stalls and a bucket of oats.

Chapter 19

How desperately we all desire to know just how things progress at the Earl of G—'s country home. Alas, we were not so lucky as to be invited. Instead we must make do with the scandal available in Town.

Tête-à-Tête, 24 December 1788

"The shooting contests are about to start. Get your coat and meet me in the gun room."

George glanced over her shoulder at the Earl of Morpeth. He'd already laid aside the magnificent velvet coat he'd worn earlier and was now wearing a loose shooting coat of buff leather.

She glanced around the courtyard. All the sportsmen had changed already. She'd been so distracted playing second hostess that she'd missed them all slipping away to exchange their coats.

Bright winter sun poured in through the glass canopy that enclosed what was once the central courtyard of the house. Blazing fires in the enormous fireplaces on either side of the courtyard cut the chill.

George wove her way through the crowd of guests. Sofas, chaises, and chairs had been arranged near each of the fireplaces. The elderly guests had been settled upon them to gossip and drink the hot rum punch which was being liberally distributed by the army of footmen employed at the Court.

Once out of the courtyard, she ran lightly up the convenient set of servants' stairs to her room. She hurriedly pulled on her fur-trimmed redingote and hat, swapped her shoes for sturdier boots, and then made her way down to the gun room. It was filled with men. They milled about, looking at Lord Glendower's extensive collection of firearms, loudly debating who would be the winner of the various contests that day.

Sydney stood up on a bench and bellowed to get everyone's attention. "All right then! There will be multiple categories today for both rifle and pistol. Targets have been erected on the far side of the house and my father is out there right now making sure everything is in readiness. Please follow Lord Morpeth out the side door; everything should be waiting for us."

The snow had been swept aside and straw thrown down on a path out to where bales of hay had been set up on end with painted canvas targets draped over them. Morpeth offered her his arm and led her along the still slippery path.

When they reached the line of waiting footmen, all standing ready with the guns for the competition, she dropped Morpeth's arm and tightened the tippet around her throat, shivering inside her coat as she adjusted to the cold.

Lady Glendower had clearly spent no small amount

of time on the targets, which were painted to resemble flying pheasants, running hares, and playing cards.

Those inclined to the first competition claimed a rifle from one of the footmen and took their place facing the targets. The others stood off to the side, indulging in the hot rum punch that had been provided. The first rounds were fired, each shot loud enough that George could feel the sound rattle through her.

Clouds of smoke mingled with the men's breath only to be blown away by the breeze. The second round of men took their shots, the competition quickly taking its toll on the pheasants and hares.

Morpeth took off a pheasant's head from forty paces, and then handed the gun to a footman to reload. George stepped forward for the third round. She sighted, called out, "Hare's eye," and fired, hitting the hare just beside its eye.

"Not much of a lady, are you, hellion?" Brimstone smiled at her, steaming mug in hand.

"If I were it'd have been me dead in the mud by the side of the road, not some filthy highwayman."

Ivo's chest seized.

What the hell was she talking about?

George had been ignoring him since yesterday when they'd returned from Leicester. The arrival of her second bulldog had made it all too easy for her. She might as well have been cloistered.

George turned her back to him as she stepped up to take her turn. The breeze ruffled the fur of her hat, filled his lungs with the scent of summer.

When they were done here she was going to damn

well talk to him if he had to drag her away kicking and screaming.

His own shot went woefully wide and he stomped over to Bennett and reclaimed his punch. The hot copper warmed his hands, making the leather of his gloves feel a part of him. Even from a dozen steps away he could hear Brimstone chuckle. An indulgent, possessive sound that made him want to bash his head in with one of the rifle butts.

The gentlemen continued to blast away while Ivo fumed. Two more rounds made it clear that only Morpeth and Bennett were truly in competition. When the smoke finally cleared and the targets were examined, Bennett was proclaimed the winner.

Ivo tried not to look surprised when George won the second contest of the day. No woman should handle a dueling pistol with such accuracy, or such aplomb. She'd bested all the gentlemen present, himself included, in only a few rounds.

Ivo glanced around at their fellow competitors; none of the men seemed put out by being beaten by a woman. Most of them were busy slapping her on the back, offering their congratulations, or trying to convince her to sell the pretty pearl-handled pistol she'd used.

The final contest of the day began, but he couldn't seem to keep his attention on it. George was busy acting as judge, writing the men's names down on the cards they had shot, her enjoyment of the day evident in every movement she made. She wiped the back of one gloved hand across her cheek, smearing the spots of powder dotting her face.

He wanted to wipe them off. To lick them off. To pull her behind the large tree she was leaning against, put his hand up her skirts and—the tree exploded in shower of splinters.

Ivo's fantasies evaporated as pandemonium struck. Shouted accusations flew back and forth, Brimstone shoved one of the contestants, men dove in from all sides, some trying to prevent a fight, others joining in.

George's face drained of color. One hand came up to brush away the bits of wood that covered her coat. Ivo pushed his way through the crowd, shoving past the knot of tangled, angry men.

He got his arm around her waist, took her roving hand in his, and tugged her away from the tree. "Inside. Now."

She glanced up, eyes huge, amber irises shimmering behind the sudden spurt of tears. "An accident. Nothing but a silly misfire."

"I'm sure it was." He strong-armed her along the straw path, half carrying her. "Happens all the time." He could feel himself getting angrier with every step. The sickening buzz in his chest spreading down his limbs.

"A dueling pistol firing wide by thirty or forty feet is *perfectly* normal." Someone was trying to kill her and she hadn't said a word. Not to him, anyway. She'd be lucky if he didn't throttle her himself.

"Dauntry." She tried to pull away. "Dauntry. Ivo!" She planted her heels, dragging to a stop. "Slow down."

"Slow down?" He jerked her into motion again, using his superior size to force her along. "Whoever just took a shot at you has had plenty of time by now to reload. We're not slowing down. And if you dig your heels in again I'll throw you over my shoulder and carry you inside a like a sack of meal."

He dragged her into the house and shut the door

behind them with a resounding boom. She yanked
her arm from his grasp and stood rubbing it, watching him warily.

"Pick a room, George. And choose wisely, because
you've got some explaining to do."

Her chin shot up. Her brows pinched together in
displeasure. "I have nothing—"

"To say to me. I'm sure. But I have several things to
say to you, and in another minute or two I'll be
saying them in front of half of the Glendowers'
guests."

Her eyes narrowed and she brushed past him. Ivo
followed, his temper straining on its leash, snapping
at her heels. She paused beside a door at the top of
the first flight of stairs and pushed it open.

"Sydney's study." She went inside, leaving the door
hanging open behind her. "Mine to use when I'm
here."

Ivo shut the door behind him. He looked her up
and down. Tiny bits of wood still clung to her, littered the fur of her hat and tippet. Three bright
specks of blood had appeared on her cheek. She was
going to need someone to pick out the splinters. He
reached out and plucked a large bit from her tippet.
George flinched.

"Before this goes any further, I am not engaged to
Miss Bagshott. Never have been—regardless of the
marquis's claims to the contrary—and never will be."

"So your grandfather's insane?"

Ivo shook his head and brushed more fragments
of the tree from her redingote. "That's one way of
looking at it. Another is that once the old man's
mind is set, it's nearly impossible to dissuade him."

He turned away, eyes roving about the room.

Trying to distract himself from the need to shake her. The urge to pull her into his arms and kiss her.

He needed a drink. They both did. He spotted a decanter, belly full of tea-colored liquid, on the mantel. "Come and sit down by the cold hearth, have a brandy—"

"A whisky."

Ivo glanced back at her, decanter in hand.

"Just so you know," she unwound the tippet and dropped it on to the desk along with her hat, "it's whisky."

"A whisky, then. Come and have a whisky."

George crossed the room, hands patting her crushed hair back into place, and dropped into one of the two chairs beside the fireplace. She accepted the glass he held out to her, drained it, and held it out.

Ivo filled it nearly to the brim, then set the decanter on the floor beside her. He dragged the other chair closer and sat down heavily.

"Exactly how long have you known someone is trying to kill you?"

George let her breath out slowly as the whisky worked its way through her, warming her from the inside out. She put one hand up to her forehead, ran her fingers over one brow, smoothing it. Trying to order her thoughts.

"About ten minutes."

"I *heard* you mention something not an hour ago about an attack by highwaymen to your damn bulldog." Dauntry's voice came out in a growl, the vein in his forehead was prominent, displaying his displeasure like a dog's raised ruff.

"My what?"

"Don't change the subject. You know damn well who I mean."

George settled back into the chair, busk pressing into her belly. She took another large gulp, half afraid she was going to drop the glass as her hand shook.

"I've known for sure since the tree exploded behind me. I've *suspected* since I was held up on my way here. The way the third highwayman looked at me . . . I don't know how to explain it. And it makes me think the fire that killed Maeve must have been deliberate as well."

"What do your bulldogs say?"

Her bulldogs. That really was what they were, Brimstone and St. Audley.

"Brimstone says he's never letting me out of his sight. I haven't told anyone else yet. Lady Glendower will panic. Lord Glendower and Alençon will try to lock me away for my own protection, and St. Audley will second them on the action."

Muffled steps outside the door made her stiffen and sit up. The door opened and Brimstone stormed in, his concerned expression slackening into relief.

"Been looking everywhere for you." He shut the door. "We managed to get Audley to stop trying to kill poor Rivenhall, but only barely."

He crossed to stand behind her, forearms resting on the back of her chair as he leaned over her. "If he figures out Somercote here is the one who absconded with you, we'll have more black eyes and scraped knuckles to deal with."

"Better me than whoever tried to shoot her." Dauntry's gaze was locked on Brimstone as the two of them stared each other down. Two dunghill cocks in the same yard.

"You'll get no argument from me on that front."

George let out the breath she hadn't realized she'd been holding and took another shaky sip of whisky.

"But George should get back to the party before she's missed. I'll take her to her room to change and escort her down. You can claim her from me in an hour or so, and then Layton will take her to dinner. After that—"

"That's enough." George glared up over her shoulder at her friend.

"And after that St. Audley can have his turn." Dauntry's voice overrode her objection.

"Right," Gabriel said, stepping round the chair and putting out a hand to help her up. "You, my dearling, are not to be left alone, Alençon's orders. And you're to be escorted all evening only by those he and Glendower have approved."

Brimstone took her glass in his free hand and steadied her as she got to her feet. The room swayed like the deck of a boat during a rough Channel crossing.

Gabriel's brow knit as she leaned heavily onto his arm. He tossed back what was left of her whisky and handed the empty glass to Dauntry.

"Come along, hoyden." He nodded to Dauntry in an almost friendly manner and led her off willy-nilly.

Chapter 20

A decidedly wicked bit of scandal-broth is being served up by the family of a country squire. The daughter, it seems, has been jilted by a certain recently returned earl.

Tête-à-Tête, 24 December 1788

Tired but not at all sleepy, George assisted the dowager countess up the main stairs and handed her over to her maid. In her own room, she found her maid waiting with the last piece of rum cake smuggled up from the kitchens.

George ate the cake, while Ellen took the copper kettle from the hob beside the fire and emptied it into the basin on the vanity. She allowed Ellen to help her out of her dress, watching the steam rise, tendrils clouding the mirror.

She slid into her favorite quilted wrapper and sat down before the vanity to wash her face and hands. The hot, wet cloth stung her cheek. Powder had concealed the marks made by the splinters, but they remained there all the same. Unwelcome reminders of the events of the past few weeks.

Powder, rouge, and kohl washed away, George curled up in front of the fire with Beckford's *The History of the Caliph Vathek*. She was almost done with the book. Maybe when she finished she'd be ready for bed?

She turned page after page, tired eyes skimming over the last of the story:

> *Such was, and such should be, the punishment of unrestrained passions and atrocious actions . . . Thus the Caliph Vathek, who, for the sake of empty pomp and forbidden power, had sullied himself with a thousand crimes, became a prey to grief without end, and remorse without mitigation . . .*

The final words of the wicked caliph's story faded away. She turned the last page and stared at the blank verso page, suddenly wide awake, then rose and stepped into her slippers. She flipped through the few volumes on the mantel, but nothing sparked her interest. She wasn't in the mood for poetry. Not even the randy poems of Donne or the Earl of Rochester. Dildoes and flea bites held little appeal . . . with a small sigh of disgust, she turned away from the mantel.

Dauntry was just down the hall. In the Venetian room. He was just down the hall, and there was simply no possibility of sleep tonight. By all rights she should have died today. And she could either spend the night fretting about it, or she could allow Dauntry to remind her that she was very much alive.

Slipping out of her room, she cinched her robe

tighter and headed down the hall. The house was dark, but so familiar she didn't need a candle.

She reached the door and put her hand to the knob. Light leaked from under the door. He was still awake. She twisted the knob and the door swung silently open. Dauntry glanced up from his seat before the fire. His expression was neither welcoming nor offended. It was wary.

She shut the door behind her and stood dumbly just inside the room. He closed the book he'd been reading with deliberate precision. As he stood, the fire cast his shadow over the room, flickering over the bed, the wall, her. Casting her into darkness until he stepped toward her.

The stomach-turning jolt when he touched her told her she'd made the right decision. Bergamot flooded her senses, made her long to bury her nose in his neck. His hands slid over her, arms wrapped around her, locking her tightly against him. His mouth came down on hers, his lips finding hers easily.

Ivo felt the shiver that ran through George as he kissed her. He pulled her to him, hands sliding around her, down her back, around her ribs, settling at her waist.

He'd been too wound up to sleep. His mind wouldn't stop churning, picturing George dead at the base of that big oak. Amber eyes dim before he could reach her. Dead in the mud beside her carriage. Dead in a country inn before he'd ever touched her . . .

His whole body was shaking, with need, with desire, with fear that she'd pull away. She stepped back, pulling him along, and came to rest against the door. Ivo leaned in to her and allowed his still unsteady hands to slide down her sides. He gripped her hips, hands clenched in the thick fabric of her robe. He wasn't about to let her slip away.

George gave an impatient shove and pulled back from him, her eyes staring up into his. Her gaze was locked on him as clearly as the insistent proof of his desire pressed against her belly.

If he hesitated, she'd be gone. She was like a bird, tempted to steal a bit of bread from a child's hand, ready to take flight at even the slightest movement.

George watched him warily, head slanted back and away from him. He kicked off his slippers, and she smiled, triumphant. Nothing more than a flash of teeth in the moonlight.

Her hands went to the front of his banyan and loosened the belt. She pushed it off his shoulders, and he allowed it to slide off and pool at his feet. She grinned at his intake of breath as the warm silk left his body, left him naked in the firelight, unmistakably eager.

She bit her lip, slid her arms around his neck, and drew him to her. Hands slid into his hair, fisted and pulled. Ivo dragged her to the bed. Hissed as she bit his neck, hard. Her mouth slid down his neck, hot and wet, teeth in play all the way. Without letting go of her he fell back into the enormous curtained bed, sprawled beside her, one leg crossing her hips and holding her in place.

She kissed him hungrily, tongue twining with his. He slid one hand inside her robe. It was a heavy, quilted wrapper, decidedly in his way. He rolled off her slightly, leaned back on one elbow, chuckling as he tugged at the belt.

"Where did you get this thing?" He pushed the of-fending garment open, distracted by her circling one of his nipples lightly with her thumb. Little jolts of lightning were coursing through his body, starting in that nipple and exploding in his cock.

"It's warm," George replied, sliding one foot provocatively along his bare leg. "And it's not as though I was planning on anyone seeing me in it when I packed it."

Ivo laughed again at the slightly petulant note in her voice, then returned to the task at hand. Tonight he wasn't going to rush; he had all the time in the world. Tonight he was not going to be the trembling creature he'd been at Oundale, completely at her mercy. Nor the overly eager lover in her town house. Tonight he was prepared to give as good as he got. Tonight was about making sure she'd never be able to ride away from him again. Never be able to deny him again.

With her wrapper loosened, there was only one layer more between them, of lawn so fine it couldn't hide the peaks of her nipples, or the shadow at the apex of her thighs.

Never taking his eyes from hers, he ran his hand down the front of her, caressing her breast, circling the slight indentation formed by her bellybutton with his thumb. He straddled her, making sure she could see the rampant state of his cock. Leaned down to kiss her again, pressing that same appendage into her belly.

Her hands slid down his ribs, circled to his back. She twisted beneath him. Nails grazed his back, her breathing degenerated into short pants.

Ivo slid his body slowly down hers, hands tracing her curves as he went, mouth following his hands: down her neck, along her collarbone, across her chest to her breasts, where he stopped to suckle through the sheer material of her gown. He nipped at her belly, at her hip bones, slipped one hand up under the hem of her nightrail and pushed it up to her waist as he continued down to her knees, licked the ticklish backs of them before working his way up her thigh. She murmured something incoherent as he parted her thighs and lightly bit the tendon on the inside of her leg.

George gasped as Dauntry pressed his mouth to her, parting her with his lips and tongue. She moved one hand down to rest lightly on his head, caught up in the sensation.

She arched, peaked nipples rubbing against the cold, wet fabric of her nightrail. He worked his way slowly, tantalizingly, teasingly up to the throbbing peak near the top of her cleft, locked his mouth over her, teeth clearly evident as he sucked swollen flesh into his mouth.

In seconds she was mewling, an incoherent flood of sounds dragged from her throat. She couldn't hold still under his carefully orchestrated assault. Her hips began to twist, her feet strained against the bedclothes.

Not yet finished, he brought one arm back around her thigh and up over her body, and with his hand splayed out across her belly, held her down. He sucked harder, flicking his tongue over her, pushing his chin against her. The pressure reminding her that soon he'd be inside her. Soon she'd experience this all over again.

The trace of beard that darkened his cheeks was rubbing her raw. Tomorrow she'd have scrapes all along the insides of her thighs, and she didn't care. It felt too good to care. It was delicious. As was everything else he was doing.

But she wanted him inside her.

Now.

She clenched one hand in his hair and tried to dislodge him. She yanked, and he reached up with his one free hand and gripped her wrist, tight.

Her climax was almost upon her. Her feet had begun to tingle. Every ounce of her being was contained in the small bit of flesh on which Dauntry was lavishing all his attention.

She gave a choked gurgle as her release swept over her and she tried not to cry out. The room flickered and went utterly black for a moment.

George took a deep, shuddering breath. She shook off his now slack grip, reached down and pulled him up to her by his hair.

This time, he came willingly, lazily retracing his route with his lips, skimming her body with his hands, taking her nightgown up and over her head. He tossed it away into the dark as she drew him up for a satisfied kiss.

George kissed him back, tongue pushing past his, and her hands down his back, feeling rock-hard muscles. He was holding himself back, and she didn't want him to. She wanted the second glorious release that his body promised her, but she was loath to take the lead away from him.

Dauntry was so obviously enjoying asserting himself. And it was wonderful to simply give herself over entirely to someone else. To trust so implicitly.

He nipped at her earlobe, teased her with his lips, teeth, and tongue. George moved her hips against his, giving him just the slightest bit of encouragement. She could clearly feel the hard length of him against her mons. She brought her knees up slightly, shifting so that he was now pressed against the hot, slick folds he'd so recently been caressing. Play was wonderful, but she was done playing.

The sudden movement of her hips, and the low moan she gave as he bit her neck, were all that was needed to get him to understand her need. With the slightest readjustment he slid into her with one long, hard thrust, stifling her moan with a deep kiss.

George locked her feet behind him. Wrapped her arms around him. Held him against her as they established a rhythm. Every thrust filled her, left her gasping.

He knew exactly how to ride her, how to wind her up into a ball of pure need and desire. He gave an extra little buck of his hips at the end of each thrust, grinding into her.

She arched beneath him and flung her head back.

Ivo gave himself over to sensation. To the simple act of two bodies meeting, need and pleasure trumping all else. George was so hot, so wet, he was past coherence anyway.

If he could just keep her in bed for the rest of their lives everything would be perfect. Here, there wasn't anything to worry about. Here, he didn't seem to be able to do anything wrong, and anything she did that shocked him could only be to the good.

He vaguely felt her nails digging deep into his back. She was whispering softly into his ear, but the words were muffled. He changed the angle of his thrust and suddenly she was crying out beneath him, strangled, near sobs issuing from her. She clenched around him as she found her release again. The added sensation of her climaxing around him was all he need to attain his own, and with a few more deep, rocking thrusts he came and then stilled atop her, his breath coming in ragged gasps.

Propping himself up on his elbows, he kissed her again. A long, slow, satisfied kiss. He just wanted to lie there with her, in the small, secure confines of his room. To keep her where she was safe.

Beneath him she sighed, not sadly, but contentedly. She kissed him back, not allowing him to roll off her when he attempted to do so. She held him in place, thighs strong from years of riding, easily able to keep him where he was.

"Aren't I a bit heavy?" He was crushing her down into the bed. She couldn't be comfortable.

"Not at all." She gave him a soft, lips-only kiss. "This is one of my favorite things in the world."

"Well then . . ." Ivo returned to kissing her. After a few more minutes, he pulled himself off her despite her protests, reached out to twitch the bed curtains shut, and settled back in, wrapping himself around George so that they drifted off entwined, the comforter pulled up nearly over their heads.

It was barely dawn when the sound of the tweeny building the fire woke George. Her eyes snapped open, and Ivo could see the exact moment when she remembered where she was. He'd been awake for what seemed like hours. Just lying there, watching her in the dim half-light. They were lying facing one another, less than a foot apart on the pillow. He smiled and lifted one finger to her lips.

She opened her mouth and sucked his finger in, tongue moving over and around it. Ivo grimaced. She *knew* he couldn't respond, not with the maid busy stoking the fire.

He'd been enjoying watching her sleep, studying the faint spray of freckles that dusted her nose, the curves of her cheekbones and lips. He'd never really seen her when she was still. George was never still. Asleep, she appeared soft, almost girlish. The illusion vanished as soon as her eyes opened. Asleep, she was merely pretty. Awake, she was magnetic.

The maid finished laying the morning fire and slipped quietly out of the room, only the faint sound of the door handle turning to alert them that she'd left.

Dauntry's smile slowly warmed, one side sliding up wickedly. George bit down on his finger slightly and he yanked his hand away. She laughed as he rolled her underneath him, and with what seemed like no effort at all, positioned himself between her thighs. With one quick thrust he was inside her, and then he was moving, sending chills all the way down to her toes.

It was totally different than what they'd just done the night before. Thrilling, intense, and utterly primitive. George quickly found her release, was driven to it again before Dauntry reached his own, spilling himself into her with one final, drawn-out thrust.

They lingered in bed, curled up sleepily together, Dauntry lightly running one hand possessively up and down her back, until George, sadly practical, forced herself to move. She pushed back the bed curtains, clambered out, and began looking for her nightrail.

Ivo groaned and propped himself up on his elbows to watch her. Light leaked through a gap in the curtains, caressed his skin, caught the deep red highlights of his hair as it spilled over his shoulder and trailed down his chest.

She pulled on her nightrail and robe. Dauntry climbed out behind her and slipped into his banyan.

"Time to go?" He ran his fingers though his hair, pulling out tangles.

"Time to go." George pushed her feet into her slippers and cinched up her robe. "Peek out and make sure the hall is empty."

Dauntry opened his door, glanced up and down the hall, pulled her in for one last, hard kiss, and then thrust her out the door. George hurried down the hall to her own room and collapsed into one of the chairs near the fireplace.

Crawling back into bed, Ivo smiled to himself. He was forgiven. That was all that mattered at the moment. She'd come to him and she'd held nothing back. It hadn't taken six nights . . . it had only taken three. Four, if he was forced to count the disastrous evening after the Devonshires' ball.

If he could just convince himself that what had happened yesterday was nothing more than an accident, the world would be perfect.

An engagement would allow him to keep her close, to pack her off to Ashcombe Park if necessary. It might even serve to scare off whoever it was that was trying to kill her. Regardless, he'd feel better with her safely under his protection both publicly and privately.

Chapter 21

*We are sorry at this time of year to continually sound
the gong of doom, but it seems to be the way of things.
A certain Mrs. P— appears to have exchanged her viscount for a mere baronet.*

Tête-à-Tête, 25 December 1788

Coming down the stairs to breakfast, George was
nearly knocked down by the Morpeths' boys and
Caesar. Christmas morning guaranteed an extra-
special effort on the part of Mrs. Stubbs and the
kitchen staff.

Instead of being served separately in the nursery,
the children would be allowed to join the adults in
the breakfast parlor. There would be chocolate as
well as the usual tea, coffee, and ale. Sticky buns and
Mrs. Stubb's special cinnamon bread would round
out the breakfast offerings of toast, eggs, cold beef,
and her father-in-law's favorite steak and kidney pie.

George arrived just after the boys and quickly grabbed a sticky bun for herself. Lady Glendower was presiding over the table with Sydney seated beside her, his own plate loaded high with cold beef and eggs.

He'd probably already consumed several sticky buns before her arrival. Lady Morpeth wandered in and quirked a repressive brow at her offspring, who immediately settled down to consume their sugary breakfast.

Victoria accepted a cup of tea from Lady Glendower and took a seat next to George. "Morpeth tells me we had some excitement yesterday?"

George met her gaze silently. The breakfast parlor was *not* the place for this discussion.

The countess sipped her tea, eyes wide with interest. "Yes, we did. My bulldogs have it in hand."

"Your what?" Victoria choked, practically spiting tea back into her cup.

George bit her lip. Why had that term come so readily to her tongue? It was hardly complimentary to her two closet friends. "My two devoted cicisbei. Bulldogs is Somercote's term for them, not mine, but it does seem apt."

"Very." The countess took a careful swallow of tea. "Morpeth wants to speak to you later today. Something about putting you under lock and key, I imagine."

George chewed a bite of sticky bun, allowing the sweet, tacky dough to soothe her frayed temper. How to respond? All of the boys were likely thinking along the same lines by now . . .

"I think Brimstone has much the same plan, as does my father-in-law, Alençon, St. Audley, and probably anyone else you ask." She finished her cup of tea and passed it to Lady Glendower to be refilled. "I'm not of a mind to be indefinitely stored away."

Victoria gave her the same look she gave her sons when they were being difficult.

"Nor am I likely to allow the boys to fight my battle. But you needn't worry, Torrie. I promise not to take any undue risks."

The countess shook her head, but let the subject drop.

After breakfast, the family gathered in the main drawing room to exchange gifts. The delicate Egyptian sideboard was almost completely obscured by carefully labeled bandboxes, brown paper parcels, and tissue-wrapped bundles tied up with string. Mostly they gave each other token gifts, but there was always an abundance of presents, token or not.

They'd been joined by their closest friends: the Morpeths, Colonel Staunton and Simone, Carr and Alençon, Lady Beverly, all of Sydney and George's childhood cohorts, and Dauntry, who'd come in with Lady Bev.

Dauntry gave her a sly half-smile as he helped his godmother to a chair. George wasn't yet sure what to make of last night. It hadn't been merely night four of the promised six. Something had been different. Was it because she'd gone to him? Or was it because her recent brushes with death had made the encounter all the more precious?

She couldn't be sure, except that it was different, and it had left her unsettled. On edge. Disturbed. She bit her lip, giving up on trying to puzzle it out, and retreated to the sideboard to begin distributing the gifts. The children were all waiting to assist her. George read the tags, and handed the gifts off to be delivered to their recipient.

When the mountain had been distributed, and each person was surrounded by his collection, George released her assistants, who promptly fell upon their own piles like soldiers looting a fallen town. The adults turned to their own gifts with slightly more circumspection, but equal glee.

Sydney was already wearing the new hat she'd bought him as he continued to assault the packages that surrounded him. It was one of the newly fashionable round hats, with a tall crown and flat brim. It was very smart. Very trig.

In her own pile were tributes from all her friends. A sword stick hidden in a tasseled parasol from Alençon. A lovely silk folding fan from Carr, along with a note insisting that somebody had to remember that she was a lady. A small pistol with a mother-of-pearl grip from Brimstone. A delicate lady's watch from St. Audley, designed to pin to her bodice, or be worn with a chain. The Morpeths had given her a fur-lined carriage rug, and Charles a ridiculously expensive reticule, with a filigree top showing a stag pursued by two wolfhounds.

Her in-laws had commissioned a painting of Caesar. He was shown lying sphinxlike at the door of her town house, his usual happy grin replaced by a majestic, far-off gaze. George smiled and inquired how ever they'd managed it.

"We conspired with Smythe to arrange for Stubbs to come over and do the sketches while you were out," Lady Glendower answered, clearly pleased with her gift's reception. "We had a little one done of Bella for Simone, too. Dog paintings are suddenly all the rage."

The group was happily showing each other their gifts, trying on hats and gloves, fluttering fans and

paging through books. George was indulgently in-
volved with Hay as he showed her his presents. He
suddenly went mute, looking up past her, eyes wide.
A hush had fallen over the room. The sound of her
shifting her weight on the chair—the rustle of silk,
the creak of wooden joints—was loud even in her
own ears.

She straightened and turned to see Dauntry standing awkwardly behind her. He met her gaze briefly,
swallowed hard, glanced back over his shoulder, and
returned his attention to her.

George's breath caught. Everyone was watching
them expectantly. Her pulse raced as she repressed
the urge to flee the room. She glanced at Lady Bev,
then at Bennett, who nodded encouragingly at her.

Damn him.

Her hands clenched into fists and she thrust them
down into her skirts to hide them. Her nails bit into
her palms, her knuckles cracked.

Damn them both for putting Dauntry up to this.
She had no doubts as to whose door to lay his
sudden start. He would never have been so stupid on
his own.

George ground her teeth and tried to remain
calm. She was not going to have a scene in front of
everyone.

She was not.

With the moment upon him, Ivo was suddenly not
so sure his choice of a public declaration was such a
good idea. This morning, lying in bed with George's
scent still lingering on the pillows, it had seemed like
the simplest thing in the world. Like the most logical
thing in the world. But now, with all her friends and
family watching, and George herself looking ready to

shy like a nervous horse, doubt welled up, flooded his chest.

He took a deep breath and broke into his proposal. He got the whole thing out, no stumbling, or stuttering, and their audience broke into smiles and sighs, but the look on George's face stopped him cold as he reached for her hand.

That was not the expression of a surprised, but happy, bride-to-be.

Her eyes were narrow, her nostrils flared. Her lips were pressed together, the corners turned slightly down and the edges white. Her skin had taken on a mottled flush, anger pinking her cheeks.

She rose, dodging his hand, and took a step back from him.

"That's not a proposal, it's a bid, and I'm not a mare on the block at Tattersalls." She took another step back, bumped into Hayden, and then turned and hurriedly exited the room, skirts rustling in obvious agitation.

The heels of her shoes rang smartly on the floor as she stormed down the hall. Ivo cursed under his breath and took off after her, only to be stopped by Alençon.

"I wouldn't do that just now, my boy," the duke said softly, steering him back into the room by his elbow. "She's not likely to become receptive any time soon. And pushing your point will simply make matters worse."

Lady Morpeth looked shocked. Brimstone was shaking his head in disbelief, disgust written all over his face. St. Audley looked ready to kill him.

He'd made a mull of it. Damn it all.

Ivo allowed the duke to thrust him down into a chair and bring him a drink. And then another, and another. It wasn't yet noon, and he was well on his way to being thoroughly cup-shot.

He didn't remember the party breaking up or the gifts being cleared out. He just sat, and drank, and brooded. He'd judged wrong. He was sure she'd be expecting it. Sure she was ready and willing.

There had been such accord between them that morning, such understanding. She'd come to *him*. That had to mean something, didn't it?

She bedded him readily enough—his anger and humiliation suddenly changed course—but she wasn't willing to trust him with anything more. Wasn't willing to give him anything more.

He had only a vague memory of being bundled off to the billiard room to continue drowning his sorrows; the rest of the day simply became a blur. A blur in which Lady Bev chastised him, Bennett sat and listened to him drunkenly try to explain his motivation and reasoning, and George put in no appearance at all.

Chapter 22

Can it be that the vivacious Lady B— has replaced the ever lovely dowager Lady G— in a certain duke's affections?

Tête-à-Tête, 25 December 1788

After spending the morning listening to a drunk and clearly despondent earl, Brimstone made his way upstairs with a luncheon tray and forced his way into George's room with a key obtained from Mrs. Stubbs.

His quarry was curled up in the window seat, as she always was when upset. Only his quick reflexes and thorough knowledge of the reception he was likely to receive saved him from being struck in the head with a well-aimed shoe.

"Go away, Gabe," George hissed, sniffling at the same time. "I don't want to eat anything, and I don't want to see any of you. I know you put him up to it, damn you all."

Brimstone kicked the door shut and put the tray down.

"I can't tell you some of our friends haven't been busy playing Cupid, but you'll have to acquit me of any such crime."

He plucked the glass of brandy from the tray and joined George in the window seat, ousting her just enough to climb in behind her.

"Come here, sweetheart." He handed her the glass and gathered her up against him. George resisted for a moment, going stiff, then relented and collapsed in a heap on his chest, spilling brandy all over the floor.

"How could he?" she asked, her voice catching between sobs.

"Shhh, darling." He patted her back, letting her have a good cry. When she'd settled into mere hiccups he dried her face and settled them both more comfortably in the window box. He hadn't seen George cry in years. Not since she was a girl and her pony had to be shot when it broke its leg in a rabbit hole.

He'd missed the first few weeks after Lyon had been killed, and by the time she'd come home, she was over the shock of it, and had retreated to a more private grief. Anger, he'd fully expected; tears from George rather scared him.

Tears were worrisome.

"He's a man, love, and at our best we're all idiots, especially when it comes to women. He thought he had a brilliant plan. Thought it would please you. Maybe even thought it would keep you safe. It's not his fault he's the only one brave enough to get on with it."

"Liar," George retorted, still sniffling. "Nothing to

do with bravery, none of the rest of you is in love with me in the least." She hiccupped then looked up at him. "You wouldn't be dumb enough to make such a public declaration, would you?"

"No, my dear, I wouldn't, but I've known you since you were a brat with no front teeth, so I've the benefit of experience. Poor Somercote's badly bitten, and Lord knows I can't fault him for his taste. The real question is, what do you want? Eh-eh-eh." He held up a hand to halt her protestations when she pushed away and turned her head to face him. "It's no use telling me you don't love him. I've seen you together."

She hunched a shoulder and turned her face so he couldn't see her expression clearly. "I know what I don't want. And I don't want to be made to look the fool in front of my entire family. And I don't want to married for the sake of keeping me safe from some madman. Maybe I'm being ridiculous, but I wish I felt like he'd actually asked me, and not like he made the assumption that my answer was a foregone conclusion."

"No question he fouled it up, love. No question at all." Brimstone sighed. He and the rest of the boys were in for far more work than they'd anticipated.

Somercote didn't have a clue as to how to manage George, and if he couldn't figure it out, Gabriel wasn't at all sure that helping him to marry her would be doing either of them a favor. Not to mention that they still had to deal with a murderous black cloud on the horizon . . . Who in the hell would want to kill George? He, himself, had had the odd urge to strangle her over the years, but this was different.

Sadly, Somercote was cut from a far different cloth than their little band. He was, to put it bluntly, a good man. Perhaps too good a man. George required a man who was willing to be a bit of a scoundrel when the situation called for it.

George had had the bit between her teeth since before she'd put her hair up, and he didn't think that likely to change. Somercote was certainly drawn to the flair George displayed—many men were—but the charm of her outrageousness might fade quickly once she was his wife.

Ivo groaned as the curtains of his bed were flung back and light flooded in.

"Up!"

The covers were yanked away. Cold air washed over him and then his banyan hit him full in the face. He groped for it and managed to pull it on without falling out of bed and onto his pounding head.

Brimstone stood a few feet from the bed, fully dressed and glowering. The smell of coffee greeted Ivo as he stumbled toward the fire, the icy floor making him hurry toward the hearth rug.

In general, he never got so foxed as to earn himself a sore head the next day, but it was becoming almost a regular occurrence of late. He'd spent an inordinate amount of the last two months at least half-sprung, and a good deal of it nearly ape-drunk.

"Do you have any idea what you're letting yourself in for?"

Ivo sank down into one of the chairs and poured himself a cup of coffee with unsteady hands. "In for?" What the hell was George's bulldog on about?

Brimstone just shook his head and sat down across from him, one long leg crossed over the other, foot swinging.

"Do you want her badly enough to not just over-look her faults, but to count them as virtues? Do you understand that she'll never make a model wife? That any attempt to make her into one will result in one thing: a runaway wife. And that her friends will support her in her flight? *Do you understand*?"

Ivo cradled his coffee between his hands, savoring the warmth in the cold room. "Do you think I'm stupid?"

Brimstone chuckled, a low, wicked sound that made the hair on the back of his neck stand on end. "No, my lord. I think you're dazzled."

Ivo shrugged before taking a large swallow of coffee. "That's not an inaccurate way of putting it."

"What I can't fathom, what none of us can, is why George?"

Ivo let his breath out through his teeth, blowing his lips loose in frustration. "Did George ever tell you how we met?" Her bulldog shook his head. "Ask her, then ask me that question again."

Brimstone gave him a curious look, black eyes piercing, brows raised. Firelight licked his glossy boots, winked back from the diamond in his cravat.

"On to another topic, then. George isn't to be left alone until we've settled the matter of her highway-man. I'm sure you agree?"

Ivo nodded. How could he not?

"She's hardly likely to allow you to squire her about when we return to town, but that will leave you free for other duties, like visiting Addington at Bow Street."

"So I'm suddenly approved of?"

Brimstone met his gaze, his expression serious. "It's not necessarily approval, Somercote, it's resignation."

Ivo swallowed the last of his coffee and set the cup

down on the tray. Resignation was better than ob-
struction. "So I'll handle hiring a runner, and you'll
handle George."

"Precisely. And the first action I'm going to take in
that capacity is to evict you from the premises."

George came downstairs to find everyone re-
strained and silent. Those who hadn't witnessed the
proposal had obviously heard the entire story. She
caught Lady Tilehurst covertly watching her, while
her eldest niece wore a pained expression. The idea
of being the recipient of a seventeen-year-old girl's
pity was mortifying.

Every time the door opened, everyone but George
turned to see who it might be, the air of expectation
palpable. Those who'd missed yesterday's scene
clearly felt they'd been deprived of a prime treat.

George toyed with her breakfast while chatting
about inconsequential, innocuous topics with Morpeth and Alençon, all the while waiting for Dauntry
to walk in. Her stomach was in a knot, her throat
almost too tight to swallow even tea. When she finished her toast she quickly retreated to the library,
where she spent the morning reviewing the lists of
things the tenants had mentioned at the fête.

Helping to manage the estate's concerns was a
wonderful distraction. She was busily making nota-
tions in Lord Glendower's ledger when Gabriel wandered in and propped himself inelegantly on the
edge of the desk.

"Mrs. Stubbs says luncheon is almost ready, and
Carr is preparing to leave. He's feeling decidedly out
of curl, having missed your contretemps. Second-
hand gossip of such an extraordinary nature doesn't

please him at all. So I've come to drag you back out into the world."

He stood and went to examine the shelves, giving her his back. "You needn't worry about bumping into Somercote; we threw him into a carriage hours ago and sent him on his way."

He plucked a volume from the shelf, flipped it open, and paged through it. He put it back, turned to face her again. "Give him a few days to think about what he wants and how he wants to go about getting it. Give you a few days to do the same."

George shot her friend a hard look, but all he did was stare her down, lips pressed into a stern line. He'd dealt with her for far too long to be easily snubbed or intimidated. Damn him.

"I'm serious, darling. You need to be clear. Do you want to marry him or not? No, no," he held up a hand to silence her, "but remember, you can't keep the man dangling forever." He came around the desk and extended his hand to her, ignoring the glare she gave him. "Come along, sweetheart, let's go and join the others for luncheon and say au revoir to Carr."

George sighed and momentarily wilted in the chair before taking his hand and allowing him to escort her to luncheon.

Chapter 23

*Lord S— has returned to Town long before he was
looked for. Perhaps he has already received his congé?*

Tête-à-Tête, 6 January 1789

George's coach rocked to a stop in front of her
house on Upper Brook Street. She shivered as the
door opened and cold air flooded the interior. Her
face felt the icy breeze whip past her, doing its best to
rip her tippet loose.

The steps were let down with a protesting clatter
and her ancient butler appeared to hand her from
the coach. A flurry of snowflakes swirled about them,
sticking to her eyelashes.

January in London was truly dismal. Or at least it
was when one was chilled to the bone, the hot brick
having long ago become nothing but an icy stone beneath her feet.

She clutched her hands together inside her muff.
At least she'd arrived home safely, regardless of how
tedious the trip had been. The dozen armed grooms

Lord Glendower had insisted upon must be frozen quite solid. Not to mention her coachman.

She'd make sure a vat of rum punch was sent down to the mews for them. And she'd have a cup herself. The only answer to cold like this was to be warmed from the inside.

George went straight past the empty salon and up to her boudoir where she huddled as close to the fire as she could until she was warm enough to shed her pelisse. The house was oddly quiet with no callers, almost unsettling.

She wanted someone there to chase away the shadows and silence. Brimstone to tease her, Alençon to cosset her . . . Dauntry to drag her off to bed.

No, not Dauntry.

He'd nearly ruined her with that unnecessary duel at Versailles. He'd coerced her into that damned bargain, and then he'd subverted their arrangement to his own ends. She never should have broken her rule and she never would again.

By the time she'd changed, Brimstone had arrived. She found him waiting for her in the library, shifting though her invitations.

"So not only am I under house arrest, but my correspondence is subject to your curiosity?"

His head snapped up, his expression darkened. "Everything is subject to inspection. And if you wish to fight about what events you'll be attending, I suggest you take it up with Lord Glendower, we're all under his orders."

"Doubtful." George rounded the desk and sat, pulling the scattered invitations to her. "You've never been one to take orders from anyone."

"Would you rather not go out at all? That was my suggestion. But Glendower thinks you'll run mad if we coop you up, so I'm to carefully select which social engagements you're to be allowed to keep."

"Allowed?" Her spine stiffened.

Brimstone sucked in one cheek and stared her down until she let her breath out and shut her eyes to keep from screaming.

"How long do you all intend to keep me caged?"

"Not caged, love. Safe. And I believe you'd best make yourself resigned for the duration."

"Very well, which of these invitations *shall* I be allowed to accept? Your shooting party?"

"Obviously."

"Cards at Lady Hardy's?" She flicked the sheet of foolscap that bore the invitation across the desk at him.

"Properly escorted? Certainly."

George rummaged through the sheets of paper until she found something a bit more exceptional. "Helen Perripoint's soirée?"

"I imagine there'll be more than enough of us present to keep you safe from Helen."

George ground her teeth. She was not going to be jollied out of her temper. He wasn't trying to be an ogre, but the idea of being subject to someone else's whims—someone else's control—was nearly too much to swallow.

She plucked another note from the pile. "What about the comte's invitation to the Frost Faire?"

"Valy? I might be convinced to entrust you to him. I've never seen a more devoted cub, but I'm not sure the Frost Faire is a safe place for you to go."

"You think my highwayman might have found easier work roasting chestnuts upon the Thames?"

Gabe made a face. "You've a point there. I'll present the outing to Lord Glendower as a possibility."

George sighed. She'd have to be content with that. If she pushed too far, resisted too strongly, Brimstone and the rest would have no compunction about locking her away in the country at some obscure estate or other.

Later in the day she sat under the eagle eyes of several of her friends as her usual visitors descended. She picked up the strings of town gossip, felt herself slide comfortably back into her accustomed role. It was good to feel herself again. To feel in control.

She'd been seriously off kilter for days—weeks, really—if she was to be perfectly honest. Between Dauntry and her highwayman she was tense whenever the door opened, half excited, half terrified. At least her guests seemed unaware of her agitation. And if a day filled with flirting and gossip seemed a trifle hollow, well, so be it.

A magnificent bouquet of hothouse flowers with Dauntry's calling card attached had been waiting for her, lush, wicked, and sinful at this time of year. Not to mention very expensive. The lack of any further message seemed ominous. As though it were a first, quick sally, alerting her that he was also in town, and that he was not done with her.

Brushing her hair as she prepared for bed, she deliberated upon plans for avoiding Dauntry. She would go riding in the morning, but not in Hyde Park where he might be waiting for her. Better a sedate trip around Green Park than a confrontation she wasn't ready for. Then she would make a round of morning calls—she'd been neglecting the female half of the *ton* shamefully in the past few months and meant to make up for it—then it was off to an appointment with her dressmaker, and finally a sedate supper with the colonel and Simone.

And all of her shopping, visiting, and riding would be conducted under the supervision of one of the three enormous footmen Brimstone had installed that morning.

George kept up the frantic pace for the rest of the week, even going so far as to attend a horticulture lecture out at Ranleigh Gardens and to accompany the Morpeths and their children to see a fireworks display in the Queen's gardens.

Anything was better than sitting at home wondering what the highwayman was plotting, not to mention trying to work out why. What had she ever done to inspire such malevolence?

Chapter 24

Ivo ground out his cigarito beneath the heel of his boot and strode down Bow Street, resisting the urge to turn about and demand results from Addington. The head magistrate was understandably defensive about his men's lack of progress.

A week.

They'd been following George covertly for a week and had nothing to say for themselves. They'd identified the two dead accomplices, for all the good that had done them. Black Charlie, suspected footpad and housebreaker, and Dick Ehle, escaped murderer. Two of the many criminals that strutted about Seven Dials, swilling gin and robbing the unwary.

Two dead ends.

Two men with nothing to gain by harming George, which could only mean that she was right, and they were in the employ of the third man . . . the one who'd gotten away.

Chilled, Ivo ducked into Claverson's Coffee House

and claimed a small table in the corner. A week. He rolled his head, cracking his neck.

A week of doing nothing. Inaction was killing him. Not seeing George was even worse. Not knowing with his own eyes that she was safe, with his own hands that she was warm and breathing. And on the morrow he had to return to Ashcombe Park for at least a few days.

The letter his grandfather had sent had been both direct and clear. His mother was distressed by his absence, and there were decisions to be made. That could only mean one thing: the marquis was not done meddling.

The sound of the door shutting behind his mother echoed through the room like the knell of a large brass bell. The tic behind Ivo's eye grew stronger. He held his hand still on the table, studied the moons at the base of his nails, the scar that ran across his knuckles. To put it up to his head, hold it over his eye until the sensation passed would be too overt a sign of weakness.

"I thought you'd put this affair of yours behind you?" The first words the marquis had addressed to him since he'd arrived that afternoon. The old man stretched out his hand for the crystal decanter of port and poured himself a glass as the silence between them lengthened.

"My affair, as you choose to term it, is none of your concern. You sent for me and I'm here. If the only topic you wish to discuss is that of Mrs. Exley, I'll take my leave in the morning."

"What I wish to discuss is the succession!" He slammed his glass down with enough force that port sloshed over the rim, mottling his hand like age spots, spreading like blood over the tablecloth. "And anything that keeps you from securing it most decidedly *is* my concern. Mrs. Exley is a childless widow. She's had Lord knows how many lovers. I can only assume she's barren. Even if her reputation were as spotless as could be wished, she'd not be a viable candidate for your hand. As it is . . . you can't marry her, my boy. It's not to be thought of."

"Would you feel differently if she were to fall pregnant?"

His grandfather's face turned puce. He gave an agitated twitch that left his wig slightly askew. "If Mrs. Exley is currently carrying your child I'll murder the both of you myself."

"Will you?" Ivo flicked away an imaginary speck of lint from his sleeve. "And risk the precious succession?"

The decanter hit the wall, showering the buffet with shards of glass and a sticky sea of port. "Get out. I don't want to so much as hear your name spoken until you're ready to christen my great-grandson. If that trollop presents you with a dozen rosy-cheeked daughters I don't want to so much as read about it in the *Post*. Do I make myself clear?"

"Perfectly, sir. I shall take up residence at Barton Court until such a time as the desired introduction can be made. Though perhaps you'd best resign yourself to a life without newspapers, as I can make no guarantee not to offend your notice with the announcement of a daughter."

Ivo deliberately raised his glass to his lips and took a sip. His grandfather glared at him for another moment, then rose from his chair and left the room, his tread heavy enough to alert the entire household to his displeasure.

The port dripped down the wall, slow and sticky, leaving a stain in its wake. He shouldn't have done that. Goaded the old man in such a way. But it was better to know how deeply the marquis's animosity ran, and now he knew. Nothing short of divine intervention was going to bring his grandfather round.

If he married George, it would mean a complete estrangement, and no matter how deeply he searched his feelings, he couldn't find any part of him that cared. He'd never had a warm relationship with his grandfather. As the son of a younger son, he'd been of only minimal import in the old man's schemes.

The next morning Ivo had his things crated off to Barton Court, the Gothic pile beside the sea where he'd grown up. It was a relief to be out from under his grandfather's thumb for the nonce.

George was on Alençon's arm, threading her way through the crush in Helen Perripoint's rather crowded rooms, when she saw Dauntry. He caught her eye and raised one brow questioningly, but didn't move to intercept them.

She must have stiffened, for Alençon paused. "Find a little pity in that cold heart of yours, *ma petite*," he whispered, before sweeping her over toward her rejected suitor and ruthlessly abandoning her there.

Traitor!

George gaped at her godfather as he disappeared into the crowd, the diamond clip holding the queue of his wig brilliant in the candlelight.

Dauntry reached for her, but then obviously thought better of it, letting his arm fall back to his side. He was, she saw with surprise, almost a vision of sartorial magnificence; from his beautifully cut coat, to the paste buckles of his evening pumps, his appearance was perfection. His valet must have finally won out, for this was not the casual, shrug-himself-into-his-own-coat gentleman who normally passed for the Earl of Somercote.

George cocked her head as she considered him. He seemed only mildly interested to see her. Confronting her was seemingly not his reason for attending.

It was too bad, really. A good fight was exactly what she needed, and Brimstone had consistently refused to give her one. He and St. Audley were treating her as though she were as delicate as a Sèvres teacup. It made her want to lash out, verbally and physically.

Her mouth quirked up as he glanced about. Searching for rescue? She couldn't be sure. He did look cornered. She placed one hand tentatively on his arm, knees nearly buckling as a wave of lust roiled through her.

"Awkward?" It didn't matter that she was still angry with him, she wanted him every bit as much as she always had. Perhaps she even wanted him all the more for having denied him—and herself!—these past weeks.

"Unexpected," he ground out, voice gravelly, as if he hadn't used it since she'd seen him last. All around them the room and its occupants seemed to recede, like the background in a theatre when the lights shadowed the actors into a mass. Nothing else existed.

"You could ask me to dance?" George slid her hand over the tense muscles of his arm, tugged him toward the swarm of people mincing about the polished floor of the parlor. "It would give us something to do besides standing silently while the gossiping hordes look on."

"I think I'd rather have you join me for a drink." He tucked her hand securely into the crook of his arm and led her toward the refreshment salon.

As they pushed past a raucous game of blind man's bluff that had spilled into the hall George found herself being yanked into one of the many curtained alcoves scattered throughout the house.

Her back hit the wall as the curtain swung shut behind them. Dauntry crowded her back into the farthest recess of the small nook. Her skirts took up most of it. Normally it held a very large Chinese vase, but Helen wasn't likely to leave so likely a spot for dalliance otherwise occupied on a night like tonight.

"I thought you wanted a drink?" George tipped her head back, senses swamped with bergamot and heat.

He cupped her chin up with his hand, holding her in place. "I want you." His thumb swept over her cheek, kidskin slick and soft.

"You appear to have me."

He gave a dismissive snort. "For as long as I can keep you trapped in this alcove." He pressed closer, so large he seemed to fill the small space. "If you'd just listen to reason . . ." He tongued the lobe of her ear, bit down hard enough to make her gasp.

"Two nights. That's what's left of our bargain."

"Oh no, love." He ran his thumb over her lower lip and she bit it in revenge, bearing down until she had a firm hold on the seam of the glove. He pulled his hand away slowly, leaving her with the glove. George spat it out. "What was the rest of it?"

"Two nights." Her skirts began to rise on one side as he bunched them up with his bare hand. She gritted her teeth, humiliated by how badly she wanted him to touch her. By how much she'd missed him. "Two nights. When and where you want them."

"What else?" His naked hand slid over her bare thigh, his tongue curled behind her ear.

"Nothing . . ."

"Something." His second hand gripped her hip, thumb digging into her. "There was one more stipulation."

"Six nights—"

"And you're not to offer so much as a kiss to any other man until our bargain's finished."

"Are you claiming a night here and now? In an alcove with nothing but a curtain between us and all of our acquaintance?" She shivered, excited by the prospect, terrified he might say yes. That she might acquiesce.

He chuckled, nose pressed to the sensitive skin behind her ear, warm breath stirring her hair, hand slipping between her thighs. "Not at all. Groping in corners hardly counts." He pushed her knees apart with his own and began to circle her clitoris with his fingers.

"Unless," he paused and she gave an embarrassing mewl of protest, "unless you were to argue that either one of us being brought to release should count? That would make what I'm doing now very foolish indeed."

He ran one finger over her and her hips rocked. Insane as it would be, she desperately wanted to reach down, free him from his breeches, and have him take her here, up against the wall. She craved the animal intensity of it.

Her hand slid down his chest, seemingly of its own volition, and suddenly he was pulling away, hands out from under her skirts, tugging the painted silk down to cover her.

"It's just occurred to me that the wisest thing I could do under the circumstances is restrain myself."

"What do you—"

And then it struck her. He meant that if he left those nights unclaimed he'd own her. He could keep her celibate indefinitely. She would have the choice of acceding to his control or breaking her word.

"You bastard." She shoved him back until he foundered up against the opposite wall, growing even more incensed by his allowing her to do so. He didn't resist at all. He was that enamored of his new plan. "That's not what I agreed to."

"That's exactly what you agreed to, my little wanton. And I promise you this: the only way you'll ever have any other man in your bed will be if you break your word. Does your word means nothing?"

Beyond response, George stalked out of the alcove, blundered into the middle of the game taking place in the hall, and was immediately caught by the blindfolded Comte de Valy.

He smiled as his hands closed on her waist. "I would know that perfume anywhere! It is Mrs. Exley." The crowd cheered and the young Frenchman removed his blindfold and leaned in to claim his kiss.

From the edge of the crowd Dauntry caught her eye. She turned away and gave the comte a far warmer kiss than the game required.

Valy kept his hold on her as she broke the kiss. "As usual, you have on the dress that puts all the others to shame. It is so rare to see an English woman with such Gallic flair. C'est magnifique!"

George smiled and accepted his praise with a nod of her head. Somehow the comte frequently managed to praise and denigrate with a single breath. It was a gift of sorts. But nowhere near as insulting as what Dauntry had just said to her.

Brimstone appeared behind the comte to claim her for their promised set. George took his hand and allowed him to return her to the parlor.

Dauntry was ahead of them, calling for his coat. George watched him leave, anger nearly choking her. As soon as the door had shut behind him she threw herself into an orgy of flirtation, fervently hoping her antics would be prominently displayed in the gossip columns. It would serve him right to have to read reports of her amorous adventures over his morning coffee.

Chapter 25

*Numerous reports of a raucous game of Blind Man's
Bluff put the Comte de Valy among the pack vying to
be next in Mrs. E—'s good graces.*

Tête-à-Tête, 16 January 1789

Philippe handed Mrs. Exley down from the hackney and gritted his teeth as her lumbering footman climbed down behind her. She never been accompanied by a servant in the past.

If he'd had her all to himself, a world of possibilities would open: a hole in the ice leading to a watery grave in the muck of the Thames, a blow to the head allowing him to do anything from strangling her to fucking her to selling her to the lowest sailors he could find—he shivered as visions danced through his head, taunting him.

None of the fates he'd been debating would be hers today, however. Today she was being attended by the largest footman London had ever seen. A hulking brute with the cauliflower ears of a pugilist.

His livery coat strained across shoulders it had clearly not been designed to encompass. Damn those clumsy peasants who'd so botched what should have been an easy job. He was now hemmed in by velvet-encased oafs.

Seething, he led her down the stairs that normally led to the churning crowd of watermen. Today they had been replaced by a swarm of peddlers, hawking everything from ribbon and oranges to hot cross buns and gin. Copious, swirling, stinking amounts of gin.

Loud voices, obviously of low origin, assaulted him from every side. Hands plucked at his pockets, searching for a wallet, a coin, a handkerchief.

Philippe shoved them away, jabbing the slowest boy with the pointed end of his walking stick. The boy squealed and glared, piglike eyes malevolent beneath a cap of greasy hair. A filthy little guttersnipe.

"Throw them a penny."

"*Non.*"

"No?"

"Very well." Better to keep her mollified, happy, trusting. He dug into his pocket and flicked a ha'penny at the boys, being careful to send it as far from the fat, glaring one as possible.

He bought a small sack of roasted chestnuts and peeled them as they walked. Rowdy audiences had formed around the makeshift stages that had been erected on the ice. They cheered the bawdy performances.

Mrs. Exley paused before a puppet show. A particularly obscene Punch was busy molesting a nun on the small swag-hung stage.

Philippe peeled another nut and popped it into his mouth. He held the scalding flesh carefully between his teeth and blew. How long was he going to have to stay here? This entire day was turning into a huge waste of time.

Judy erupted onto the stage, beating Punch and the nun with a cricket bat. The crowed gave a roar of approval. Philippe chewed, counting the minutes until he could escape.

The comte handed George down from the hackney. She smirked into her tippet as a pained expression crossed his face when Hay bounded out after her. Her bodyguard-cum-footman climbed down from the box, his weight causing the well-worn carriage to squeak and squeal in protest. Still looking as if his senses were deeply offended, the comte slid back into the coach and shut the door behind him. George could almost feel sorry for him, if he'd been less of a prig.

Dismissing the man she and Hay had been torturing ever since they'd joined forces on the ice, she turned her attention to her godson. The boy's grin turned to laughter as George led him up her steps and into the house. Whatever the comte had expected when he'd invited her to attend the Frost Faire, it had not included the infantry. Children were decidedly not his forte.

"I can't imagine you're in the least bit hungry after all the treats you consumed today." George ushered Hay up to the main drawing room. "So we won't bother with luncheon. Don't you dare tell your mother I let you eat nothing but gingerbread and chocolate."

Hayden assured his godmother that he'd never betray their secret, with such a serious face that

George was unsure how he could maintain it. "Imp." She ruffled his hair and pushed him into the drawing room.

Inside she found Brimstone playing chess with Colonel Staunton in the otherwise deserted room. His eyes lighting up, Hay made straight for them. He drew up a chair beside the colonel and absently petted Caesar while he observed the game.

"What have you been up to, my boy?" Brimstone moved his knight, putting the colonel's rook in jeopardy.

"Bullocking Aunt George's Frenchman."

Both men laughed and Hay prattled on, relating their day's adventures. He was still talking when his father appeared some twenty minutes later.

"I knew once he was here you'd never dislodge him. Come along, you young scamp, your Aunt George has basked in the glow of your admiration long enough. You'll make all her suitors jealous if you stay any longer."

When the earl had taken his son off, George threw herself down on the settee. "Any word on when I might be allowed out of doors without what looks like a cadre of dockworkers at my heels?"

Brimstone chuckled. "Don't like the looks of Addington's men?"

"I could care less what they look like. Having Adonis and Paris constantly peering over my shoulder would be just as irritating."

"I highly doubt that." The colonel tipped his king over, conceding defeat. He crossed the room to take a seat beside her. "And I'm sure you'll agree that a bodyguard or two is preferable to being shipped away to Scotland?"

"Vastly." George did nothing to hide the sarcasm in her voice. Of course it was better, but only just.

"Cribbed, cabined, and confined."

"Keep your damn quotes to yourself, Brimstone." She turned her head to look at him over her shoulder. He was busy readying the chessboard for its next game, setting all to rights in his fastidious way. "Unless you've something more instructive than *Macbeth*?"

"Sadly, no, sweet termagant. Nothing of interest to report from your expedition upon the frozen Thames?"

"Nothing besides what Hayden has already told you. The ice was overrun with players, chestnut roasters, and sellers of gin. But not a murder to be seen."

"Which I know frustrates you to no end, but we mere men would prefer the criminal caught without his taking another shot at you."

"As would I, but I'd settle for some more active plan in which he were allowed that shot if it would relieve me of my hulking shadows."

"Another fight I'll leave to Lord Glendower." He rose from the chess table and sketched her a bow. George made a rude sound in the back of her throat. "For the colonel and I are otherwise promised for the evening, and we've just time to make our engagement if we leave now."

The colonel likewise stood and the two of them strode out of the room. Their steps echoed in the hall as they descended the stairs, claimed their coats, and left her to brood.

It had been two days since Helen Perripoint's party, and she'd not seen so much as a nosegay from Dauntry. Damn him.

She crossed the room and peeked out the window,

watching her friends stride off down the street, the two of them already deep in conversation.

She turned to warm her hands at the fire. Dauntry couldn't really mean to go through with his threat, could he?

Chapter 26

We must apologize most profusely concerning our reports regarding the incomparable Mrs. P—. She has not, in fact, traded down for a baronet, but up for a duke.

Tête-à-Tête, 16 January 1789

Ivo sat uncomfortably in the Morpeths' red and gold salon, tea untouched, mind racing. The countess had called a council of war and George's defenders had come out in force.

Her bulldogs were present, as were her father-in-law, Bennett, Alençon, Carr, Colonel Staunton, and her brother-in-law, Viscount Layton.

They were agreed that simply waiting out the killer wasn't going to work. Some action had to be taken. The question was, what could be done to flush him out? Under what circumstances could they both protect George while luring her enemy in to the open?

His own thoughts were muddled and impaired, whirling with plans of his own.

A simple declaration would not do the trick; George

would very likely decline it. Nor would another public display be in his best interests. Putting her on the spot again could only be disastrous. A bold gesture was called for, but just what constituted bold when it came to George was open to debate.

Ivo was struggling to follow both the discussion taking place around him as well as the one raging in his own head when the door opened and they were joined by Morpeth.

"Need I even ask what you're plotting, my dear?" the earl inquired, crossing the room and perching on the arm of the settee beside his wife.

Victoria looked at him crossly. "You know very well what we're up to, Rupert. You were invited, after all. And if you're going to join us, the least you can do is enter into the spirit of the thing."

"Oh, I do, my dear, but I have my reservations about dangling George about like so much bait, not that my objections are likely to win out with this unholy coalition. So, do you want to enlighten me? What grand scheme have you hatched between you?"

"Well . . ." the countess began. "Lord Frampton's masked ball at Vauxhall seems too good an opportunity for the killer to pass up. The crowd, the fireworks, the dark walks. Ideal for his purposes, wouldn't you think?"

"Perhaps too ideal?" the colonel said. "A knife in the crowd, everyone masked."

"What's the alternative? To keep her confined until he burns her house around her ears?" Ivo realized with a start he'd spoken aloud and the entire room had turned to look at him.

"Honestly," he continued, "Addington's men have gotten nowhere. It's a waiting game. We're waiting for the highwayman to make another attempt, and he's waiting for us to let our guard down. And eventually both of those things are going to happen, preferably not at the same time. The masque might be our best hope."

Chapter 27

Is it our imagination, or does Mrs. E— appear not in her usual spirits? Could it be that she has finally been the first to be dismissed? What man could be so foolish?

Tête-à-Tête, 3 February 1789

Brimstone gave a low chuckle as they arrived at the door of Number 6, Dover Street. George threw him a stern look. The party of starchy ladies they'd just passed were clustered on the sidewalk, the girls scurrying behind their mother like rabbits scenting a fox.

Even now, as they stepped through the portal of that august men's sanctuary, the ladies were straining to catch a clearer glimpse. Should she have Gabriel lead her back out to take a little bow, perhaps to sign the guidebook the mother had been clutching?

She could picture the entry the girls would make in it later: *Saw the famous Mrs. Exley entering Manton's on the arm of a dissolute rake. Her gown was beautiful, but how can she? Father would never permit.*

The poor little dears. They had no idea what threats the wide world held, what delights it offered. And they never would, by the look of them.

Inside, Bennett and Morpeth were waiting, along with the proprietor. Her brother-in-law was examining a fowling piece, while St. Audley looked on, both their faces serious as they evaluated the gun. Sydney tested the balance, switched hands, switched back, and then was finally persuaded to hand the piece over to St. Audley, who promptly set about doing exactly the same thing.

They'd be indignant if she were to openly compare them to ladies in a draper's shop, but that was exactly what they put her in mind of.

George smiled and accepted a glass of ale from Bennett before unpacking her new pistol. Brimstone had acquired it for her the day before, something small enough for her to carry about her person, to conceal within in a pocket, but deadly all the same.

Today they had reserved the famous shooting gallery so she could practice firing it. Those who weren't examining guns in the shop were busily engaged in the shooting gallery. Some of the gentlemen had brought their own guns, while others were busy testing those that the Mantons had for sale.

George spent the afternoon chatting with her friends, smoking Bennett's cigaritoes, and drinking the excellent ale Brimstone had provided. Her little gun was a work of art: one round that fired straight and true. She had no problem at all hitting her desired target.

Tonight was the night.

The trap had been carefully set. Her regular visitors

had all been appraised of her attendance . . . All that remained was for the highwayman to show his hand.

Would he? Was the opportunity they were presenting as irresistible as they'd imagined?

Had they all turned a series of unrelated events into a conspiracy that didn't exist?

She'd dressed carefully, purposefully wearing her usual amber, heavily embroidered in gold. Over this, she draped a plain black domino. Even with her loo mask hiding the upper half of her face she was easily identifiable.

The ride to Vauxhall passed quickly enough, since the road was not choked with the throngs that flocked to the gardens during the season. The city flashed past the small carriage window like a series of vignettes. George tried to breathe steadily, to control the quaking sensation roiling her stomach.

Soon enough she found herself being helped from the carriage by a serious-faced Brimstone. He'd forgone a domino, and wore only a simple black loo mask. George smiled up at him as he claimed her hand.

"Good evening, Gabe," she said, slipping her arm into his and stepping aside to allow the earl and countess to exit the carriage.

"Good evening, my Lady of Mystery," he responded, leading her into the gardens in the wake of their hosts.

The gardens were nearly overflowing with masked guests. It must have cost Lord Frampton a fortune to rent the gardens out for the night. Normally, Vauxhall wasn't open in the winter months, but Frampton wanted to puff off his latest find, a plump little soprano from Poland, and so he'd arranged with the proprietor to open it for one night only, at his expense. He'd issued gilded cards of invitation to the *ton*, and notices had been inserted in the papers, advertising a Venetian masquerade, the cost of admission for those without a card being enormously steep at a guinea.

George glanced about as Brimstone escorted her to their box. Scandalously clad members of the demimonde mingled with the ladies and gentlemen of the *ton*. Wealthy merchants and barristers took their supper boxes next to the lords and ladies.

London had been quiet of late, and everyone was looking for an escape from the dreary weather. The gentry and merchant classes flocked to those few occasions when they could be assured of rubbing elbows with society. George felt a flicker of anticipation deep in her chest, blooming, filling her, undercut by a shiver of fear. Was he here tonight? Was he out there in the dark garden, waiting? Or was he mingling with the colorful crowd, watching her?

The walkways were lit with colorful globes and the musicians had already begun to play. The mob of bright masqueraders was seething with suppressed merriment. Everyone waiting for the fireworks to set the evening off, or searching for someone or other in the crowd. It felt like the evening before a battle. Everyone just a little too gay, a little too loud. It was exhilarating in a way a simple *ton* drum could never be. The evening had an edge to it.

Gathered in the large supper box the earl had rented were most of her friends. Each of them easy for her to identify, even hidden behind their dominos and masks. They were gathered in a knot: tense, wary, ready.

All except Dauntry.

Alienated or not, she'd expected him to be present. The same part of her that was searching the crowd for the highwayman was tense with the hunt for Dauntry as well.

George claimed her seat and then the earl called for their supper. While they all consumed the paper-thin wafers of ham and tiny roasted chickens that Vauxhall was so rightly famous for, George could feel her body becoming more and more tense, back rigid, shoulders hard, legs shaking with the need to move, to fight, to run away. With the need to act.

The small pistol Brimstone had bought her lay cold and solid against her leg. A reassuringly hard reality cloaked by petticoats.

A man in a puce domino stopped just a few feet from them and bowed, leg extended, eyes glittering in the light thrown by the lanterns. George forced herself to smile, to nod her head flirtatiously. To behave normally. Every man who looked at her, who paused, who bowed, who smiled, or eyed her through his quizzing glass was suspect.

When their meal was finished, and everyone was picking at the last of the sweet biscuits and cheese cakes, St. Audley stood, swept George a profound leg, and held out his hand. "Come along then, dance with me."

Taking his hand, she allowed him to help her up and to lead her into the rotunda, where the dancing was taking place. Scores of couples were already assembled in the large ballroom, and as the next set got underway, George quickly found herself parted from St. Audley. She gave herself over to trying to guess the identities of the other dancers. Some of them she recognized. Others were harder to place. She was almost convinced that the lady in the brown domino was Lady Jersey, and the man in crimson Baron Ott, but she couldn't be sure. Sometimes a

man's hair, or a woman's laugh, or some other distinct characteristic—such as St. Audley's mismatched
eyes—would give them away, but mostly the masqueraders who cared to do so did a fairly good job of dis-
guising themselves. And at a semi-public masquerade
such as this, a large number of the guests were simply
unknown to her.

Circling back through the set, George could see St.
Audley only a few partners away. This meant the first
set was almost through, and they could either stay for
another, or retire to the box.

George was parched, and the room was hot and
stuffy for all that the night was cold. On the sidelines
stood Brimstone, Bennett, Morpeth, Alençon. All of
them watching, waiting, as tense as she was.

The music ended and they made their way back to
the nearly deserted box. St. Audley caught their
waiter and ordered punch. He took a seat beside her
and they sat and simply watched the crowd mill
about on the lawn between the rotunda and the
pavilion.

As they'd made their way out of the rotunda, she'd
spotted Dauntry, standing quietly off to one side, his
attention riveted to her. She'd known the moment
he'd appeared. Even now she could feel his gaze, like
moth wings fluttering against her skin.

He'd worn all black, with a silvery, mouse-gray
domino draped over his head and shoulders. She
swallowed with difficulty, throat tight. Rejected, he
was here.

It was St. Audley's job to entertain her, Brimstone's to take her out and then seemingly disappear, chasing after some temping Paphian. Lord
knew there were plenty of them about. At this very
moment, two of them were sauntering right toward

Dauntry, dominos artfully draped to expose their wares, nipples rouged and rosy in the candlelight.

She couldn't concentrate on who else might be watching her when she knew Dauntry was. Nothing else was able to invade her senses. Hell, nothing else even seemed to matter.

George drained her cup, letting the warmth quiet the shaking of her hands as the alcohol settled her stomach. St. Audley sipped his drink, eyes flitting over the crowd. The first vivid burst of fireworks exploded overhead and Brimstone appeared at the edge of the box as if by magic.

As the crowd oohed and aahed, clapped and cheered, he slid his hand around her waist. "Come along, Georgie, let's go for a walk. Crowd's too thick for me."

George swiveled her head around and looked up at him. She extended her hand. This was it. From this moment it on it was all for show, all for deception; one dangerous gamble.

"Lead on, Bottom," she commanded. "I've half a mind to fall in love with you tonight."

"Not Bottom. Surely you're not so cruel. Let me be Puck! Let me be Orsino. Let me be Petruchio."

"I'm afraid the role of Petruchio is already taken."

Brimstone snorted and led her down the dark Lovers' Walk, the two of them weaving their way past other couples bent on more romantic assignations.

"What about Romeo?"

"Dead."

"Hamlet?"

"The lady's dead in that one. Go back to comedies."

They stopped at the grotto and George stood staring at the water cascading down into the small pool, lost in thought. Brimstone paused beside her, his hand squeezing hers.

Was the highwayman here? Had he taken the bait? Or was all their playacting for naught?

A pretty little fille de joie sidled by, stopping momentarily—as she'd been paid to do—and giving Brimstone a saucy, come-hither smile. This was it, the moment of truth . . .

"How about Ariel?"

"Ariel? I think Bottom was correct after all, off with you." She gave him a nudge and laughed when he swept her a deep, courtly bow before hurrying off after the girl's disappearing form.

George turned back to the water. Gabe wouldn't go far, and the rest of the boys were out there too, lurking in the dark paths.

This was it. Her knees trembled and she tensed the muscles of her thighs to stop them shaking. All she could do was wait. Wait and hope her highwayman was desperate enough to have followed her.

Ivo stood on the dark path that led to the grotto, cloaked in the embrace of evergreens, and watched the theatrics play out. George's gown rustled in the silence, Brimstone's shoes ground the gravel of the walk audibly as he stepped around her.

Their banter flowed easily, edged with the wit and education their whole class worshipped. It felt genuine, right down to George's exasperated expression and her bulldog's slightly drunken walk.

Ivo ran the palm over the pommel of his dress sword, the cold metal reassuring even through the leather of his gloves, the sharp, deadly reality that rode his hip oddly calming.

The Cyprian toddled away, mincing along one of the many paths that converged in the grotto. The improbable gauze flounces of her gown beckoned in the breeze of her passing. Brimstone staggered after her, disappearing in the twists of the path; the paste buckles of his breeches and shoes sparked in the darkness even after he'd merged with the shadows, then winked out.

George turned back to the waterfall, slid the hood of her domino off to settle about her shoulders. The column of her neck held him frozen in place. Pale, delicate, naked from the bone at its base to the nape of her neck. The colored light thrown by the lantern caressed her skin, turning it blue and pink and yellow. It refracted a riot of color in her hair, highlighting every strand that had escaped the powder.

He stole up to her, lost in the curls that twisted at her nape, the sweep of her shoulders, the angle of her head. He wanted to touch her. Needed to. Couldn't control the desire to press a kiss between her shoulders, a sensual landscape of subtle hills and valleys.

He stepped close, caught her round the waist, and pulled her back to him. He pressed his lips to the spot that had been taunting him. "Petruchio's taken, is it? What about Oberon?"

George stiffened then went slack as he spoke, sagging back against him. "Damn you, Dauntry. I thought you were *him*."

"Sorry to disappoint, love."

"You're ruining everything. Go away."

He was. And he didn't give a damn. Suddenly he didn't care so much for their scheme, for leaving George unprotected for even a moment. Anyone who wanted to get to her was going to have to go though him first. That was the way it ought to be. The way it would be.

He ducked his head, nose to the soft, bare patch of skin behind her ear. Jasmine filled his nostrils, flooded his senses, curled around him and held him as securely as a chain.

She was his, whether she was ready to admit it or not. His.

The second his grip relaxed she broke away and darted off, sparing him no more than a chastising glance. Ivo raced after her, chased her through the twists and turns of the path, nearly losing her in the dark. Only the occasional glint of the gold trimmings of her gown gave her away.

She spun around a corner and he lost her entirely as an amorous, giggling couple blundered into him, knocking him back.

Damnation!

By the time he rounded the corner she had disappeared entirely. The path forked around a large tree, gravel scattered all around its roots. Ivo dove down the right path, praying he was right, that George would have chosen the darker of the two, the one without lanterns bobbing welcomingly along it.

A startled exclamation—clearly feminine—sent him racing, heedless of branches, pebbles, roots. His domino snagged and he threw it off, leaving it hanging in his wake.

George stared wide-eyed at the man in the peacock blue domino. Her breath caught in her throat, choking her. Her eyes burned with the need to blink, but she couldn't look away.

Moonlight wove its way through the canopy,

glinted off polished metal, outlining the deadly curves of the pistol gripped in his right hand. As long as she held his gaze he wouldn't shoot. She was sure of it. He was savoring the moment. He'd make it last for as long as she allowed him to.

He wanted more than just her death. That much had been obvious all along.

After a moment his pistol wavered, dipping slightly, but not falling away. The lanterns high in the trees threw a strange crimson light over them both, casting shadows in odd places, making it impossible to see what little of his face was bare below his Venetian-style mask. His lips and jaw were eerily missing, but she knew those eyes.

Why couldn't she place them?

Why was it so much more frightening to know she *knew* the man trying to kill her? She felt suddenly damp inside her clothes. Her shift clung to her legs, the night air turned her dewy skin to ice.

"Time to go, my lady." His voice dripped with sarcasm as his tongue wrapped around the title and spat it out.

"Go?"

He didn't respond except to indicate with the pistol that she should move. George swallowed as the world around her refused to return to life. Like a clockwork toy that had wound down, it was stuck, motionless.

She took a step back, willing the world to continue. Her hands began to tingle. Her heart was clawing its way up her throat. Where were the boys? Where was Dauntry? He'd been right behind her . . . and here she was, the bait on the end of the hook.

"I'm afraid I don't understand, monsieur. I think you must have the wrong lady."

He smiled at that, just a quick flash of teeth that glinted in the light. "I don't think so. I have exactly the right whore, and I have her exactly where I want her. Or I will in just a few moments. There's a carriage out the side gate, waiting just for you." He gestured again with the gun, stepped closer, anger radiating from him like heat from a forge.

George lifted her chin and placed one hand on her hip. All she had to do was reach into her petticoats, down into the pocket that rode against her hip. Her own pistol waited there, loaded, ready to blast any foe. "You force me to repeat myself, sir. I do not know you. You have the wrong lady."

He closed the space between them with swift angry strides, lowering his gun as he took hold of her arm with his free hand. "You know me and you knew my father. Or have you caused the death of so many men that you can no longer remember them all?"

"I don't know—"

"*Vous savez!*" His grip tightened, fingers digging into her, pressing down on the bone. She held her breath to keep from wincing. "Paris. Six years ago. You clipped your leash to his collar and led him around like a pet monkey. Right under your husband's nose, and then another of your lovers killed him in a jealous rage."

George went cold. This was about Blanchot? Why did everything in her life seem to spiral back to that night?

"I don't—"

He dropped her arm and backhanded her across the face hard enough to send her flying. Her head cracked against the unforgiving marble knee of Aphrodite. Her vision blurred, went black, then swam sickingly as the lights danced overhead.

She landed in a sprawl on her back in the under-growth, feet and arms tangled, hair and gown snag-ging, trapped like a wild thing in a snare.

Her face burned, inflamed beyond the heat of a blush. The hot, coppery taste of blood filled her mouth. She swallowed it down, struggling to get her arms free, to get her hand through layers of petti-coats and into her pocket.

She'd had next to nothing to do with Blanchot's death, but she was more than willing to be responsi-ble for this one.

Her assailant bent to grab hold of her again. His domino slid, revealing the sleeve of his coat. A very distinctive sleeve: pale blue leopard-spotted velvet. Only one man would ever wear such an outrageous coat and he'd been running tame in her house for more than six months. The Comte de Valy.

George scrabbled back, lashed out with one foot, missing her target entirely, sending her shoe flying off into the dark. The comte grabbed her ankle and pulled, and then he was hauled off her and sent flying himself.

Chapter 28

Tonight all of London is poised to witness the ridiculous display Lord F— is making of his imported mistress. Oh, to be deaf . . .

Tête-à-Tête, 13 February 1789

George was down on the ground, a man in a blue domino bent over her, struggling to get a grip on her. Ivo flung back the enveloping folds of his own garb, freeing his sword arm. The metallic scrape as he drew his sword stopped the man cold. Made him straighten and turn.

George continued to flail in the undergrowth. She was all right. Scratched and shaken, but alive. The expression on her face—fury combined with deadly intent—told him everything he needed to know.

Ivo's breath shuddered out of him, relief flooding through him. The man in the blue domino wasn't going to be able to say the same for long. Ivo was going to kill him. Rend him limb from limb. And he was going to enjoy every unchristian and uncivilized bit of it.

He stood steady on his feet, waiting for the man to draw his own sword . . . waiting for the moment when the clash of steel would bring them close enough for him to taste the other man's fear.

The man brought one arm up, a gun clutched in his hand.

Ivo ground his teeth. Anger flushed through him, blood rushing past his ears, pumped by his furiously beating heart. He flexed his hands, imagining them about the other man's neck.

He set his jaw, teeth clenched to the breaking point. One shot. That's all he had. One shot, and then Ivo was going to kill him.

The man's arm straightened, the gun steadied, then the crack of the shot broke the silence. Ivo braced himself even as fireworks exploded overhead. The man in peacock blue crumpled without a sound, simply folding in upon himself, the loose fabric of his domino fluttering out, settling around him like a shroud.

Ivo turned to where George lay, skirts hiked up and tangled about her legs, one shoe missing, one stocking down around her ankle, a smoking pistol in her hand. Men burst in from all sides: her bulldogs, Bennett, Morpeth, a very frazzled-looking Alençon, wig askew and full of leaves.

Pandemonium ruled, but every nuance flooded through him, as though each moment took an eternity. George met his gaze, her mischievous dimple briefly flashing in her cheek.

Unharmed and undaunted. That was his love.

Ivo took a breath, afraid he was going to embarrass himself and vomit. His body felt oddly weak. Two steps and he was pulling George up, ripping her loose from the undergrowth, dragging her free. His mouth met hers. Hot. Insistent. Impatient.

She sagged against him, hands limp on his chest. She broke the kiss and dropped her head to his shoulder. He was vaguely aware that their friends were circling, that they were speaking amongst themselves in low tones, voices crashing over one another.

He dropped his head, resting his cheek against the top of her head, inhaling the scented powder that coated her hair. "I've got you, love. I've got you."

She pulled back, pushing hard with her arms. Her eyes were wet. Shimmering. One spilled over and the tear raced down her cheek, leaving a pink track of exposed skin as it washed away the powder. She opened her lips, but nothing came out.

"George?" His grip slackened and his eyes searched hers. Panic flood her face. Mysterious and inexplicable. Why, just this once, couldn't she be more like other women? She loved him. He knew she did. Why was it so hard—so impossible—for her to admit it?

She wrenched herself out of his arms, took a step away from him, and then another. Time collapsed as she retreated. St. Audley stepped between them, blocked him out. The viscount glared over his shoulder as he tugged her out of the glen.

Ivo stalked after them, senses snapping with anger, on the verge of simply strangling the viscount as he'd like to have strangled the man who was now dead. Only steps ahead of him, they emerged from the darkened walk and into the crowded grove where Frampton's soprano was performing.

She'd lost her mask during her flight and her domino trailed behind her like the wings of a fabled beast. The viscount shouldered his way through the mob, pressing forward toward their box. They came to a halt when they encountered Lady Morpeth, and St. Audley gave way as George was enfolded into the countess's protective embrace.

Ivo paused, the crowd swirling about him: loud, raucous, pulsing with energy and life. St. Audley trailed behind the women as Victoria led George back toward their supper box, and they momentarily disappeared from sight. Clenching his teeth, Ivo pushed his way through the crowd, heedless of the dirty looks from those trying to listen to the singer.

Rattled, George wrapped her domino about her, clutched it to her, tried to disappear into its folds. She could hear Lyon's voice echoing in her head. He'd have called her a stupid little fool. She could almost hear the exact inflection he'd use. He'd have liked the earl, damn it all.

Lyon would have been horrified about all the time she'd wasted. She'd needed a good shaking. Needed it badly. And now here was Dauntry arrived to turn her world topsy-turvy.

She couldn't keep putting him off. He'd appeared as though she'd conjured him up from the darkness. Kissed her like some demon lover. Saved her again . . .

She allowed St. Audley to press a glass of steaming hot punch into her icy hands. Her chest felt hollow. Her eyes burned, unshed tears pushing for release.

She'd almost died. *He'd* almost died. That would have been infinitely worse. Loath as she was to admit to the emotion, she loved him. Marriage to Dauntry would be a risk, might just be an unmitigated disaster. They'd likely fight—and frequently.

But she wanted him, and she wasn't going to get him on any other terms. She only had to say one simple word to claim both him and the life he offered. One word. And she couldn't seem to say it.

His grandfather and past scandals be damned. The world owed her a little bit of happiness. A little joy. She'd had enough losses and sorrows. Was she really prepared to allow Dauntry to be one more?

Frustrated, she blinked back the tears that threatened and swallowed as much of the punch as she could take in a single swallow. Giddiness and panic overwhelmed her. She couldn't breathe, couldn't think. Her heart was racing, and her fingers tingling, almost numb.

She actually felt faint. She never felt faint!

Lyon would be ashamed of her. She was ashamed of herself. Dauntry's stricken face swam before her, blotting out the manic, predatory expression in Valy's eyes when he'd touched her.

The press of the crowd and the din of the musicians pushed in on her, making her head swim. She was safe. She was free. And all she wanted to do was collapse in a heap and cry.

Chapter 29

It is impossible to escape the news that the Lady
Corinthian appears to have joined the Turk's harem.
It is a sad day for Englishmen everywhere . . .

Tête-à-Tête, 13 February 1789

Ivo strode past Lord Carr, who eyed him knowingly
but forbore to step between him and his quarry.
George was seated, staring quietly at her hands while
Lady Morpeth hovered over her, patting her and tut-
tutting like a mother hen with only one chick. St.
Audley paced at the back of the box, expression dark
as a storm cloud.

"Out!" Ivo barked, ignoring the viscount's threat-
ening stance.

"But . . . but . . ." the countess stammered.

When she failed to give way, Ivo snarled and
pushed past her. Without a word he hauled George
up out of her chair and tossed her up and over his
shoulder. He shoved the viscount back with his free
arm, sending him sprawling into the chairs, then

turned and marched out of the box, making for the gates.

He was done with this.

Done with George's indecision.

Done with his own.

They were leaving. Now. He wasn't going to propose again. Nor was he going to allow her to prevaricate. She wouldn't be allowed any avenue of escape, not if he had to kidnap her and flee for the border this very night.

She was *his*, damn it.

Not causing a scene be damned. His grandfather be damned. Her bloody bulldogs be damned!

He pushed past a startled woman in a purple domino and shouldered aside her escort, deaf to their remonstrations. George rode his shoulder, oddly quiescent. Only the tension of her spine alerted him that should his grip slacken she'd be off and running like a doe pursued by hounds.

George watched the crowd at Vauxhall watching her. Watching them. Dauntry's shoulder was hard against her hips, muscles rolling under the silk of his coat. His hands were locked about her thighs, holding her fast. One side of her hoops had collapsed between her hip and his head.

They must present quite a sight.

He was making a scene that would not soon be forgotten. A wonderful scene. A glorious *on-dit* for the scandalmongers.

Something that would overrun the gossip surrounding a well-known French aristocrat being found murdered in the garden, or floating in the Thames, which was far more likely given her godfather's maddening efficiency and the close proximity of the river.

Over the heads of the crowd she saw their friends in hot pursuit and began to laugh, the sound bubbling up out of her uncontrollably. A few of them actually looked concerned as they wove through the milling crowd. As if Dauntry were far more dangerous than her highwayman had been.

She raised her head, bracing her hands on Dauntry's back. He'd lost his hair ribbon, as well as his domino and mask. Dark curls spilled over his shoulders, twisted down his back. There was not a chance that most of the sea of revelers didn't recognize her. Didn't recognize them.

She could almost feel the gossip swirling around them like midges on a hot summer night. The entire *ton* would be buzzing with it by morning. But, as she'd be the Countess of Somercote before she was likely to see any of them again, it really didn't matter.

Cynical and wrong as it might be, a marriage and a title would sweep this all away. Make it nothing more than a mildly amusing story. Gossip was only truly savory when attached to scandal.

Dauntry marched straight out the gates, past the stunned and titillated faces of the hordes, and down the street to the top of the Vauxhall Stairs. He slung her down off his shoulder and set her on her feet, one hand still locked about her arm, pressing down on bruises he wasn't aware of.

George forced herself not to flinch. He wouldn't forgive himself if she complained, if he knew.

"Well, curst Katharina?" He let go of her, raising one hand to brush a curl away from her eyes. He swept it back, hooking it behind her ear, fingers tracing the curve of her ear, trailing down her neck.

"Yes, Petruchio?"

"Yes—the very word I've been waiting for." He

bent his head and kissed her again, his eager hands locking her to him.

George pressed close, twined her hands in his loose hair, and kissed him back.

A few houses up, Brimstone stopped to watch George and her bedeviled suitor. The sound of running feet echoed loudly in the dark. Shouts and shrill laughter spilled out of the gardens.

"Well?" Bennett inquired as he and Morpeth caught up with him. "Is he kissing her or beating her?"

"Would it make any difference?" Brimstone shot his cuffs and turned back toward the gardens, suddenly overcome with thirst. There was nothing more boring than happily united lovers.

Epilogue

Barton Court, August 1793

Curled up indecorously in her favorite chair, George watched two-year-old Dysart play with his wooden horses. Caesar, a look of long suffering on his graying face, was being put to use as the hill Dy's chargers were running up and down.

The distinct sound of a carriage rolling along the gravel drive—the crackle of wheels shifting rock, the steady gait of the team—eased its way in through the open window, grew louder as the clock ticked on the mantel and the birds chirped outside in the warmth of the afternoon.

Dy's head snapped up and one of his beloved chargers fell unnoted to the carpet. He stood and ran to the window, the skirts of his dress flapping. George stood and shook out her gown, peeling her shift away from her damp skin. She scooped up her son and held him so he could peer out the open window.

"Our guest is arriving. Shall we go and meet him?"

Dy nodded, dark curls bobbing. He clutched his favorite horse to his chest.

With her son balanced on her hip and Caesar trailing along beside her, George made her way down the main stairs to the entrance hall.

The portrait of Ivo's father smiled down upon her as she passed it. As did the one of her father, and those of past Dauntrys too numerous to count.

Ivo had gone to town to meet with his solicitor, and George had sent a long overdue invitation to Ashcombe Park. She hadn't been sure the marquis would come, but something had to be done. Someone had to swallow their pride . . . and this time around it had been her. The estrangement between her husband and his family had gone on long enough.

The front door was thrown open by the butler and the marquis appeared in the open doorway, backlit by the afternoon sky. A tall, steady figure for all that he was well into his eighties.

Caesar's hackles went up and George shushed him, running a hand down his back to smooth the hair back into place. She snapped her fingers and the dog obediently prostrated himself on the floor.

Lord Tregaron stepped inside, wig precisely set, as if he'd just stepped from the hands of his valet, not from a carriage after a jolting thirty-mile drive. He leaned upon the elegant walking stick clutched in his right hand a bit more than she remembered, but not so much that a casual observer would notice.

"Do you have Somercote trained as well as that beast?"

George bit the inside of her lip to keep from smiling. The old man was very much as she remembered him from their few, brief encounters. Haughty. Angry. Like a cat rubbed the wrong way.

"Well, girl?" His bushy brows rose as he tipped his head back and glared down at her from his superior height. His cocoa-brown eyes, exactly like his grandson's, bored into her.

"I'm wondering how to answer you, my lord. If I say yes, you'll think your grandson a fool. If I say no, you'll think me one."

The old man gave a bark of laughter and stripped off his linen surtout, handing the full-skirted coat over to the butler, along with his hat and gloves. "That my heir?"

George glanced at Dysart and bucked him up farther on her hip, getting her arm under him. Dysart looked back at her uncertainly, his free hand clinging to the front of her gown, chubby fingers soft against her skin.

"I told that stubborn grandson of mine all would be forgiven when he presented me with an heir."

The marquis's gruff tone put her forcibly in mind of her husband when he knew he was in the wrong but was loath to apologize. A family trait, that. Or, perhaps, simply a masculine one. Her own father had been much the same.

"I doubt that my husband feels in need of forgiveness. But if you'd like to meet your great-grandson, I suggest you follow me to the sitting room." She turned and crossed the hall, not looking back to see if the marquis was following.

Dysart twisted in her arms to face back over her shoulder. "I have a horse."

"So you do," the marquis's voice sounded close behind her. "Do you have him in the saddle yet, girl?

As I remember, one of your few accomplishments was your seat."

George smiled, not trusting herself to respond with anything but a peal of laughter. It wasn't a compliment, but for the marquis it was damned close. She'd have him eating out of her hand by the time Ivo returned.

Ivo tossed Cobweb's reins to a groom and vaulted from the saddle. He eyed the large carriage squatting in the middle of the stable block with misgiving. The Tregaron arms emblazoned on the door panel left him in no doubt of who was paying a visit.

How had the old man known when he'd be away? If he'd upset George in any way . . . He clenched his teeth and stalked toward the house, picturing the dramatic scene that no doubt awaited him inside.

Gravel churned beneath his boots, a vicious grinding that gave him a tingle of perverse pleasure. When he reached the house a nervous-looking footman directed him to his wife's sitting room. He'd be lucky if George had only cracked the marquis on the head with a decanter.

He threw open the door to the large, west-facing salon and stood staring dumbly at the quietly domestic scene unfolding inside. There was a loaded tea tray, remarkably intact, on the table next to George. The marquis was dangling his quizzing glass in front of Dysart, like a child playing with a kitten and a string.

His grandfather looked up, but the old man gave no other outward sign of surprise. George raised her brows ever so slightly, one corner of her mouth curling up with just a hint of a mischief-making smile.

Dysart dropped the marquis's quizzing glass and

ran shrieking toward him. Ivo stepped into the room and scooped him up to keep him away from his mud-splashed boots.

"No need to stand there, my boy."

Ivo held back the retort that came to mind and carried his son back into the room. The moment he sat, Dysart squirmed down and darted to the marquis to reclaim the quizzing glass.

"Your wife and I were just discussing her upcoming house party." The old man reached out one hand to adjust the skirt of Dy's dress. "I was thinking of sending my carriage to fetch your mother."

Ivo glanced at George. She cocked her head with what looked like coquettish sweetness. He knew the smile that lurked at the corner of her mouth all too well to be fooled. It was pure triumph.

He relaxed into the settee and flung out one arm so he could twine his fingers into George's curls. Lord, he loved his beguiling witch of a wife.

Author's Note

The late 1780s is a period which fascinates me. It's tumultuous on multiple fronts, multiple continents, in ways both micro and macro. 1787 marks a major milestone for the still fledgling United States: the signing of the Constitution. Uranus, Oberon, and Titan are discovered by Herschel. Mozart's *Don Giovanni* is performed for the first time. In 1788, England's George III experiences his first bout of madness, ushering in the Regency crisis which will last for the next twenty-plus years. London's *Daily Universal Register* becomes the *Times*. The first convicts are transported from Britain to Australia, and Sydney is founded. 1789 marks the beginning of the Revolution in France, and the world will never be the same. The guillotine is invented. Mrs. Radcliffe's first horror novel, *The Castles of Athlin and Dunbayne*, is published. Fashion is also undergoing a major transformation, the likes of which will not be seen again until the flappers burst onto the scene more than one hundred years later. Hoops have been discarded in favor of false rumps, and soon even those will be gone as the fashion turns toward a Greek ideal. Vigée Le Brun has already painted the scandalous portrait of Marie Antoinette in her *Robe à la Reine* and the fashion has taken England by storm. The Duke of Devonshire is openly living with his wife and his mistress (the duchess's best friend). The young Prince of Wales is illegally married to the Catholic Mrs. Fitzherbert, and has likely already sired an illegitimate son. The Whigs and Tories are locked in combat in Parliament, each marshaled behind their leaders, Charles Fox and his former protégé, William Pitt.

It is this world that I have tried to give you a glimpse into—a world poised on the brink of almost unimaginable change. I hope you have enjoyed the journey, and I hope you'll join me for many, many more. For information about me and my upcoming releases please visit me on my Web site: kalenhughes.com. To join me in my daily search for historical accuracy and verisimilitude, please visit my blog: History Hoydens.